Sarah's Destiny

Books by Vicky Adin

The Cornish Knot
Portrait of a Man

Brigid The Girl from County Clare
Gwenna The Welsh Confectioner
The Costumier's Gift

The Disenchanted Soldier

The Art of Secrets
Elinor
Lucy

THE ANCESTORS BOOK 1

Sarah's Destiny

VICKY ADIN

Produced for Vicky Adin by AM Publishing New Zealand
www.ampublishingnz.com

Front cover image Adrienne Charlton

To buy copies of Vicky Adin's paperbacks and ebooks:
www.vickyadin.co.nz, www.amazon.com

* * * * * * *

To my granddaughters.
May they know a great love in their lives.

* * * * * * *

Main Characters

Sarah Daniels – 1834–1907
Jacob Daniels – innkeeper, her father
Betsey – her mother
Sarah's sisters – Mary Powell b. 1812
           – Harriet Williams b. 1826 (lives in Wales)
Ted – Mary's son
Aunt Nettie – Betsey's sister
Molly – kitchen maid
Ethel Binns – housemaid and companion
Amos Baker – assistant barman
Ada – scullery maid
Eli – barrel boy

Husbands
John **Clements** 1823–1860
Richard **Hunt** 1816–1905

Children
Mary Jane 1856–1859
John Jacob 1859–1954
Mary Ann 1864–1896
Sarah 1866–1870
Alfred 1868–1925
Beatrice 1872–1918
Sidney 1873–1916

Family Tree

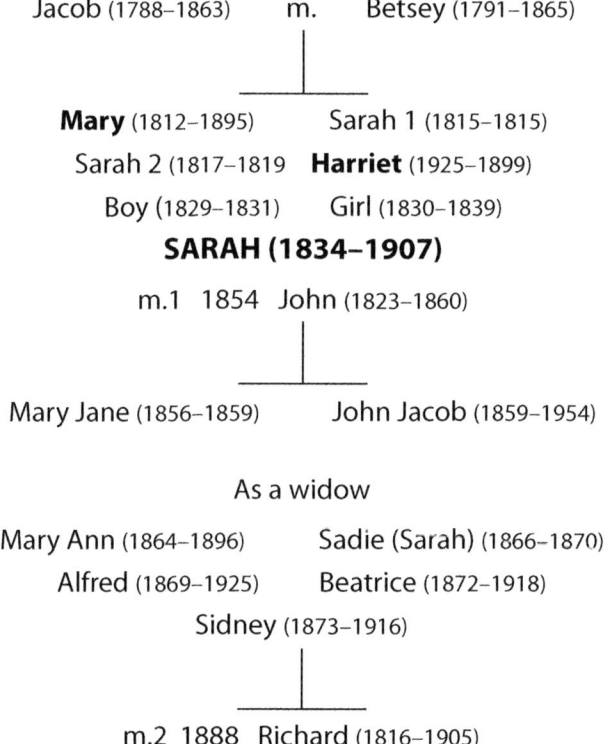

Jacob (1788–1863)   m.   Betsey (1791–1865)

Mary (1812–1895)   Sarah 1 (1815–1815)

Sarah 2 (1817–1819   **Harriet** (1925–1899)

Boy (1829–1831)   Girl (1830–1839)

SARAH (1834–1907)

m.1 1854 John (1823–1860)

Mary Jane (1856–1859)   John Jacob (1859–1954)

As a widow

Mary Ann (1864–1896)   Sadie (Sarah) (1866–1870)

Alfred (1869–1925)   Beatrice (1872–1918)

Sidney (1873–1916)

m.2 1888 Richard (1816–1905)

Glossary

This story is written in British English, and uses British slang and contractions, some of which are unique to the Bristol area.

A'feard – afraid

Al'right, me luvver? – hello/you all right mate

Babber – endearment, baby, friend

Backalong – in the past

Betwaddled – confused

Dreckly – directly or straight away

Ere – used at the start of a sentence

Gert – great

I'nit – isn't it, or other random sentence or question tags e.g. won't I

Kid – a term of endearment

Kiddie – a child, or someone younger than you

Maid – word for woman/female/girl

Mind – used as emphasis at the end of a sentence

Room and found – lodgings and food given as part of or in lieu of wages

Scrumpy – apple cider

That's the badger – that's what I meant/was talking about

Trows – flat-bottomed boats with collapsible masts to get under bridges

Welsh Back – the wharf and quay where the boats crossing the Severn from Wales could dock

Whadya – what do you [think/say], or what are you [doing]

Yer tiz – here it is

Part One

The Innkeeper's Daughter

1
The early years

Welsh Back, Bristol
March 1851

Sarah Daniels closed her eyes and breathed in the familiar odours of the river carried on the breeze, the sharp tang of salt and the earthiness of tar and wet timber, and decided she loved her life living and working at The White Hart Inn along the Welsh Back.

Most of the time.

She loved the hustle and bustle of the wharves, listening to the gulls caw, and watched the mariners working on the numerous seagoing craft trading their wares on the River Avon. She'd hear the habitual creak of rigging and the ropes singing, as the ships rocked at anchor in Bristol's floating harbour, and feel at home.

Some days the sounds sparked a hankering to know more about the world outside her haven. Not that she was complaining. She enjoyed the chatter of the weather-beaten sailors who came to her father's inn every day, and saying hello to any new customers.

And she loved her family.

Most of the time.

She took one last deep breath and retraced her steps.

"Get us a pint, Sarah me luv," called one of the familiar seamen in his lovely sing-song Welsh accent. "I'll give ya a reward, me beauty." He winked at his mates and squeezed her backside as she sidled past on the sticky flagstones, collecting up the tankards.

"I don't need the sort of reward you're offering Jacko, but if ya do that again, you'll wear the blessed pint." She flashed the brightest of smiles, which put a sparkle in her dark eyes, but she meant every word. Her rich mahogany waves swung loose from the yellow ribbon she wore, and swirled around her shoulders as she turned to fulfil her task.

The others leaning against the counter guffawed. "Serves ya right, Jacko. Shouldda known better." Sarah was their favourite. Pretty as a picture, and charming, most of the time, but cheeky with it. By now they knew she wouldn't stand for nonsense.

"Don't let her dadda catch ya, mind," said one scrawny salt, draining his pint pot and waving it aloft. "Another, Jacob, my good man."

While the innkeeper, Jacob Daniels, was a kindly man, he kept a tight rein on the many boatmen who lodged upstairs. "As long as you behave yourself," he replied, happy to encourage those unloading their flat-bottomed trows at the wharf, known as Welsh Back, to eat and drink heartily in his establishment.

Sarah had grown up with the smell of beer and salt water, and the sweat of hard work. She considered it a good life and had never known loneliness, despite not having siblings close. Her companions were the trowmen who plied their trade back and forth, ferrying mostly slate, timber, and coal across the Severn Estuary from the ports of Chepstow, Newport or Cardiff in Wales and up the Avon river to Bristol's floating harbour.

She'd never known the docks backalong when the tidal flow left boats lying in the mud and silt. Four decades on, the water was a constant depth and ships found a safe harbour created by a series of locks and sluices, and a feeder canal. The trowmen's specially designed boats were equipped with masts that could be lowered to get under the bridges and up to the nearby wharf, colloquially known as the Back.

"Sarah, luv. Can ya get us some of your cheese and pickles?" All day long people demanded something of her. "And a piece o' pie."

Sometimes, when she'd been younger, she'd played along the cobblestones with others like her, children of the licensed victuallers along the Avon riverside, or ran wild on the green in Queen's Square. These days she was needed full time at the inn.

"Sarah!" called her father. "Give us a hand, will ya, luv? I need another barrel and a firkin."

There were days when the unrealised promise of siblings who had passed before she was born rested heavily on her shoulders. The youngest of seven, and named Sarah in memory of two who hadn't survived, she could never make up her mind if she was blessed or cursed with the name, but since she'd turned sixteen last December the expectations of her ageing parents extended to her doing more than her fair share of work. Mostly she regretted not having her two remaining sisters, Mary and Harriet, nearby to share her innermost worries.

And these days she had plenty of those.

"I'll get it, Da, don't fret none. I can manage."

She had long since mastered the art of rolling the 36-gallon ale barrels across the cellar floor on their edges to their place under the bar, and attaching the pipe from the beer engine. For some of the fancier ales, Da mostly bought the nine-gallon firkins, which made life easier, but he needed barrels under the syphon handle. Neither of them could manoeuvre the largest hogsheads, a difficulty that cost them good money.

"Ah, you're a good lass, that ya are. Be careful, mind."

Sarah reassuringly patted his arm as she went past. "Where's Ma?"

A worried frown marred Jacob's brow. "Having one of her turns. I told her to lie down. Let the girl prepare the pies."

Sarah swallowed a sigh. Ma's melancholy was getting worse.

"I'll check in on Molly on me way," she said as she disappeared towards the kitchen, contemplating the busy night ahead of her, but that had always been Sarah's lot.

At an early age, bewildered and forlorn herself, she'd learnt how heartbreaking loss changed a person. Listening to her despairing mother weep for one more daughter, Sarah watched her become increasingly doleful. Around her, the local women had keened in consolation at the death of yet another child – Betsey's fourth – including a precious only son who'd passed long before Sarah had come into the world. Betsey had donned her black clothes that day and had worn black for evermore. Since then, Sarah had become her parents' only shoulder to lean on.

Passing through the kitchen, she found Molly hard at work. "How's it all going? Are ya managing well enough?"

The young servant girl blushed and bobbed. "Oh, aye. The pastry's all done and the stew pot's a bubblin'."

Sarah was impressed. She might only be fourteen, and tiny, but Molly was a quick learner and worked hard. Ma had taught her well. She just needed to keep her eyes off their Ted, her sister Mary's boy, who lodged with them. It wouldn't do for the girl to find herself compromised, especially since Ted'd be more than willing, given half a chance.

"Well done, me girl, and ya don't need to bob to me," Sarah said sweetly. "I'll be back to help later if the mistress don't come down."

Sarah continued her way to the cellar to shift the barrel and collect the firkin. By the time she returned to the front room, the lunchtime crowd had eased, the men returning to prepare their vessels for the next trip.

She heaved the firkin onto the bar and pressed her sleeve to her forehead to wipe away the sweat, clearing stray tendrils from across her face. She looked down at her brown woven skirt and crumpled apron, now streaked with dirt, and eased her shoulders within the cotton blouse sticking to her back. "You al'right for a minute, Da? I'd like to tidy m'self up a bit. It don't look like Ma'll be down today, so it'll get hectic later."

"Good as gold, luv. Go make yourself pretty. It'll be quiet now for a couple of hours, mind. Why don't ya have a wee bit of a lie down yourself. You've been up since before dawn."

She placed a hand on her father's shoulder and kissed his whiskered cheek. "So have you, Da. I'll be fine. Won't be long."

"Ah, you're the best, my girl. I couldn't do without ya, that I couldn't."

Sarah watched him pick up a rag and wipe the countertop, trying to hide his rheumy eyes. Her da was such a gentle soul at heart, despite his trade and the seafarers who surrounded him, and she knew he was feeling his age. She promised herself she would never leave him, never let him down, despite her yearning to know of places beyond the Back.

Sarah returned to the barroom as quickly as she could. She'd washed and changed into a black skirt, clean apron and fresh cream blouse with a pretty collar, coiling her hair up and holding it in place with a tortoiseshell comb.

Her sister Mary, who was a clever dressmaker, had made the blouse for her. Sarah sometimes wished she was taller, like her sister, and straighter. Mary carried herself with such elegance, while Sarah, darker in looks, thought she looked more like a Welsh incomer.

She smiled inwardly when she saw her father had nodded off while sitting in a captain's chair behind the bar. Two men sat at one of the new tables by the window, supping their ale and quietly chatting.

As she approached the men, one turned towards her. Her heart skipped a beat as an unexpected and unrecognised feeling tingled her skin. She was mesmerised by his looks: tanned but not burnt to brown butter, a moulded rather than chiselled face, neither clean-shaven nor bearded. His cap sat at the back of his head, allowing his sun-lightened hair to curl around his ears and flop over his eyebrows.

"Name's John," he said with a grin that lit his startling eyes, as blue as any sky she'd seen, and sent her heart into a greater flutter. "And who might you be?"

"Give over, Johnno," said his companion, scoffing. "Everyone's known Sarah since she were a nipper."

And he wasn't wrong. By sight, Sarah knew both men, regulars from the boats, but she'd never had anyone look at her like that before.

John's voice interrupted her appraisal. "What? Nah. This gorgeous creature afore me can't be the same scrawny kid that used to roam the cobbles." He stood then and was suddenly inches away. "I'd never've guessed." She could feel his breath on her cheek as he leaned forward and inhaled, taking in the scent of the olive oil toilet soap she used, made locally by Fripp & Thomas. She clutched the sides of her skirt to keep her hands steady.

Sarah cleared her throat and took a step back. "Can I … can I um, get ya anything? More scrumpy or summat to eat?" she stammered.

He sat down, drained his cider and held the vessel out to her. "How can I resist 'aving your sweet hands resting on the same pot I been clutching?"

She gingerly took the tankard, carefully avoiding the touch of his fingertips, and returned to the bar where Jacob stood frowning.

"Did ya get prettied up specially for him?" he nodded towards John, who sat with one ankle resting on his knee, watching her every move.

"No!" she whispered aghast, but couldn't resist turning her head for a sneak look. "I didn't know they were in town, much less here."

Jacob's mouth formed a thin line. "Well. Watch your step, my girl. He's lookin' for a diversion, and it better not be you."

Instead of handing her the cider to deliver, he came out from behind the bar and walked over to the two men, placing the scrumpy carefully on the table. "If you're lookin' for lodgings, we're full, so drink up and be gone if ya wanna find a place tonight."

"Ah, landlord," said John raising his arm in a toast. "Cheers. Tis a gert brew you serve at the White Hart. And I think you've done wonders with the new kit-out. Be sure to compliment your dear wife and 'andsome daughter, but could we get a pie to go with our pints afore we leave? Whadya think, Tommy? Hungry?" he asked his companion.

Tom grinned sheepishly. "Aye, that's the badger, if'n you've a mind, landlord. Right starvin' we are. And another pot of scrumpy too, if it ain't too much trouble."

Jacob knew better than to upset his clients. A bad word would soon spread amongst the seamen, and he needed their patronage. It had cost a pretty penny to put in the new reflector sconces around the walls, and the fancy paraffin lamp with its tall chimney hanging above the bartop that Sarah had wanted, but, he had to confess, she'd been right. With a pulley rope tied against the wall, it had made a big difference when lowering it to extinguish the flame and raising it again when relit. The light was much brighter, and the new paraffin wax candles meant the air was nowhere near as smoky.

He stared at the two men a second longer. "Money first, then," he agreed as he held his hand out for the coins.

Jacob sent Sarah to the kitchen to fetch the pies. Molly had been busy, but the batch intended for the evening supper was not yet ready. Sarah found a large pie from the day before in the larder and cut off two hefty slices and shoved them on a tray in the already hot oven. Hoping to heat them quickly, she added more wood to the firebox and fanned the flames, which brought Molly hurrying to take over as smoke billowed into the room.

"Let me, miss. She's a tricky beast at times." Molly quickly poked the fire, flapped the long grey apron worn over her grey dress, to disperse the smoke, and opened the flues, seemingly without effort. Dark-haired and pale-faced, the girl looked like a wraith who'd blow away in a good gust of wind.

Sarah stepped back without a word, knowing her haste had caused the problem and only because of how flustered she was. "I'll be back shortly," she murmured and fled out the back door to gather her wits.

What had just come over her?

She knew of Tom and John from long ago, but they'd been young men back then who couldn't be bothered with little girls. These days, they worked the larger shipping vessels that travelled farther afield than the Channel trows and were often away for long periods of time. But they'd been regular customers once and sometimes lodgers over the years.

Her father's reaction to John's attention had come as a surprise. She wasn't a little girl any more and sooner or later would be expected to marry. But how could she do that and keep her promise to her father?

In her dreams, her fantasies about the future, she had hoped that one day she would fall in love – whatever that was – and live a better life than the drudgery she saw around her. Women weighed down by overwork, with too many children, and too much loss; women who were downtrodden and miserable.

She wanted ... She quashed those thoughts before they were fully framed. There was no point in dreams. The reality was she had responsibilities, and if Mary and Harriet were anything to go by, hard work and pregnancy would be her lot in life too.

* * * * *

She'd not seen John or his mate for several days. Busily wiping down tables and stacking the empty tankards and dirty plates, she wondered if she would see him again or if he'd already sailed. Humming to herself as she worked, she jumped when he came up quietly behind her and whispered hello in her ear. She spun around to face him, and felt her skin heat up and her heart flutter. He stood so close she leaned backwards trying to put space between them, one hand still clutching the damp cloth pressed against her chest.

"Are ya not pleased to see me?" he asked with that captivating grin.

She glanced around to see who might be watching but no one was paying them any attention. "Um, well, yes, if you like. Is there summat I can get for ya?"

"I can't stay, ma sweet pea. Just came to say farewell. My ship sails on the tide, but I couldna leave without seeing ya again."

"That's nice." She turned to pick up the pile of plates she'd gathered as her heart fluttered. "Have a good trip then," she added, her back to him.

What was the matter with her? She wasn't usually so put out.

"Is that all ya can say to a man about to embark on a dangerous journey?"

"Dangerous?" A sense of panic that he might not return filled her with dismay. She dropped the plates back on the table with a clatter and swivelled around to face him again. "Is it really? More'n usual?"

"No more or less," he reassured her with a wink, "but every trip has its dangers. Wish me well, sweet Sarah." He took her hand in his and held it to his lips.

She pulled it away, not knowing what to think. This wasn't behaviour she was used to. John wasn't some smooth-talking swell, one she would distrust on sight; he was a mariner, a local, someone she knew. Why was he talking like that?

"Go well, and may you have fair winds and following tides." She murmured the traditional blessing, knowing how superstitious sailors could be.

After a quick glance around, he dropped a brief kiss on her cheek before walking out the door.

She stood staring after him through the empty doorway, her hand on her face where his lips had touched her skin, wondering if she was experiencing those feelings of love she'd heard so much about. Surely not; he was several years older than her and nothing like the man she imagined in her dreams.

2
Mary's intervention

May 1851

The weeks passed and thoughts of that fleeting moment before John left were swallowed by the busyness of Sarah's days. "How ya feeling, Ma?" she asked as she took her mother a cup of tea first thing. "Molly's already in the kitchen." She pulled back the curtains to let in the morning light, pausing for a moment to look out at the masts piercing the sky up and down the river she loved so much. Briefly, she let herself think of the mast John sailed under and when, or if, he might return.

"What ya looking at, girl?" her mother's croaky voice asked.

"Just the ships at anchor."

"Hmmph," came a guttural response. "After a boy, are ya? Well, be it on your own head, girl. Tis a lonely life you're choosing if'n you plan to be tied to a mariner."

Sarah pulled her gaze from the window and crossed to the bed. "Not at all, I'm not. And there be plenny-o-time to think on that later. Now, will you be about making our favourite pies this day?" she asked as she fussed around her mother.

Helping her to sit up, plumping up some pillows, and pushing aside any ideas about John, Sarah tidied the bedclothes before handing over the cup and saucer. Even when he returned, he might not call to see her. Silly of her to think otherwise.

"She's a good maid, that Molly, but nay, I feel so cast down I don't think I'll venture below today."

Sarah sighed inwardly, responsibility weighing on her shoulders. She had no idea how to help her mother, but what she did know was that without her up and around, her own workload increased tenfold. When Ma lay abed, Sarah found herself constantly up and down the stairs at her beck and call.

Betsey laid her head, encased in a lace nightcap, back on the pillows, the teacup and saucer tilting precariously sideways. "I feel so tired, Sarah, I can barely lift me arms." Her eyes closed and Sarah rescued the china before it fell. They had few enough pieces of good china as it was.

"'Tis sad ya feel so poorly, Ma. I miss your teachings around the household."

She kissed her mother's brow. Betsey's eyes remained closed as she murmured, "I've nuffin' left to teach ya, my girl. It's up to you now."

Sarah wasn't sure what her mother meant. What was up to her? The workload certainly was, but not much else.

"You'll be feeling right as rain soon, Ma. I'm sure of it. Think about all the lovely times we've had. I hear Mary's coming up on the train for a visit next week. Gert news, i'nit?"

She hoped news of Mary's visit would cheer her mother. There was only the three of them now. Not that Sarah really knew her sisters well. Mary was over two decades older than her, and had married the year of Sarah's birth. She lived in a village near Bath with her stonemason husband and their family.

"She's coming to see Ted, is she, lovey?" asked Betsey, her once-white nightgown tightly tied at the throat. "That lad is such a let-down to your father."

Two years younger than Sarah, Ted had been sent to live with his grandparents a year or so back. In that time, she had grown fond of her nephew. He made her laugh.

"That ain't fair, Ma. Ted's just naturally clever with his numbers. It's good he's been 'prenticed to learn the ledgers the right way."

"But while he's doing that, he's not doing what he's supposed to be. He should be helpin' your father."

Sarah's eyes watered. Betsey rarely gave her credit for any of the work she did and certainly not the business side of things. She could never imagine a woman running an inn. Their place was in the kitchen and having babies. But if having and losing babies was all there was to life, then Sarah didn't want a bar of it. "I do me best," she whispered.

"Aye, I know you do, girl, but you'll find a fella soon nuff and be gone. Just like your sisters, and then what, I ask ya? What's left in life after they've all gone? When all the little ones are gone."

Betsey's head dropped forward as her mind drifted to the past.

Sarah slipped from the room as gentle snores indicated her mother had found a different sort of peace.

Her folks had lived in Mary's village for a while, after the two younger Sarahs had died, or so she'd been told. 'To get away from the memories,' Ma had said.

Da had been a grocer in those days, selling fresh foods to the markets. Sarah's middle sister, Harriet, halfway between Mary and her, who she rarely saw now as she lived far away in Wales, was born there. Then another tragedy beset them.

'We lost our boy, our precious only son,' Ma often bemoaned. 'He weren't even two when 'e was taken from us. Taken too soon.' And she'd wipe her tears and withdraw into the darkness that held her.

'We needed to start a new life,' Da had explained. 'Something to give us hope and a future.'

Da and Ma returned to Bristol and set themselves up in an inn, leaving seven-year-old Harriet to be raised by Mary. The two older sisters were close, despite the age difference. Sarah, being that much younger again, they treated as a child. But she wasn't. Not any more.

Even so, she was glad Mary was coming and hoped her sister might be able to say something to stir Ma.

And maybe she could ask Mary about John.

* * * * *

"Course you can do it, Ma," said Mary, showing everyone the news articles about the Great Exhibition at the wonderful new Crystal Palace in London. "We'll all go together on the train. It's not too long a journey."

"But what about Harriet?" whined Betsey.

Mary kept a happy smile on her face. "It's too far for Harriet to come up from Wales, and besides, she's big with child and has too many youngsters underfoot to consider it. Sarah should come, though."

"Oh, no. That wouldn't do," snapped Betsey. "She needs to stay at home with your father and help him. I won't leave 'im on his own."

Sarah held back a retort of resentment at the rising disappointment. The Crystal Palace sounded amazing, with all its glittering windows. She didn't know anything about the industry displays or any of the science, but she'd never know if she didn't go to places to learn. "Wouldn't it be amazing if Queen Victoria or Prince Albert was there," she enthused.

"It would indeed." Mary winked. "I could always ask Aunt Nettie to come in for a few hours to fill in for Sarah. She really should come with us, Ma. It'd be such an experience for us all."

Aunt Nettie lived out at Bitton, more than seven miles away, so if Nettie could find time, and transport, to get away from the family's cordwaining business, then why wasn't *she* allowed, fumed Sarah inwardly.

Betsey pulled her woollen shawl more tightly around her and grimaced. "She's too young. She knows nuffin'."

"And neither will she if she's not able to visit new places." Mary pushed her plea. "I'd like Sarah to come with me. It's been ages since we had time to talk."

Sarah didn't know how Mary kept so calm. She wanted to scream. Ma was being so unreasonable, and unfair.

"Well, that's not my fault," huffed Ma. "If I agree to go – and I haven't said I will yet – then I want Nettie to come with me. There's plenty of time for Sarah, but Nettie's getting on now."

"All the more reason. This is a once-in-a-lifetime opportunity, it says. I'll get my Ted to help Da. It's his half-day, so there's no excuses."

Mary smiled in triumph when there was no further rebuff to her plan. "That's settled then, we shall all go. On Wednesday. I'll get four tickets."

Betsey glared at her. "I'm surprised at ya. Taken in by all that frippery. Waste of money. Well, I'm not going!"

But she did.

* * * * *

"Look at all these people," said Sarah, as the four women pushed their way through the crowds lining the station platform. "Are they all getting on the train? Will there be room for us?" Nerves were getting the better of her common sense in her eagerness to get there.

Mary placed a reassuring hand on her arm. "Most of 'em are here to watch the train leave. They can't go themselves, but wanna see who can afford to go to London for such a special event. I must say you are looking very pretty today."

At a cost of one shilling each entry fee, plus the train fare, today was going to be an expensive day out, but Mary had persuaded them all around and cajoled the money from their menfolk.

"Yer tiz, Ma," said Mary as the train rumbled to a stop in front of them. "You and Aunt Nettie climb aboard and make yourselves comfortable."

Once they were settled, it was only a matter of minutes before they heard the whistle, and the train began to move. People waved to them as they departed and Sarah's spirits lifted. Nothing this exciting had happened to her before, if she discounted John.

She'd not had the chance to ask Mary what it all meant, but she hoped they'd have some time alone as they wandered around. It looked like Ma and Aunt Nettie would be inseparable.

Where Mary got her confidence from was a mystery to Sarah. Thrust into the throngs of London, the noise and constant movement unsettled her, but Mary soon had them off the train, into a hackney and entering the great Crystal Palace building.

"Oh my, Mary. I've never seen anything like it in me life. Look at the trees growing inside, and those enormous plants over there, and the fountain!" She did a twirl, hand on hat to keep it in place and, flushed with excitement, didn't notice the admiring gazes from passing strangers.

Wide-eyed, she tried to capture everything in one turn. People billowed all around her, but the place was so vast she didn't feel hemmed in.

"Stop gushing, Sarah. And keep your voice down," hissed Ma. "We don't want everyone to think we're country bumpkins who don't know no better."

Exasperated, Sarah linked her arm through Mary's as they made their way around the displays. The machinery demonstrations that attracted quite a large male crowd held little to no interest to Ma as she and Aunt Nettie strode on past, but then Sarah heard her mother gasp.

"Isn't that the most beautiful vase you've ever seen? I must have one."

"The sign says it's called *ma-jol-ic-a* work by Minton," said Nettie, sounding out the unusual name.

"It's gorgeous, but it looks very expensive."

"Never mind that. I'll be making enquiries, I will. Now, what else is there to see?"

Sarah subdued a grin as Ma and Aunt Nettie once again sailed forth, skirts swaying as they hurried to see the exhibits from India and New Zealand, as well as those from Sweden and Norway and various parts of Europe and Asia. Their sudden enthusiasm let her off the hook.

They oohed and ahhed at the Koh-i-noor, reputedly the largest cut diamond in the world, and at the similarly large rectangular pink Darya-ye-Noor diamond, said to be the rarest, but they spent much of their time at the daguerreotype stand learning about photography.

Mary whispered, "What's the chances Ma will insist we all need our images captured?"

"Very high," agreed Sarah, nodding towards their mother who was already sitting in place to have her photograph taken. She tugged on Mary's arm, leading her away. "Could we look over here for a moment?"

"What's caught your eye, little sister?"

"Nothing, really. I wanted … well, that is …" she paused, suddenly uncertain. "Can I ask ya summat? Um. Personal."

"Course ya can, kid. What is it?" Mary took both Sarah's hands in hers. "Whadya want to know? You look flummoxed."

Sarah nodded. "The truth is, I rather feel that way. Summat happened and I don't know what it means."

"Go on, this sounds interesting, but let's keep walking so Ma don't call us back."

Linking arms again, they continued their stroll and disappeared into the crowds.

Mary listened intently while Sarah stammered out her concerns.

"I've never felt anything like that before. I didn't know a body could … well, um, tingle, I suppose, in, ya know, places …" Her voice faded to a bare whisper. Sarah turned her head to hide the distinctive pink flush.

She sensed Mary trying to control laughter beside her. Miffed, Sarah demanded, "What's so funny?"

"Nothing, my sweet girl, nothing at all. I'm glad to know you're growing up and becoming a woman. Those feelings will help you find the right man, cos whoever he is, however good he sounds, however important he may be, he'll not be the man for you without them."

Sarah opened her mouth to say something and shut it again, suddenly speechless.

"It's quite normal, Sarah," Mary said, patting her younger sister's hand. "Shall we find the others and take tea?"

3
Growing up

Welsh Back
September 1852

Sarah stood at the inn door looking wistfully across the Back to the various sailing craft going about their business. A full year and more had passed since the unforgettable visit to the Great Exhibition, and Sarah wondered what would become of her. Not that she would ever be one of those wealthy young misses with their airs and graces, attending the London Season, but she did yearn for some excitement. Something to change the monotony of the days, and she wouldn't mind a pretty new dress, but that wasn't likely either. She never went anywhere to justify the cost.

She'd be eighteen before the year was done and would soon be an old maid if she didn't find a husband before long. Except, if she took a husband, how would she fulfil her promise to her da?

She could hear the slap of rope against the masts and shivered in the cool breeze flapping the sails as a warning of the cold, dark months ahead. The more summer faded, the harder she tried to shake off the gloomy thoughts of late, worried in part that she was catching her mother's woefulness, even though she had little to complain about. While Ma still had her melancholy moments, she was much better, thanks to Mary's intervention last year. She was back in the kitchen, teaching Molly more about running an efficient operation. Ma said she enjoyed cooking, but apart from that, she left the running of the business to Jacob, and he left much of it to Sarah.

Was that what she wanted from life? Being tied to the inn, responsible for the care of her parents, doing the same chores day in and day out, never to know anything different? Seeing the Crystal Palace had shown her so many unusual and inspiring things that, since then, she'd felt … not quite trapped, but not free either.

"Will I see ya in later, Mister Bob?" she called to one of the many sailors working the ropes and unloading goods.

He waved back. "Sure will. Lookin' forward to one of your special smiles and ya ma's cookin'."

For a man of his age, Da was keeping in very good health and maintained a cheerful visage for all the customers, but Sarah knew she was the drawcard. She could flirt and banter with the best of them, and, in truth, she enjoyed the jesting. Not only did it increase business, but it took her mind off John and his infrequent visits.

She let out a sigh and returned to cleaning the tables ready for the lunchtime arrivals. She didn't know what to make of the situation with John. Every time she'd seen him, it had been the same. He – full of chatter and charm and hints. She – pretending it didn't matter, while her body betrayed her with its shivers and gooseflesh. But their meetings had been so fleeting and so far apart.

'I'm only home for a few days, me darlin', afore me ship sails again,' she'd recalled his words often in the months since he'd last called in. 'Ah. But it's good to see ya, my little grown-up Sarah. You make me 'eart sing.'

But then he'd be gone again, sometimes for months on end, and all she had was memories. She tried not to let her imagination run away with ideas that led nowhere, but there were times she dreamt that one of those masts would take her away to somewhere exotic.

"Have ya seen the news?"

Her dispirited thoughts were instantly swept away as her nephew Ted raced into the inn waving the *Bristol Times* above his head.

"Whadya talking about, lad?" asked Jacob.

"Wellington. He's dead."

Sarah had no time to catch her breath or gather her thoughts to say anything before several more men came rushing in babbling about the same news, in their rough dialect.

"Beer, landlord!"

Jacob started pulling handles and Sarah quickly distributed them, trying to pick up snippets of conversation to work out what had happened.

"He were old, mind. Well over eighty."

"But 'e were a gert man, mind. A good soldier."

"An' a politician."

"He weren't no good at bein' prime minister, in ma opinion, but, aye, he were a gert military man. I'll give 'im that."

"True. True. A real hero to me, 'e was."

Sarah gathered empty mugs and delivered full ones as the room filled with more and more people who had come to tell their stories and share their memories.

A one-legged old man limped in on his crutch. Medals hung from faded ribbons on his jacket several sizes too large for his gaunt frame. "Fanks to 'im we're still British 'n that upstart Napoleon got 'is comeuppance."

He set himself up in the corner between the fireplace and the bar and began to talk about his campaign days with His Grace. "Clever general, 'e were. I r'member one battle when 'e outfoxed 'em all …"

"Who're they talking about, Da?" she asked quietly while waiting for the next batch of scrumpy to be drawn.

Jacob never took his eyes off the beer he was pouring, intent on not wasting a drop. "The gert man hisself. The Duke of Wellington."

"I don't remember him. Were he prime minister?" Sarah dipped the empty mugs in a bucket and rinsed them before stacking them up ready for Jacob to refill.

"Before your time, girlie. Back in the late '20s 'n '30s. Earned himself the nickname 'The Iron Duke'. Some say cos of the iron bars he put on his home to keep protesters out; others say cos he were a hard man. Tough on 'is men. Too set in 'is ways and right stubborn he were about things. Hated the Jews and favoured the Catholics. Now, enough gabbing. Get these delivered."

Carrying two tankards in each hand, she took them to the drinkers, still listening for odd bits of conversation, sometimes stalling by wiping up spills with the cloth tucked into her apron.

Another man, sporting an eye patch, had joined the old soldier, and the two were deep in conversation when she delivered their ale. She glanced at the fire she had lit earlier that day to see all that remained were dying embers. It would take some effort to resurrect it, but she doubted 'twould be needed now. The room was warm with so many extra men, and the air already thick with the odour of unwashed bodies, stale brine and pipe smoke.

"He weren't popular with many after he refused to support that Reform Act."

"That were twenty year ago, man. Don't be 'arpin' on. Was the right thing. Who wants women and riff-raff voting?"

"But tain't fair. Every man should 'ave a say in gov'ment. They work for us."

Someone laughed. "Fine thing, if'n it were true. They just line their own pockets and be damned with the rest of us."

But she still didn't get a sense of why one man's death was such big news. Every time she paused to listen, someone asked for more ale and once one started, they all began to order bread and cheese, or a slice of pie, or a stack of roast meat. She found herself racing between kitchen and bar, trying to be all things to all people while not slipping on the increasingly wet, sticky floor.

The heat rose higher within the confines of the thick stone walls and, even though the door was open, little breeze flowed through. She wiped her forehead with her sleeve and gathered more jugs of ale. Jacob would be pleased at the extra income, but the crush of people was testing her patience. She didn't usually feel this betwaddled.

Then the singing started. A croaky voice began to hum a strain of music. The old veterans stopped talking and a few picked up the tune. She recognised a section from 'Rule Britannia', but the words were different, and then the melody changed again and she heard a piece that sounded like 'For He's a Jolly Good Fellow'. She listened as the voices gathered strength, memories kicking into place, and now it sounded more like 'God Save The King'.

They say that I don't belong
Say that I should retreat
That I'm marching to the rhythm
Of a lonesome defeat

But the sound of your voice
Puts the pain in reverse
No surrender, no illusions
And for better or worse

When they turn down the lights
I hear my battle symphony

She found Ted in the midst of the throng, leaning on a bench, drink in hand, listening.

"Hey. You could give me a hand, 'n all, ya lump."

"T'nit marvellous, Salls?" said her nephew, ignoring her comment. "Remembering a hero like that."

Sarah bumped him sideways with her hip and reached for the empty mugs and platters on the counters. "Twould be if'n I had time to make out what's going on. What're they singing anyway? It's sounding the same to me." She had to stand on tiptoe to hear what he was saying above the din.

"Sections from 'Wellington's Victory'. Beethoven wrote it back in 1813 after Wellington defeated Bonaparte at the Battle of Vittoria. It's too long and too hard to sing all of it, so they just do the best-known parts."

She looked blankly at him. "What? How d'ya know all that?"

Ted shrugged. "How do I know anything? I read. I ask questions. I listen." He grinned cheekily.

"Huh! Lucky for some."

She was thankful that she could read, but she had so little time to herself, let alone spare moments to listen to discussions and ask questions. Sunday mornings were her best chance. She'd begun attending the weekly book readings after church a few years earlier, when her reading wasn't so good. She had learnt new words and new ways to say them. Not that they were much use in the pub. But she liked to say her words properly. These days, she could afford her own copy of the stories and was quite fluent, even if she did say so herself. That hour was the best hour of the entire week.

This year, they were reading Charles Dickens's *Bleak House* in the monthly serials, but she found it was living up to its name, being very desolate and dreary. She much preferred his *David Copperfield,* which they'd read a couple of years back. She could relate better to the young character who struggled through some hard times but found love after all.

Sarah longed for love. For better times, when something delightful might happen and … she blocked her thoughts before they started to run away with her again. It was no good wishing.

She still liked to read *David Copperfield* now and again when she had enough light and time before her eyes closed from exhaustion.

She shrugged. With her hands full of dirty mugs and dishes, she headed to the kitchen, answering those who called for more ale as she passed, wishing once again for the choices men like Ted had.

* * * * *

For the next couple of months, as she went about serving the customers, all she heard was talk about the state funeral Queen Victoria planned for the duke on 18th November.

"It's gonna to cost a fortune, mind. £10,000 I heard," said one in a group of six leaning on the counters, swallowing ale faster than she could deliver it.

"He deserves the best, whatever it costs. The Queen is insisting 'e be buried in St Paul's Cathedral, no less."

"But didn't I 'ear he wanted to be buried at Walmer Castle?"

"Where's that?" Sarah asked, remembering what Ted had said about learning new things.

One of the men who sailed the coastlines wiped his lips with his sleeve before speaking. "One of Henry VIII's old forts down Kent way."

She didn't really know where Kent was. She'd never travelled that far. They went to Bath sometimes when she visited Mary once or twice a year. And she'd never forget her one and only trip to London. She stared longingly at the masts outside the window, thinking she'd like to travel one day and see more places.

"Sarah!" Her father's voice pulled her away.

"Sorry, Da. I got caught up listening to news about the duke's funeral."

"You don't have time for that, lass, and tis nuffin' to you, anyway. None of us'll be going."

"But we can read about it in the newspapers," she suggested.

"What's the point? We all know what 'appens."

She could hardly argue with him about that. People died all the time, families grieved, the bodies were quickly buried, and people soon went about their business again. Why did a duke's funeral seem more important? There was nothing as heartbreaking as losing one of your own, someone you loved, but listening to them talk about this stranger, you'd think he'd been someone close.

Throughout the week leading up to the funeral, the newspapers were full of it. Sarah glued her eyes to the reports every moment she had. The enormous solid-bronze funeral car, and the twelve matching black draught horses drawing it, each with a dramatic plume of black ostrich feathers; the exact route – not that she knew which way was which, nor had she seen many of the landmarks mentioned; the thousands of troops involved in the procession; and the throngs of people at St Paul's Cathedral for the service and interment. And Queen Victoria's involvement and how upset she'd become.

The whole affair fascinated and annoyed Sarah at the same time. Why couldn't she see all these wonderful things? Why were people like her expected to know their place and behave accordingly? Was her life so mapped out she had no say in what happened?

4
The promise of love

November 1853

"Al'right, me luvver? How's me favourite maid?"

Sarah twirled at the sound of the voice she had longed to hear. She smiled sweetly but tried not to show the surge of emotion she felt at the sight of the man she'd pined for.

"Al'right yourself," she said, noting John's full beard, dirt-encrusted hands and weary face. But his eyes still sparkled the way she remembered, and her heart beat faster than ever when he stepped towards her. A calloused finger gently stroked her cheek, and those tingles she'd been so frightened of once, stirred her into life. "What brings ya back after so long?"

"Ye."

She scoffed. "It's been many a month, and many more afore that, laddie. Ya must've met up with lots of other barmaids in your travels, but I've a feelin' your favourite girl is the one standing closest to ya. When d'ya get in?"

"On the night tide. Came as soon as I could, and aye, I've been to lots o' bars and met a great number o' barmaids in many parts o' this strange world, but none that hold a candle to ye."

Taken aback by his fancy words, Sarah replied, "Well, it's nice to see you too. What can I get ya?"

"Some scrumpy would be good, 'n a room, a shave and a bath?"

"I can give ya two of those." She handed him the pint she expertly poured and pointed to the stairs, trying to quell the thought of him lying under the same roof as her. "Third room on the left is free. How long ya staying?"

"A few weeks, I hope."

So too did she.

Not that she'd let on, but she'd carried a torch for John for three long years and never faltered. She always remembered Mary's words when she was barely sixteen. And her sister had been right; none of the men who'd made a play for her, none who had caught her eye, none that her parents encouraged, had made her feel the way John did.

But then much of her life had not changed since then. Her mother was as querulous and melancholic as ever, her father stoic. Their options were few. Without Sarah more or less running the inn, where would they be? Oh, the licence was still in her father's name, and her mother ostensibly still ran the kitchen, even though Molly, loyal as ever, did all the work, but in truth, there wasn't anything Sarah didn't know about the business. She couldn't leave them. Not then, not now. "Sorry, whadya say? I was away with the fairies, that I was."

John grinned in that special way and her insides melted. "I were saying, there's no place like 'ome, and this is 'ome to me."

Sarah laughed, trying to hide the blush infusing her entire body. "Get away with ya now. Tis just as it's always been. A humble inn offering the best it can, just like all the dozen others roundabouts."

"Aye, that's true, but none of 'em have you at the helm."

Lost for words, Sarah couldn't find the usual banter she used for any suggestive comments the regulars threw at her, but this was different. These were words she'd longed to hear. Could she dream, after all?

Before she could speak, the moment was lost.

"Ah, John Clements. Good to see ya back again, lad," said her father.

He reached out and the pair shook hands. "Thanks, Mr Daniels. It's good to see ya. I were just telling Sarah that a moment ago."

"Pour us an 'alf, Sarah luv. I'll sit with John a wee while if ya can manage."

"'Course I can, Da. Yer tiz."

Sarah sighed in relief when she saw her da and John take the table by the wall closest to the bar. She'd be able to listen in while she worked. And listen in she did, ears keenly attuned to John's voice while he talked about all the exotic ports, foods and spices, furniture and fabrics that could only be bought in foreign lands. She remembered some of the things she'd seen at the Great Exhibition back in '51, and while part of her yearned for knowledge beyond these four walls, she knew in her heart she was destined never to experience any.

In between serving the steady stream of customers, answering her mother's calls from the kitchen and delivering food to the tables, she missed some of John's stories. Maybe if he was here for a while she – and he – could find time for him to tell her some tales himself.

Her ears picked up a change of tone.

"I've only got one more long trip in me, Mr Daniels; eighteen months at most. Then I wanna settle down. Work the local waters. Tis a tough life. All 'ard work, and lonely too, with only crusty ol' tars for company. I don't wanna become like them."

Da said something she didn't catch.

John chuckled. She loved the throaty sound. "Nuffin' be as good as 'ome, Mr Daniels. Nuffin'. And no sight as gert as the shores of good ol' Britain and hearing the voices of people ya know and luv."

"Good to have ya back. I'd best get back to work," said Jacob, rising. "Get yourself cleaned up and settled. We'll talk more later."

"What was that all about, Da?" she asked innocently.

"Just chatter. Catchin' up on the news both here and abroad. Nothing to worry your head about."

She didn't believe him, but let it go. For now.

Sarah was beside herself with joy when she learned John intended to take on shorter, more local trips for a few months while the shipping company readied the ocean-going ship for its next long journey.

"Like I said to your da, I've one more big trip in me, and then I'm 'ome for good. But for now, 'twill be a nice change. Like a rest, 'twill. We can get to know each other better. Would ya like that?"

Sarah pulled at a tendril that had fallen beside her cheek and tried to look coy while her heart soared. "That'd be nice."

His eyes, redolent of the sea, shone as his smile broadened and her insides trembled. "Aye. I think I'm gonna like being around more. It's gonna be different, I can tell ya that. These docks are a marvel. Peaceful and calm now inside this 'ere floating harbour, 'n no more risk of getting stuck in the mud at the bottom when the tide goes out. But navigatin' that river, the estuary and the channel beyond is still tough goin'. Those tides can be a killer."

She looked at him sceptically. "Don't everyone know that? Even I know the tides can vary by more'n thirty or forty feet in the channel."

He didn't look pleased at being corrected. "Aye, everyone what's lived in these parts knows that, but it's the current what catches people out. The pull is fast, specially when the moon's full. It's not for the faint-hearted."

"If it's so dangerous, why d'ya do it?"

"For the money, course. Can't settle down else." He winked. "Don't you wanna see me round more often?"

"Course I do, silly," she blushed.

Their banter continued as he came and went. Sometimes, he'd be gone for a few days, sometimes she'd see him every day. As the months passed, she felt comforted knowing he was close by and longed to see him come through the door, knowing they both slept under the same roof.

With each wink, each smile, each subtle touch, she gave more of her heart to him.

April 1854

Sarah's eyes flicked open to see fingers of moonlight streaking across her cotton counterpane through the tiny window in the attic. Alert now, she listened for the sound that had disturbed her. She usually slept through all the comings and goings of the sailors who stayed at the inn. The old building often creaked and groaned at all hours of the night, but this was different. This was closer.

She lay perfectly still, listening intently. A slight scratching noise. A tiny squeak. Instinctively, she knew the sounds were coming through the wall directly behind her. Her eyes were drawn to a merest change in the shadows and dilated as she saw the door at the foot of her bed open a chink. She watched as the gap widened enough to let a figure in and close again. Every nerve end twitched, and she felt sure the thumping of her heart could be heard by whoever had entered.

She'd had many a drunken and lost sailor crashing into her room in times past, thinking they were going to their own bed, but this was too furtive to be a mistake. Her throat tightened, and she felt incapable of sound, until her nostrils detected a scent she knew.

"John?" she whispered.

A second later, a hand clasped over her mouth and a weight sank onto the side of the bed, a shadow blocking the moonlight. He leant forward and whispered into her ear. "Aye, tis me. I 'ad to see ya. We sail on the tide."

Her eyes did the talking, questioning. Why? He wasn't due to leave yet.

His lips began to caress her ear, her neck, her chin, her lips. "Quick change-a plans. Just 'cross the Atlantic, sweet pea," he explained as he explored. "A few short months and I'll be back. Oh, Salls, 'twill be hard to leave ya. Can you give a man summat to remember?"

She sank back slightly into the pillow. "We shouldn't be doing this," she hissed.

"I can't leave without your sweet kiss," he mumbled against her skin. "Are we not near on promised to each other?"

"Are we?" Her skin tingled with anticipation as much as her heart beat guiltily in her chest.

He simply nodded as he nestled deeper against her throat. His calloused fingers gently ran up and down her arm, across the front of her nightdress, undoing the ribbons and down to her tummy button. She moaned with a burning intensity she didn't fully understand but knew she couldn't resist. Her arms crept about his neck as she offered her lips to his. She melted into a kiss like nothing she'd ever experienced, her body spontaneously arching, craving more. Much more.

He left as quietly as he'd come and only she would ever know he'd been there. She'd been a girl when he came and was a woman when he left. She clutched her arms around her, trying to retain the feeling of joy, the warmth, the overwhelming fervour of emotion and passion that still enveloped her. She lay there, the damp soreness between her thighs reminding her of every delicious moment.

How she went about her daily duties without everyone asking what had caused her to be so perky she didn't know, but she was determined to keep this secret to herself until John came back to claim her.

Didn't he say as much? Just a few short months and he'd be back, and she'd be his for all the world to see.

But her da noticed. "Full of the joys of spring this morning, are ya, lass?"

"And why not, Da? The sun's a-shining, birds're singing and afore long all the trees'll be in full leaf. What reason is there not to be happy?"

Jacob chuckled. "No reason at all, lass. No reason at all."

The day passed in a whirl as she chatted to customers, never giving a moment's thought to all the talk of war in the Crimea, a place she'd never heard of. Neither did she take any notice of her mother's grumps over the slightest thing.

"Whadsup with ya, girl?" she demanded as Sarah flitted in and out of the kitchen bringing empty plates back and carrying full ones out to the customers. "Can ya no stand still for one minute and do a proper job?"

"Sorry, Ma. I thought these plates were ready to go. Shall I stay and fill more?"

"No. No. Stupid girl. Take them while they're 'ot or else we'll get complaints."

"I'll help with the dishes then, when I get a moment. That'll save ya."

"You will not. That's Molly's job. Your job is to keep the customers 'appy. Now be off with ya."

Sarah was too happy to even get cross with her mother's contrariness today. At least she was in the kitchen and not moping in her room, as was still her wont from time to time.

The euphoria lasted for several weeks as she counted them off, hoping John'd be back before the end of summer so they could be wed while the weather held. Midway through June she began to feel queasy some mornings and often had to run to the privy or worse, sometimes use the chamber pot, and then try to sneak down without anyone seeing her so she could empty it. Thankfully, whatever the problem was soon passed and she felt content and satisfied with herself most days.

But time was slipping by and there was no word from John. It looked like a summer wedding was unlikely after all.

Sarah was in the kitchen one early August morning, tasting morsels of the food spread out on the table. A bit of pie, a sweet cookie, a dainty sponge. Ma and Molly were such good cooks, she thought, as she sampled some more. She was constantly hungry these days and had developed a taste for the local scrumpy to quench her thirst when the air turned sultry after a summer storm.

"Tis so hot," she moaned, loosening the buttons at her neck, swallowing another pot.

"A good cuppa would be better for ya than that there scrumpy, mind," said her mother filling the teapot.

Sarah smiled inwardly at the contrast between Ma and Molly. Ma, who enjoyed sampling her own food and had a figure to prove it, quite overwhelmed the girl, while Molly remained as thin as ever.

"No ta, Ma. It makes me feel even hotter."

She stood by the kitchen door seeking whatever breeze might be had but soon turned back to the table for more to eat.

"And you'd better stop that eatin' too. You're getting podgy." Betsey glared at her daughter. "If I didna know better, I'd say ya were with child. That I would."

Sarah froze. Her hand halfway to her mouth.

She dropped what she was going to eat and brushed her hands together to clean them of crumbs. "Podgy!" she exclaimed as indignantly as she could as realisation hit home. "That's not a nice thing to say. Not at all."

Sarah lifted her skirts and pounded up the stairs to her room. She shut the door, leaning back against it with her eyes closed, fighting back tears. Endless thoughts swept through her brain. How could she have been so stupid? And why hadn't she seen the changes? She'd never even considered the possibility. The more she thought about it, the more reality sank in.

She was carrying John's child and had no idea where he was or when he'd be home.

What should she do? If her mother had spotted it, so would others. Should she confess her sin to God? But how that would help her situation she had no idea. If she told her mother the truth, how would she react? Sarah blushed with shame. The thought of letting her da down was more than she could bear. He thought the world of her, and she had promised to help him run the inn. She couldn't do that with a big belly or a squalling baby.

"Dear God, help me," she muttered, fully aware that she was in a predicament of her own doing, and had to stand on her own two feet to deal with it. But how?

One thing for certain, she couldn't hang around in her room all day feeling sorry for herself. She washed her face and combed her hair, retying the ribbon before she returned to the barroom. At least she could ask some questions and see if anyone had heard of John or his ship.

"What's the name of his ship, lass? He might've got caught up with these doings in Crimea."

Sarah withheld the gasp as panic set in. She couldn't lose him, not now – not to some stupid battle. He was a merchant trader not a naval man. Her mind scrambled for an answer. He'd not told her the ship's name. Only that he'd be away for a few months but that was four months ago. How many was a few?

"You know me, Mr Tanner," she teased, "I'd forget me own name if someone didn't call me by it every few minutes. He's been on so many, I can't say which one is which, but I do remember this one was different. This passage was across the Atlantic."

"Then he'll be safe from the battles at least. I'll ask around for ya, Sarah," he winked emphasising her name. "He can't be far away."

Sarah hoped so. Whatever was happening between the Russians and the Turks was more than she could bear to think about, but if he wasn't in that part of the world, maybe all would be well.

Her mother didn't make any other scathing comments in the days that followed, and Sarah relaxed a little, although she did tighten her stays a smidgen and determinedly did not eat anywhere near as much. Especially when her mother was looking.

"You're looking right rosy these days, ma girl,"

said her da, adding to her nervousness. "Real healthy. Enjoying life, are ya?"

"I am that, Da. Why wouldn't I be? I've a gert life and the best da in the world."

She kissed his whiskered cheek and patted his chest. Did she really look that different for him to comment? Had anyone else noticed?

She sent up another prayer that John would come home soon.

5
The test of love

She saw him before he saw her.

Standing behind the bar, partially hidden in the shadows, Sarah instinctively turned when new customers arrived. As if in answer to her prayers, John appeared in the doorway, looking left and right. She thought he'd come looking for her, but he headed towards two men at one of the trestles. She couldn't hear what was being said, but John was obviously angry. Before long, arms began to wave. One man pushed John, and fingers were pointed.

"Now then, lads," said Jacob kindly when he saw trouble brewing. "I think you should all leave afore whatever this is gets out of 'and." He held his arms out, directing all three of them to the door. "Come along, now. You'll be welcome back later after you've sorted your problems."

Surprised the men left, if not meekly then amenable to Jacob's request, her spirits sank as she watched John go. She was in such a turmoil. Nauseous with worry, her body ached, she wanted him so much. But after what she'd just witnessed, she was fearful, and her heart reached out to his. If he loved her, surely he'd sense her need. Her mind reeled. What would she say to him? How would he take her news? Would he be pleased or angry?

Whatever his reaction, she had to tell him. She hoped and prayed he was the man she thought he was and would make an honest woman of her. But was that what she wanted?

Hours passed before Sarah saw John again, but she'd been so busy with customers she missed seeing him arrive. Only when he came up behind her, after she'd put several tankards on the table for the drinkers, and whispered in her ear did she realise he was there.

"Shall I see you later tonight, sweet pea? Be together like last time? I've dreamt of nuffin' else."

Her eager body spun ready to greet him while a lump of fear choked her throat. Before she could speak, she stopped. He looked awful. He needed a haircut and a shave, and the smell of the ocean and tar still clung to his clothes. There was a cut above his eye and a bruised lip. She wanted to reach out and touch his face, to ease his wounds, but he looked too narky. She guessed he'd been in a fight, but more than that, the colour of his skin frightened her. Even his eyes seemed to lack their usual lustre.

"Johnno, oh John. It's so good to see ya," she finally croaked. Nevertheless, she must not let him come to her room tonight. She knew she wouldn't be able to resist him and that would be a greater disaster until they'd sorted out the problem. She hated calling her baby a problem, but until she was wed, the reality was insurmountable.

"But not tonight … I don't think so. Not this time. Maybe get cleaned up first, and get some rest, then we can talk, eh," she answered bitterly.

He grabbed her arm as she tried to pass. "What?"

She stopped, glaring at him, denying the shivers that set her skin alight but frightened by his quick temper. She glanced down at his hand and looked up again, her expression fierce.

He released his grip and spoke more mannerly. "I'm that glad to see ya, Miss Daniels. Really, I am." His eyes searched her face for a sign that all was well. "Ya look right comely. I like it. A real beauty 'n all."

Determined not to let her heart, or rather her body, rule her head, she tried being offhand. "It's good to see ya home again, Mr Clements, but I'm too busy to talk right now. Tomorrow will be soon nuff."

A flash of anger coloured his face. "Ya can't be serious. After all this time. I need to see ya."

"No," she hissed looking around hoping no one was listening in. "Not tonight."

She stepped past him, muttered to her father she was going to the privy and disappeared through the kitchen and out the door into the back alley.

Was she doing the right thing, making him wait? But she couldn't let him into her bed until she was certain he would marry her.

He'd gone by the time she returned. She breathed a deep sigh of relief. At least their encounter would not be in front of her father or any of the patrons.

The rest of the evening passed pleasantly enough although, despite her usual chatter, she was on edge, constantly watching the door for when he did return.

"That's us for the night," said Jacob finally, mopping up the bar while she cleaned the last of the tables. "Take yourself off to bed, lovey. I'll just 'ave a nightcap and a quiet smoke afore I go up."

"Are ya sure, Da? I don't mind staying to chat awhile."

"Nay, girlie. No need. You need your beauty sleep."

"That to-do with Mr Clements earlier, what was that about? Did it come to summat?"

Jacob looked at her through squinted eyes. "Worried about him, are ya?"

She hitched one shoulder and promptly sat on the stool beside the fireplace. Slipping off one of her pumps, she rubbed her foot hoping to avoid Jacob's watchful gaze. "Tis a bit out of the ordinary for him, i'nit? He don't usually get in a tussle."

"No, he's not one for fisticuffs but he won't be pushed around neither. 'Tweren't much, summat to do with being 'ard done by. He'll be right."

Sarah wasn't so sure. He might have been hard done by, but he'd been in a brawl over something more than that, she felt sure. She fretted what it might be and if it would mean John couldn't or wouldn't keep his word.

She kissed her da on the cheek and said goodnight, making her way up the staircase, with its twisty landing, to her tiny attic room, wondering where she might find John in the morning and how she would begin to say what needed to be said.

She leaned her aching back against the closed bedroom door with a sigh, suddenly overwhelmed with exhaustion. After undoing the ribbon from her hair, she sat at the washstand rubbing at her face trying to brush away her troubles. A door creaked somewhere, and she leapt up with fright. What if he tried to come back tonight despite her refusal? She picked up the chair and jammed it under the doorknob. Would that hold if he was determined? Maybe not. But maybe he wouldn't come, either.

She undressed, carefully hanging her clothes on the hooks on the wall. Keeping her chemise on, she drew her nightgown over her head, making sure to double tie the ribbons at her throat. She could take no more chances.

Her body sagged into the mattress seeking relief from the tension in her shoulders and neck as she pulled the counterpane over her. Despite her tiredness, sleep eluded her. She had to stop being starry-eyed and gullible. She was no longer a young girl looking for romantic love, a pretty wedding and happy ever after. She was about to become a mother, and a wife, with luck, but there'd be no celebrations and no happy endings. Life had just become more complicated.

The night dragged on. Each sound set her nerves alight as she wondered if it was John trying to get in. She tossed and turned wishing for the morning to come so she could get this sorted once and for all.

When dawn finally heralded the start of the new day, Sarah could barely drag her eyes open or her body from the bed. Leaden, and overcome with a weariness greater than anything she'd ever experienced, she splashed cold water from the ewer on her face to ease her scratchy eyes.

She'd need her wits and all her charm and appeal about her if she was to win Johnno. He must want her as much as she wanted him, or all was lost. If he only married her because of the babe, they were doomed to failure.

The moment Sarah entered the taproom where the lodgers ate their morning meal, she found John already waiting for her. His eyes questioning.

"You're up early. No one's down yet," she said brightly as she turned towards the kitchen. "I'll get started on some food, if you can wait a while."

"Weren't waiting for grub. I were waiting for you. I wanna reason, Sarah."

She paused. The moment had come. Twisting her hands together, praying she wouldn't be sick and hoping the right words would come, she nodded.

His voice was soft but demanding. "What's wrong? Why don't ya wanna see me no more? Found another fella, 'ave ya? Is that it?"

Her heart tumbled. "No. Never. Ya gotta believe me. There's nothin' like that. But …" Her eyes pleaded with his briefly before she dropped her gaze. She bit her lip as the words refused to come.

She felt John come closer. His finger touched her chin and lifted it. "What's botherin' ya then, Salls? How can I make ya feel better?"

Her body shivered at his touch as her eyes pooled, confusion written on her face.

"Don't ya know I luv ya, 'n I want to be with ya. Are ya listening? I. Want. Ya."

She stared into his face, beseeching him. "Do you mean it? Oh, dear God. Do you really mean it?"

"Of course I do. What is it, Salls? What's wrong?" The softness of his voice and the use of her nickname gave her confidence.

"You won't think bad of me? Whatever tis?" she begged.

John took her in his arms, kissed the top of her head and promised. "Never."

Sarah's sobs of relief broke free, and she leant against his shoulder. "I've been ever so worrit, y'see, since you've been away. What if ya hadna come home. What if ya didna want me no more. What if …"

"But I'm back now,'n I do want ya. Why would ya be so worrit about it? Have I ever let you down?"

Sarah shook her head against the rough cloth of his jacket.

"Well then?"

Her face flushed the colour of crimson. "Do ya remember when ya came to my room that time?"

John held her tighter. "How could I forget? I never stopped thinking about it the whole time I were away. Tis why I were keen to see ya last night."

She looked into his eyes, begging him to understand. She didn't want to say the words out loud. She held her stomach and dropped her eyes.

He suddenly released her and held her at arm's length. Dipping down to her height, a smile broadened his face, and his eyes lit up. "Are you telling me there's a babber? Is that the problem?" he asked, waiting for her nod before sweeping her into his arms again when her tearful smile confirmed what he suspected.

"Oh, me luv, what gert news! I always wanted to be a da. We'll be a family." He twirled her round. "Let's get married. Soon. Tomorrow. Today." He gabbled excitedly while Sarah tried to gather her wits. She knew his parents were both dead and all his siblings had died in infancy and realised why he was so excited at the thought of having a family to call his own. She too was smiling now, although her face was still wet with tears. Happiness bubbled inside her. "Oh John. Are ya sure?"

He kissed her deeply instead of answering.

Relief flowed through her body. "I do so love ya," she said happily when she finally caught her breath.

"Then that's settled. We'll go see the reverend today."

Panic rose in Sarah's gut. "We can't! They'll all know what we did," her naivety and shame overcoming sense.

John looked confused, then laughed. "They'll know soon nuff, even if we don't tell 'em. You'll not be able to hide it for much longer. I knew ya looked different the moment I saw ya. I never thought 'twould be this. Come on, Salls. Let's tell everyone. Tell your folks we want to be wed, and we'll go up to the church as soon as the vicar is up."

Sarah's spirits rose in chorus with his eagerness. She wouldn't be considered a harlot after all. She would be a married woman with a man who loved her and a new babber to care for. Life suddenly looked a lot brighter.

Later that morning, with Sarah's hand clutched tightly in his, John faced Jacob and formally asked for Sarah's hand. If Jacob had doubts, he never voiced them.

"Take good care of her, lad, or you'll have her ma to answer to," he said as he extended his hand towards John.

"I told ya I suspected summat," muttered Betsey. "Her body were softening, I could see. We'll need to get a licence to stop all the gossiping. No need to waste weeks having the banns read 'n people knowing our business."

Sarah stifled a grin and kept her head down. A licence was expensive but if Ma was willing then she could be married sooner. She couldn't wait. Her body almost betrayed her as she thought of what being married meant.

"Ta to ya both," said John. "I'll straight away arrange what tis we need, but as soon as possible will suit me. I've signed on for a three-month voyage, leaving in two weeks. I weren't expecting Sarah to accept me so soon, and we'll need the money. Can I ask if'n you'll look after Sarah as you've always done while I'm away?"

Seeing the disappointment on her face, he turned to Sarah and squeezed her hand. "Sorry, luv. If I'd known, maybe things coulda been different."

She put on a brave smile and tried not to let her sorrow show. "Tis what I'd better get used to if I've chosen to marry a mariner. Just be sure you're back afore year end."

The rest of the week passed in a whirlwind. A licence was sought and taken to the vicar who agreed to marry them a week on Sunday, in the afternoon. Letters were sent to Mary asking her if she could come visit and make one of Sarah's dresses more suitable to get married in. *And,* thought Sarah, *adjust some to allow for my expanding waistline.* Mary would soon see her condition. She only hoped her sister would understand.

The inn suddenly seemed to be full of people who added nothing to the business of being an inn. Mary's boy Ted, who'd found rooms elsewhere, popped in to wish her good luck. "Are ya sure he's the right one, Sal? You're a long time married to some'un if'n he's not."

Sarah quietly assured Ted she loved John and was happy even if she avoided telling him she was expecting. Like everyone else, he would find out soon enough.

Aunt Nettie floated in and out in a buzz of euphoria. "I just love weddings, don't you?"

Sarah wondered if her mother had mentioned the reason, but gut instinct told her her aunt had not been informed of her predicament either. She felt a surprising surge of gratitude as she looked across at her mother who was talking non-stop about what she should wear and who should be invited back for afternoon tea, and what food she should serve. Sarah's head felt quite dizzy with so much noise and so many decisions.

She was thankful when Mary arrived and instilled a degree of calm to the proceedings.

"So, little sister, you're to be married. Congratulations, but I hope ya know what that means."

Sarah blushed a little thinking Mary was hinting at what happened when the two of them were alone in their bed, but they weren't her thoughts at all.

"There's nothing rosy about being wed to a sailor, Sarah. He'll be away at sea more often than home. There'll be nights you'll despair and days of loneliness. It's good and well that you'll be staying here with our folks to watch over you. You'll need them, so don't pretend otherwise. And don't mind Ma. She has her ups and downs but she'll not let you down either."

Sarah agreed. "I know. And I can manage most of the time. She's better since the doctor gave her a tonic, but she still gets her down days."

"And always will. That's her nature. Now, I can see already ya know the delights of the bedroom, but he won't be around to manage the consequences. That'll be all up to you."

"Aye, I know that Mary, but tis what I want."

Mary hugged her and kissed her on each cheek. "Very well. Let's see what we can do about some suitable clothing then, shall we?"

For the occasion, and thanks to Mary, Ma chose not to wear black for once and decided on a dove-grey dress and jacket that really did suit her. For Sarah, her sister worked wonders with a soft peach floral cotton. Cleverly placing layers and frills to conceal any signs of her rounded belly, the colour added a warm glow to her russet brown eyes. With her dark hair tied back with white ribbons and sprigs of orange blossom, she would look as lovely as any young bride could.

At last, her wedding day arrived. And not a day too soon. On Sunday 17th September 1854, the small party walked to the nearby church where Reverend William Battersby gave the blessings to make John her husband and she his legal wife.

6

When love fails

September 1854

Sarah never expected her life to remain as it had been, but neither did she expect such change.

The first few days after the vicar had given his blessing to their marriage, she and John basked in the joys of love. From the moment of their early morning intimacy until they could be reunited that night, the days moved far too slowly, never mind how busy Sarah was in the kitchen and in the taproom. Betsey had not let up in her demands, or her criticism of Sarah's lack of motivation and energy when she was found staring out the window looking for a glimpse of John as he went about his work.

But those glorious days of togetherness were brief. It seemed to Sarah that no time had passed at all before John was, once again, leaving on another voyage.

"Aye. I'm that sorry I 'ave to go, but I promised, and we need the money."

Sarah had bitten back her tears even though her

heart ached. She had to be strong. "Nay. It's what ya must do. You're a mariner, so go ya ought. But please send me a message now and then, when ya can, mind. And beg the master to make sure you are 'ome by year's end. The babber won't wait, and I want ya to see the child first."

"I doubt I'll be the first with your ma and the midwife and all the other women taking care of ya. But, aye, I'll be home dreckly. I want to hold our babber as soon as I can. Look after yourself, kid."

He'd kissed her gently, holding her face in his hands to memorise every detail. Their eyes shone with the newness of love and the possibilities to come, but finally he pulled away.

"Go well, my love," she whispered as John picked up his seabag and left without a backward glance.

Coming up two months later, she missed him dreadfully.

Sarah noticed the first change in her body soon after John had left, but only those who saw her undressed would have noticed the slight bump, even if nearly everyone she met commented on how rosy and bonnie she was looking. But a month later, almost overnight, her stomach bulged, and she was thankful for the alterations Mary had made to her clothes during her visit.

Before long, her back ached as she did her chores, her legs throbbed and her feet swelled. She wished Mary was still with them. She would understand and commiserate, and maybe explain what was going on, but Ma just told her it was normal and to get on with things. But that was easier said than done. She felt awkward and heavy. Bending and lifting became almost more than she could manage, and she was close to tears more often than she liked. And she still had nearly three months to go.

"Don't you dare lift that firkin," said her father one morning when he saw what she was trying to do. "I'll find a lad to do that for me."

"But Da. That'll cost."

"Phttt. Won't be much, and you and that babber are more important." He looked around furtively. "Pop upstairs for an hour and rest, Sarah lass. Ya ma's not about and there's few customers at the mo'. I'll be al'right. That I will."

She hugged her father, tears pouring down her face at his consideration. Working families like theirs couldn't usually afford sentiment.

Sarah let herself cry a little as she curled up on her bed, thankful to be off her feet if only for an hour, but her plucky nature wouldn't let her dwell for long on what couldn't be changed. She was soon up and doing her utmost to be her entertaining best. The patrons didn't seem at all put out by her burgeoning shape and teased her just the same.

But the tone of the conversation had changed. The talk turned to the war in Crimea and how badly things were going.

Back in September, only two days after she and John wed, a battle had erupted south of the River Alma involving the British, French and Turks against the Russians. From what Sarah could gather it hadn't gone as planned. Confusion about who was doing what and where, which direction they should go, and who was in command led to arguments and defeats.

Sarah had little concept of battle strategy, but she was learning quickly, and unlike during the Battle of Waterloo in 1815, regular news reports were being received. An Irish reporter by the name of William Howard Russell was sending daily updates to *The Times* newspaper that were critical of both the leadership and the lack of organisation. News that enraged many as the death toll mounted, and they read about the appalling conditions the injured soldiers had to endure. News that allowed people to make up their own minds about the state of affairs. And to criticise and complain.

"Y'd think they'd 'ave learnt summat from then, wouldn't ya?" Sarah heard one of the bedecked old soldiers say. "But if'n what it says 'ere is true, looks like more of the ol' *charge and hope for the best* strategy's still the plan." He picked up the ale Sarah had just given him and took a long gulp. "Didn't work then. Won't work now."

Photographs started appearing in the paper, which caused even more dissension. Some photos glorified the officers in their fine uniforms, while others showed the extent of the battle and the devastation it wreaked. Sarah shuddered, hoping John would not be on one of the ships delivering the reportedly much-needed food and medical supplies.

By the end of October, things had deteriorated. After a lengthy siege at the port of Sevastopol, the Russians launched an assault near the village of Balaklava, hoping to break the British lines.

"Can ya believe all this?" Sarah overheard a group of

men talking while they pored over the day's newspapers, although what she was supposed to believe or otherwise was lost on her.

"Them Highlanders were brave standin' up to a full mounted charge by the Russkies."

"Yeah. They nicknamed those Scots 'the thin red line' cos there were only two rows of foot soldiers what fired the volleys 'n forced the enemy to retreat."

"Must've been well-aimed shots to do that."

"Well, suppose it were either do or die," bandied a couple of the men.

The men continued to read, interspersing comments of outrage as others peered over their shoulders.

"What a mess it must've been."

"Only eight hundred of the Heavy Brigade to rout more than three thousand fleeing Russian cavalry. That's some feat."

"'Tis 'n all. Think what coulda 'appened if they'd pushed their advantage."

"Stupid buggers. Fancy stoppin' to look behind."

Mutterings of agreement and the odd exchange of opinion hardly interested Sarah as she continued to flit between them.

Papers were passed on to someone else while some, clearly reading slower than others, irritated those wanting to read it for themselves. The volume rose in the enclosed space as they emptied their tankards and called for more ale and scrumpy.

"So how'd the rest of it go so wrong?"

Sarah perked her ears up at that question. From all the discussions so far, she'd assumed the British had won the battle.

Bob picked up the paper. "Bad communication it says here. That Russell character don't pull any punches. He says: *without waiting for reinforcements, Lord Raglan senselessly ordered his remaining troops to stop the Russians from moving the guns they'd captured earlier. But the commanders couldn't see the battlefield Raglan was looking at and didn't know which guns he meant. What they saw were Russian gunners gathered at the end of the valley, but they were the wrong ones. So the Light Brigade charged down the valley, forcing the men manning the guns to retreat, and galloped on through to find Russian artillery fire coming from three sides. The Brigade lost over a third of their men and more than four hundred and seventy horses.*"

Bob put the paper down. They all remained silent for a moment as they took in what it meant.

"And all that 'appened in one day?"

"Hardly even that. It says it were all over not long after noon."

A voice piped up. "Thank the Lord the reinforcements arrived when they did 'n the French cavalry could protect the retreat."

The old timer who often sat by the fireplace, sucking on his pipe, quietly interjected. "But for what purpose? If'n them Russkies still hold the heights 'n the road, and our allies hold the village 'n the port, then the supplies ain't gonna make it to those who need it. If the cruel winter doesn't kill 'em, disease and hunger will."

* * * * *

A few weeks later, Sarah's body changed again, but something didn't feel right. The downward pressure on

60

her innards vexed her all the time. She found leaning backwards to counterbalance the bulge sometimes helped, but her back was so painful by the end of the day, she could hardly stand.

To make matters worse, she'd heard next to nothing from John. Two short, scribbled notes saying he was doing fine hardly answered her myriad of questions. At least he was safe. That was a comfort, but not knowing exactly where he was or what he was doing became a constant worry.

As the old soldier had predicted, one of the worst storms in memory hit the Crimean Peninsula in November, destroying the allied camps and sinking many of the ships carrying supplies for winter. Sarah could only hope that John was not on one of those vessels, or any of those setting off to deliver the next consignment of supplies.

Such deliveries would take weeks at best, according to Russell's reports, but meanwhile the starving allied soldiers foraged for scraps as best they could. With little or no firewood, they suffered badly from the cold, hunger, and disease – which evidently killed far more soldiers than the enemy. Even the horses and mules died from lack of food, and when supplies finally reached the base at Balaklava, they were slow to reach the troops.

The doom and gloom Sarah heard and read about did little to lift her spirits or displace the feeling of impending disaster that frequently dogged her dreams.

Whether in response to the public recognition of the hardship, or because people were looking for something to lift the usual winter melancholy, when Alfred, Lord Tennyson, the Poet Laureate, released his verse that

December, it wasn't long before she and others could recite it by heart.

The Charge of the Light Brigade

I

Half a league, half a league,
Half a league onward,
All in the valley of Death
Rode the six hundred.
"Forward, the Light Brigade!
Charge for the guns!" he said.
Into the valley of Death
Rode the six hundred.

V

Cannon to right of them,
Cannon to left of them,
Cannon behind them
Volleyed and thundered;
Stormed at with shot and shell,
While horse and hero fell.
They that had fought so well
Came through the jaws of Death,
Back from the mouth of hell,
All that was left of them,
Left of six hundred.

After a long night of carousing patrons, Sarah slowly climbed the narrow stairs to her room. Every step seemed more difficult than the last. She gasped more than once as pain struck. Finally reaching the top of the stairs, she held on to the banister for support as a wave of dizziness caught her unawares.

"Ma!" she screamed as her knees folded and she fell. Tumbling several steps, she came to a stop at the corner of the small landing halfway down. She was only vaguely aware of her mother fussing, the shrill voice piercing Sarah's brain as someone lifted her up and carried her to her parents' room. She knew Da was beside her, she could sense his calmness and hear his soothing voice, but she couldn't seem to understand his words. All she knew was pain. Wave after wave. Hour after hour. Endless pain drifting in the darkness.

Shadows came and went, but she had no idea who they were or what they were doing. She didn't have the strength to open her eyes to find out. Sounds swirled inside her head until even those faded.

"Ah, you're awake are ya, lovey?" said a voice as her eyelids fluttered. "Let's see what we have here then."

Sarah didn't recognise the woman. She let her gaze wander around the room as she gathered her senses trying to remember what had happened. Why was the woman here? Whoever she was, she knew what she was about. A fire in the hearth spread a warm and cosy glow throughout the room. The newly laundered sheets smelt clean, and she wore a fresh nightgown with a faint aroma of lavender, but Sarah's body hurt and every muscle ached as if she'd been toiling on the docks.

"The babber ..." she whispered hopefully, almost too exhausted to speak.

"Don't you worry about that for now. Let's get you

cleaned up and rested and then we'll talk, shall we? How about a nice cuppa? That'll help, it will."

Instinct told Sarah all was not well. Seeing her mother sitting pale-faced and forlorn by the window added to her unease. Her hands sought her stomach, which last night had been taut and solid – had it only been last night? She had no idea how much time had passed. She hazily remembered the grip of pain at the top of the stairs and a sense of falling but then, nothing – until now.

Fear swept through her as her hands confirmed the slack, empty space where her baby had once been. Tears began to trickle from both eyes and slide down the side of her face onto the plump, clean pillows supporting her head.

"The babber …" she repeated, desperate for an outcome other than what she feared.

The mournful wail from her mother answered her question. A deep hollow settled inside while her body shook with sobs that sucked every bit of air from her lungs.

"No-oo-oo …!" She knew the baby was no more. Her anguished howl could be heard throughout the inn.

She would never forget that moment, never forget that cool December morning when her world changed forever and whatever happiness she'd known flew away, leaving her bereft.

* * * * *

Christmas, her 20th birthday four days later, and then, a few weeks into the new year, the date when the baby had been expected, all passed without John being there.

The woman who came and saw to her, saving her life if not the baby's, had refused to tell her what it had been – boy or girl. A pact of silence had been agreed upon, and nothing Sarah had tried would shift either the midwife or her mother.

With an aching heart, Sarah went about her daily tasks as she had always done but without the spring in her step and the laughter in her voice. Her usual joy in Christmas and its celebrations was gone. She couldn't bring herself to participate in anything.

John had written, of course, but his words had meant nothing. He'd promised to be home and he'd broken his promise at a time when she'd needed him most. Someone had told him about the baby, about how she'd failed, how he had no child to come home to, and he'd chosen to take on another voyage instead of returning to comfort her. She was trying hard to forgive him, but she was finding that easier said than done.

Her mother flipped between solicitous proclamations, 'You're young, there's plenty of time for more,' or 'You gotta get on with life' or 'Every woman's lost a baby at some stage, you 'ave to get over it,' to the days when the melancholy took over and she remembered all the babies *she* had lost and took to her bed leaving Sarah with more work than usual.

She didn't begrudge her mother these low days as much as she had in the past. Not now she understood. She had her own low days, but her mother's absence didn't help. Sarah prayed that her loss wouldn't similarly dog her for decades to come. She longed for John to come home. She longed for the feel of his hands on her body and the passion they shared to bring her to life again.

"Hey, you. Bring more ale!" demanded an unkempt man with a loud voice.

Sarah glared at the stranger. He was one of the increasing number of rough-talking, unscrupulous sailors arriving through the door. Some were privateers, marauders looking out for themselves. She wouldn't trust a single one. She'd heard talk of so many men, especially those caught up in the war in Crimea or those transporting supplies, becoming villains and evil-minded. Being away at sea for long stretches, egged on by the greedy and the nasty, meant that when they came ashore they were bullying and a threat to the locals. She was seeing too many of them for comfort. Foul-smelling drunks who'd throw a fist or draw a knife as quick as look at them if she didn't keep her wits, but she was having none of his rudeness today.

"If ya want servin' y'd betta put a civil tongue in your head."

"And who're you to tell me what?"

Jacob drew his bulk up to full height as he stepped forward and growled. "She's my daughter, that's who, and if you dinna want to end up on your nose outside the door, I suggest ya do as she says."

Another of the mercenaries watching the goings on grabbed the man's arm before he could react. "Give it a miss, me old mucker. Not worth it. See?" He looked around the taproom and nodded towards the many locals watching and waiting. "Too many allies." Hardly less uncouth than his friend, his tone was at least more mannerly when he spoke to Sarah.

"Me mate's sorry, he is, and politely asks could we 'ave more ale?"

The group of five men chortled and nudged one another pretending to be put out. "Ooh, aren't we being all grand now," they teased their companion.

"Get the ale."

Sarah ignored the other less-complimentary comments muttered under their breath and brought five tankards of ale to them without saying another word. All she could hope for was that John wouldn't turn into this new breed of mariner. Doubts flitted in her head: she'd seen his temper and known him get into many a fight. Maybe his behaviour would no longer fit her expectations.

7

A sea change

February 1855

"So, you're back." Sarah struggled to keep the bitterness from her voice even while she yearned for what they once shared.

"Tis been a long journey, Mrs Clements." John looked dejected, utterly worn but with a hardness to his eyes that hadn't been there before. Sarah shuddered.

"Aye, that it has," she murmured, her voice aching with loss, "and much 'as happened since ya left. I'm no longer the girl ya knew, I'm grown now."

The twitch of his shoulder could almost have been a dismissive shrug that he thought better of. "Aye, I see that. And there's been a change in me too. I've seen things a man should never see, and a woman should never know."

"Will ya tell me about 'em?" she implored gently. "To ease your burden."

"No."

His curt refusal shocked her. About to answer back, an image of an old soldier who once had sat across the bar from her came to mind, and she recalled his words. 'War's a terrible thing, kid. Terrible. Cruelty, on both sides mind, that no man should witness, or be forced to bear. Changes a man, it does.'

Her skin crept at the memory, and she hoped the change in John was not caused by savagery, and that it wouldn't be permanent.

They stared at each other for several seconds, analysing, not knowing how to break the barrier of anger and disappointment.

Sarah capitulated first. "You'd better take your things upstairs then." She flapped her hand towards the stairwell. "Be careful on that landing, or it could be death of you too." Sarah now hated that small turn in the stairs. While it had stopped her fall, it had also taken her babber.

John lowered his eyes and picked up his seabag. He tried to touch Sarah as he passed but she recoiled, and he let his hand drop. "Sorry," he mumbled and headed up the stairs.

Sarah stood watching him. Was sorry enough? And sorry for what? For her loss; their loss? For not being here at the time? For not coming home as he'd promised? For what!

But inherently she understood he was no longer the man she'd married only a few months ago.

"We'll talk dreckly, eh?" she called after him, hoping they could find solace in being together again.

John stopped but didn't turn around. "Talkin' won't change nuffin'," and carried on.

How she got through the rest of the day, cleaning and restocking, and serving the customers their meals and copious quantities of ale, she didn't know. A lot of what she did was by rote.

"What's wrong with ya, girl? That's far too hot to carry like that," barked her mother when Sarah yelped, nearly dropping a charger plate laden with fresh roast beef and gravy. "Get a hold o' yourself."

Sarah merely shrugged, grabbed a couple of cloths and, folding them several times, carried the platter through to the waiting customers.

Her mother's shout followed her out the kitchen. "Don't you go all sullen on me!"

"What's the matter, kid?" asked one of the regulars. "You've lost ya spark of late. Come on lass, gi' us a smile."

Sarah pulled her face into a grimace posing as a smile and turned on her heel. She didn't feel as if she'd ever regain her spark. For so long she'd waited for John. For so long she had trusted him, relied on him to be her mainstay. For so long she'd loved him from afar, dreaming of their life together. Now he was back, and whatever it was that had once set her alight had waned. She felt different and scared they'd not find their way again.

The day finally came to an end, and she made her way up those dreaded stairs to her room. John's seabag was sitting on the floor where he'd dropped it. Sarah sighed, wondering whether in relief at him not being there, or disappointment. He must have gone back to the ship to finish unloading and reset for the next voyage or found himself another inn to drown his sorrows.

She began to undress, putting her apron and blouse to one side to be washed and hanging her skirt on the pegs. Unpinning her hair, she sat at the dresser.

Almost on cue, as if he'd been watching and waiting, he opened the door, pausing on the threshold to test his welcome. Again, their eyes met, assessing the moment. Sarah saw his eyes change. That hardness she'd noticed before now glinted with something far more calculating – and dangerous.

"I can't change what's 'appened. Not to you. Not to me. And talkin' ain't gonna fix it. I'm back now and you're still me wife. Through thick 'n thin we said, so let's get on with it."

Stripping off his jacket and cap, he strode to where she stood, banging the door shut behind him. His rough hands grabbed her shoulders and pulled her to him. She smelt the stench of beer on his breath, stagnant salt air on his clothes, and felt the coarse scrape of his unshaven face as his tongue sought her mouth. She tried to recoil, to speak, to regain control, but he held her tightly, his lust rising faster than her bile. Like a man bedevilled, one hand biting painfully into her shoulder, he tore at her chemise.

"Mr Clements!" she panted. "Stop. What's got into you? John. No!" The buttons popped and her breasts lay exposed. Without pause, he lifted her up and dropped her on the bed and fell on top of her. Grasping both her hands in one of his, he fumbled with his clothing while smothering her face with his lips, his tongue everywhere as she turned her head from side to side.

"Stop. Mr Clements. Please. Not like this." The more she struggled, the more inflamed he became. "Please stop," she begged, tears beginning to fall. "Not like this," she whispered, the fight draining away as he backhanded her. She lay slack as the sobs took hold.

"Shut up," John growled. "Shut the noise."

His weight lifted from her body onto his knees jammed between her legs. Ripping open her chemise all the way down, he exposed her still flaccid stomach. She flinched, every instinct pulling her deeper into the mattress, away from him, as he unbuttoned his trousers. Seconds later he pushed himself into her.

She groaned in shock and pain. Where had her gentle lover gone? What had happened to that tingling sensation she'd once had whenever John came near her? When had her desire for him dissipated? Her body tensed at the onslaught as her mind sought answers to how they had reached this point. Each thrust more hurtful than the last until he shuddered, sagged, and rolled off.

"Clean yourself up. I'll be back." He threw a linen cloth at her and walked out the door.

All the joy she'd once known, all the love she'd once held close, all the hope she'd nurtured vanished, and only a burning sensation remained.

After that night, John returned to a semblance of his earlier self. He was more considerate towards her, and she began to hope again, but she couldn't break through to him.

"I don't understand what's distressed ya so much," Sarah said after their nightly coitus as she tried to cuddle against him. "It must be more than the loss of the babber. Won't you tell me what tis? Where were ya that kept you from me? What were ya doing that's changed you so?"

He turned on his side away from her. "Leave it be, eh. There's nuffin' to know. You deal with your demons, and I'll deal with mine. I don't wanna talk 'bout it. None of it."

Nothing she said or did made any difference. If she questioned him too hard, he turned on her. Sometimes he would disappear for days on end and return with no explanation. One night he slapped her again; something new she had to learn to forgive him for. She was aware she was fortunate in many ways. Wives were often beaten for not living up to their husband's expectations, but she suspected the presence of her father kept John's temper in check. Whatever was eating him up remained his secret.

As she knew would happen, he'd been home less than a month before he announced he was leaving again. "We need the money," he said. "'Tis a six-month voyage, so don't expect to hear from me."

Sarah nodded, wished him well, and returned to life as the innkeeper's daughter.

* * * * *

Summer began to cast her benevolence, and people went about their business with more vigour. Sarah took extra time to gather their fresh supplies so she could appreciate the aroma of fresh green grass, the pretty flowers waving their heads in the gentle breeze, and the warmth of the sun easing the tension from her weary muscles.

On Sunday, after church, the vicar invited her back to Sunday school. "Have you heard that Charles Dickens's latest novel, *Little Dorrit*, is now available? The first part of the serial has just arrived. Will you join us again? You used to love reading so much, and it would be good for the younger ones to see someone of your age, married and working, reading and enjoying the stories. I'd like you to read them aloud for the children. It will encourage them."

For a brief moment, her heart hiccoughed. She would indeed like to return to read the new story to the children. It would be such a change from the endless talk of the war in Crimea, even if it did sound like the British and allies were winning, and help her avoid the influx of hardened freebooters for a time. Jacob had done his best to make life uncomfortable for them and encouraged their ilk to attend the Llandoger Trow, a much larger and older pub around the corner on King Street, but much as she'd like to take up the reverend's offer, she could not keep up the weekly meetings for long.

She knew she was pregnant again with a child conceived of bitterness and sorrow. "Thank ya, reverend, for thinking of me. I'd love to, but ya see … um, that is." Suddenly embarrassed, she wondered how to explain to the gentle man who stood before with his kindly blue eyes that she was with child. It was not something a woman discussed and certainly not with a man of the cloth. "Um. Well, thank ya anyway, but I can't."

She gathered her skirts and was about to hasten away, when the vicar put a staying hand on her arm. "I am guessing, since your husband was recently at home, that you may be, shall we say, anticipating a happy event in the future."

His soft smile reassured her. She dropped her gaze to her shoes and nodded.

"In which case," he continued lightly, "I understand your dilemma, but until such time as you feel too tired, or the walk is too onerous, then I feel you should at least start. Remember, it is God's will that we procreate."

She nodded again; her eyes still downcast.

With that, the vicar patted her shoulder. "I will look forward to seeing you next week then. God be with you, child."

"Thank you, reverend."

Sarah walked home conflicted. Part of her was happy to have the chance to do something different, while another part railed about her fate to have lost one child conceived in love, only to carry another conceived under a cloud. She wished Mary lived closer. Her letters were always reassuring, but Sarah found it difficult to confide her deepest thoughts on paper. But maybe she could write about what the vicar had offered and see what Mary thought.

September 1855

"Sevastopol is won!"

Sarah had little idea what that meant, except that the war with Russia had turned for the good. But the men seemed happy and happy men drank a lot, which was good for business even if it brought more work for her.

Ships still journeyed to and fro, transporting more soldiers to replace the dead and injured, or delivering fresh supplies to feed those still on the ground. A year or so back, when William Russell reported in *The Times* how badly the soldiers were being neglected, there'd been an uproar. It seemed incredulous that soldiers more often died of disease rather than their injuries. Since then, Sarah had read a lot about Florence Nightingale who had been sent to the Crimea with a team of nurses. She had a reputation for being a hard taskmaster, but she set about cleaning up the appalling and unsanitary conditions the injured and maimed were in. She'd been nicknamed the Lady with the Lamp due to her nightly visits to the sick and dying. Her praises were sung far and wide, and not only by Russell, for saving so many lives.

But to Sarah, something far more pleasant and pertinent was the arrival of her sister, Mary.

While Mary greeted her parents and told them the latest news, Sarah was on tenterhooks, wanting time alone with her sibling.

"It's so good having Ted home again. He's a good lad and so helpful. But he won't stay long. He's an accountant now and destined for bigger things," finished Mary with pride.

Sarah hadn't known it was possible to earn a respectable living from doing figuring for other people, but she was happy for him. He'd be going up in the world and become a gentleman in no time.

"Hope ya right," grunted Ma. "He weren't much good round 'ere."

Mary gasped, but Da interrupted before she could respond. "Now then Betsey, that's no fair, and ya know it. Ted's a good lad, and he's for better things than heaving barrels around."

Sarah wondered if her da thought that of her too. Was she for better things than being a barmaid? She doubted she'd ever get the chance to find out. The stars she gazed at so frequently wouldn't hold her destiny; hers was bound by duty.

Despite Ma's grumpiness, Mary seemed to spend an age talking with her about her ailments, worries, and moans, but finally the two sisters found a quiet time in her room to chat without being interrupted.

Sarah was almost in tears as she reached for her sister's hands, she was so relieved. "Oh, Mary. I'm that glad to see ya. I know it's only a short journey by train, but we don't see each other anywhere near nuff."

"I know it's not easy, 'n I can only stay for a wee while, Sarah, me dear, but your last letter worried me. Y've had such a hard time of it."

"I'm not sure ya know the half of it, some things I couldn't put on paper, mind."

"Such as …" Mary urged putting one arm around Sarah's shoulder as they sat side by side on the edge of the bed. "I'm here now, get it off your chest and tell me everything."

"Remember, back when we went to the Crystal Palace all those years ago, I asked about that feeling I got every time John came near me, well … it's just … it's no longer there."

Sarah promptly burst into tears and slowly, through each painful sob, talked about being let down by John, feeling a failure for losing the baby, and a fool for letting herself get with child in the first place. How she'd missed John so badly when he was away and how brutally he'd treated her when he returned. That was the hardest part.

Giving Mary all the intimate details and sharing her deepest fear.

"Oh, dear God. No," said Mary. "Oh, Sarah I wish I'd been here to help you through all that." Mary continued to offer sympathetic and understanding murmurings as Sarah went on.

"Whatever there was between us has shifted, and I'm not sure I even want to see him again. He frightens me." Sarah shook her head. "But I know he'll be back one day. I can't get it out of me 'ead. Ma's always grumbling about how useless I am, and I feel so guilty for breaking my promise to our da. I said I'd always be here for him, and now I'm expecting again. What if I lose this one? What will John do then?"

"Oh Sarah, lass. You can't take everything on your shoulders. None of it is your fault. None. Do you hear me? And if John tries anything like that again, he'll 'ave me and Da to face up to. As for Ma. Don't take it to heart. It's just her way. She don't mean half of it."

The girls chatted for an hour or more with Mary encouraging and reassuring Sarah before she had to leave to catch the train.

"Now, you write as often as you can. Tell me all about how you get on reading *Little Dorrit*. I think it's a wonderful idea. I will come back as soon as possible. Now, promise me. Stop blaming yourself, look forward to the babber, never mind the circumstances. I'm sure things with John will work out better after the little one is born."

With that, Mary was gone and Sarah, feeling more confident and cheered by Mary's good sense, returned to being the daughter of the inn. A position she loved.

8
The joys of motherhood

July 1856

"Welcome, little one," murmured Sarah. "I'm going to call ya Mary Jane after me sister and your old great-grandmother." Sarah gave some thought to when her grandmother had passed and decided it must have been five years since. She smiled as she watched the baby lying in her arms make faces in her sleep. Grandma Jane had been a kind and gentle soul, who worked herself to the bone to feed and care for her family. Sarah still missed her granny, but, "Mary has been my anchor and given me much joy," she whispered. "I hope you will too."

Sarah shut out the hurts and disappointments of the last year and tried not to think too much about how John had changed. Whatever had happened to him – and he got angry whenever she tried to find out – it had changed her too; and their marriage.

When he did come home between voyages, she often felt he couldn't wait to set off again. While there hadn't been a repeat of 'that night', as she called it, when he'd been so rough and cruel, neither was there the thrill of being together. Their lives had become superficial, exchanging pleasantries, avoiding arguments and satisfying his needs in the bedroom. Beyond that, she cared for Mary Jane and helped her da as much as she was able, while John ventured off on the boats.

One evening, John seemed in a better mood.

"We used to have such good times together, Johnno. Can we try again, do ya think?"

"What's wrong with things the way they are?"

"We, um, we've lost summat. We couldn't wait to be together once. I'm not sure that's the case any more. Do ya still look forward to seeing me?"

"S'pose." He shrugged his shoulders and stared morosely into his ale.

Sarah decided his answer wasn't a flat no and he hadn't walked away, so she pursued her point. "Backalong, afore we were wed, you told Da ya had one more big trip in you. Eighteen months, ya reckoned, and then ya'd be home for good. Remember? Is that still true? Are ya thinking of giving up sailing, or at least the long hauls?"

"What's with all the questions? I bring back nuff money, don't I? What's it matter to you how long I'm away?"

"Don't be silly; course, it matters. I want us to be a family. Remember how happy we were and how excited we were at having a babber? I know things didn't work out the way we'd planned, but we have a new child now. Doesn't she count?"

Another shrug. "Course she does, but things have changed since then. And I can't be a proper da if I'm not 'ere."

Sarah swallowed a sigh of frustration. That was exactly her point. Why was he being so difficult? There were many quicker trips like those across the Atlantic, or even the Baltic or Mediterranean crossings, which were shorter than the long hauls he was doing.

"In that case, couldn't ya sign on for shorter journeys?"

He lifted his head and stared at her. His cold eyes glinted in anger. "Leave it Sarah, or by God I won't be held to 'count. I do what I 'ave to and that's that." He thrust his chair back. The loud screech of the legs against the flagstones bruised her ears, but not as much as his departing back bruised her heart.

* * * * *

After the ferocious February storms, all the talk at the inn had been about the devastating loss of lives when several sailing ships had been wrecked. One, the *Grand Duke*, came to its watery end just off the coast of Wales with the loss of twenty-nine lives; so close but too far to be saved. The merchant ship, just like the ones John worked on, had been returning to port after delivering goods far and wide.

Sarah walked around in trepidation, listening to the men as they debated the reasons for so many tragedies. Some shook their heads over the foolhardiness of one master and bemoaned the actions of others. Her stomach felt full of crawling insects, and her nerves jangled so close to the skin's surface she jumped at unexpected sounds. John might have been on any one of those ships. What would she do if she lost him? Although what good he was to her these days was doubtful.

The only upside, if there was any upside to death, was the arrival of the regular mariners sailing their trows across from Wales. With them they brought the strains of a new Welsh song called 'Glan Rhondda'.

"What's it all mean?" asked Sarah as the men sang the rousing chorus about country and the days of old that echoed around the walls and crept into her heart.

"It's about the land, me *cariad*, the land of our fathers, me mother's home, and *heireth*," explained one of the older hands.

"*Heireth*?" Sarah tried rolling the word on her tongue. "What's *heireth*?"

"Belonging," he uttered between gulps of ale. "A yearning," before bellowing out the chorus again.

"Gwlad! Gwlad! Pleidiol wyf i'm gwlad.
Tra môr yn fur i'r bur hoff bau,
O bydded i'r hen iaith barhau.

Home, home, my heart yearns to be home," he sang.

The tune settled into Sarah's brain, and she often hummed it to herself, feeling a kinship she didn't entirely understand but found uplifting.

Within days came the devastating news that two American clippers transporting emigrants across the Atlantic to a new life had been wrecked. Both ships were lost without trace, and the bodies and souls of near on five hundred people were left drifting in limbo.

Not that long since, she had thought the Atlantic trips were the best as they took John away for the shortest length of time, but now, she hoped he would never sail the Atlantic again. Despite their difficulties, she loved him still and wanted him home. She couldn't get the images of all those poor drowned souls out of her head and looked forward to Sunday when she could go to church and pray.

Even though she only had a vague idea of God, she found comfort in the religious rituals and she knew reading another chapter of Dickens's *Little Dorrit* would bring her solace. Every month a new instalment of three or four chapters was released, and every week, she would read one of those chapters aloud; although she had often read well ahead for her own pleasure beforehand.

"Thank ya, reverend, for letting me read to the children."

"You do it so well, Sarah, it is me who should be thanking you. You bring the stories alive, and the children are keen to listen and learn."

At the end of March, the sailors were once again spending up large and celebrating the official end of the Crimean War after three long and reportedly bloody years. The signing of a treaty in Paris also ushered in new rules of wartime commerce, including a ban on privateering. Hopefully now, or so the men said, they could get back to fair trading under far better conditions. Sarah was equally happy with the news for different reasons.

She'd hated serving the privateers when they came into the inn. They had a cruel arrogance about them. Often nasty, bad-mouthed and bad-tempered, they treated other sailors, and her, with disdain. She could almost guarantee a fight would break out when they were present, and their premises would get damaged yet again. But their arrival was a mixed blessing. They always brought money and lots of it, and usually their appearance heralded John's. She often wondered if he was mixed up with them somehow, but she saw no evidence of any additional coin or goods to confirm her suspicions, and her heart had leapt at the first sight of him.

But that was then.

Now, only a matter of months later, his presence perturbed her. He carried an air of menace and was always looking over his shoulder, always on edge, always short-tempered. She still had no idea what had happened to change him; was it something he'd seen that had unmanned him, or was it something he'd done? Or was he being threatened? Either way, she had even less idea what to say or how to help. All she knew was that she needed to become more self-reliant, and soon. Her parents needed her, her daughter needed her, and increasingly she knew she couldn't trust John for anything.

* * * * *

Eight months after Mary Jane's birth, Sarah found herself back into the full swing of managing the inn. While Jacob liked to pretend he was a young man, the truth of the matter was that he was already into his late sixties and had a bad foot. Aunt Nettie was a godsend. Five years younger than her sister, Nettie knew how to cheer Betsey up when she was in one of her moods, which seemed to Sarah to be worsening by the day. Never mind how well Sarah cared for her daughter or how hard she worked, Ma moaned.

"Ere, never used to be like this in our day, mind. Did

it, sister? We'd never have done such a thing then. Really girl, you're 'opeless. Just hopeless."

"Now, now Betsey," interrupted Nettie. "Times change and Sarah's a lot on her plate, she has. Rock the babber in her crib for a minute while I make us a nice cuppa."

Nettie adored the little newborn, and between them, the two sisters took over the child-minding duties, leaving Sarah free to work.

"Is Mary Jane being spoilt by those two again?" asked Jacob as Sarah bustled around doing chores faster than he could think what needed doing next.

"Probably. But Ma and Aunt Nettie do a proper job of keeping her occupied," she frowned. "But she's an odd little thing."

"Whadya mean, odd? She, she looks a pretty wee moppet to me."

Sarah paused in her cleaning; her thoughts mirrored in her expression as she bit her lip. "I don't know exactly. But she's almost too quiet, too placid. I thought babbers were supposed to squawk and squeal a lot."

"Aye, they can, and many do. Some of your siblings were that way, but not you. You were a serious tot who studied the world around ya before ya did anything."

"You can hardly say that of me now," muttered Sarah, resuming her work. "If anything, I don't think enough."

"Are ya worrit, lass?"

"No, not exactly, just hoping it don't mean she's sickly, that's all. I'm going up to do the rooms."

Sarah escaped her father's gaze, not wanting to say what was deep in her heart. She *was* worried. Not that the child was sickly, but that she was morose. That the poor child was cursed with her grandmother's disposition or her father's bile, neither of which would serve her well in life.

Every time she climbed the stairs, Sarah remembered her first effort at motherhood and the failure it had been, but since the birth of Mary Jane, she felt more assured, more like a real mother and an adult in her own right, now she'd reached the age of twenty-one, even if she was still under her parents' roof.

The days and weeks fell into the same routine: cleaning, restocking the bar, doing the books, settling Molly, their kitchen maid, after Ma had scolded her over something trivial again, serving the clients and falling into bed late at night, thankful that Mary Jane was tucked up asleep in her crib.

Some nights she stood by her child's cot and watched her in awe. Her flawless skin gleamed in a sliver of light and was so soft to the touch. She wished upon every star, the Bible, and the souls of her departed sisters that the child would thrive and do well in life.

She climbed into her lonely bed hoping sleep would come before her thoughts overtook her. She hated those nights when she revisited her life over the last two years and considered what she could have done differently. Her mother and Mary had both warned her about the uncertainty of life with a sailor, but she'd paid no heed. Would she now? There were so many things she would change if she had the chance.

Attracted to the noise, Sarah rushed into the kitchen.

"Mistress Nettie's hid the bottle," whispered Molly,

crouching in the corner while Betsey, her eyes wide and staring, ransacked the area, sweeping anything in her way onto the floor. Several bowls lay smashed amongst the tangle of cooking utensils and a rolling pin threatened to trip her up. Molly would have quite a job cleaning up all the flour dusting the flagstones.

"Ma!" shouted Sarah as she hastened to prevent the contents of the Welsh dresser plummeting onto the stone slabs. Momentarily distracted, Betsey turned towards her daughter with a desperate stare, allowing Sarah to get close enough to take her hands and still her swinging arms.

"Where is it?"

"Shall we sit, Ma, and have a cuppa? You know you always like a cuppa at this time of the morning."

Sarah nodded to Molly, indicating she could come out of hiding and put the kettle back on the heat. Sarah helped her mother into her favourite chair and sat on the stool beside her, taking her hands in hers again. "What is it that ails ya this morning, Ma?"

Betsey raised her red-rimmed and bloodshot eyes. Sarah noticed how small her pupils were. "I can't find me medicine," she answered in a shaky voice.

"It'll be around somewhere. We'll find it later, but here's a nice cuppa tea," she said, taking the cup and saucer from Molly's hand and mouthing a thank you. "I've put lots of sugar in it, just how ya like it." She added an extra spoonful for good luck, hoping the sweetness would help restore her mother's well-being.

Betsey said nothing but took the saucer and briskly raised and lowered the cup to her lips. She found the first sip too hot and tipped some of the tea into the saucer and slurped it from there before finishing what was left from the teacup.

"Did ya enjoy that? Would ya like another?" asked Sarah.

Betsey nodded several times before suddenly lifting her head. Her eyes were unnaturally glassy, just like Sarah had seen John's eyes on occasions.

"I'm going up," Ma said defiantly and abruptly heaved herself out of the chair and disappeared through the door, leaving Sarah and Molly staring after her.

"What happened with the mistress, Molly?"

"Um. I don't wish to talk out of place … but she's not been 'erself of late."

"In what way?" Sarah urged the girl to say more.

"Sometimes she's all bustling and I can 'ardly keep up with her orders. Other times, she sits in the chair and says nuffin', just stares at the wall."

"Does she often shout at you?"

Molly nodded.

"What does Mistress Nettie say?"

"Oh, nuffin' to me, miss. It's not me place to talk about the mistress with Mistress Nettie."

"So, what bottle did she hide? And where?"

Molly blushed. "The new medicine."

Sarah perked her ears up. "What new medicine? Do you know where it is?"

Again Molly nodded. "In pantry, at bottom behind the barrels."

Sarah breathed a sigh of relief that Betsey hadn't found her way into the pantry and destroyed a year's supply of jams and jellies, and pickles. She soon found what she was looking for and read Laudanum on the label, but also words she'd never noticed before: Poison and Opium.

Sarah's heart thumped. Did this explain her mother's strange behaviour of late? She knew laudanum was commonly used and recommended by doctors and chemists to alleviate any manner of complaints, but opium? She'd heard a lot about the dangers of opium and seen the effects on some in the taproom. "Do you know how much she takes?"

"No, miss. Not exactly. She keeps it in her pocket mostly and adds it her to tea or ale. She says it's a lifesaver, makes her feel better, but it tastes nasty."

Sarah pulled the cork and sniffed, pulling her head back and squawking in disgust. "Ugh." She'd need to speak with Aunt Nettie and find out why she hid it, if it was as harmless as everyone made out.

Maybe they could devise a plan to get Ma off the dreadful stuff. It obviously wasn't doing her any good. Sarah thought about the dullness she'd seen in her mother's eyes and a similar image flashed across her mind. Was John using laudanum too? Or worse, opium? Was that what caused the changes in him?

Sarah didn't know for certain, but she had a gut feeling it was the cause of all the problems.

Back in the bar, Sarah was surprised to see how busy it had become. She had no time to mention Ma's behaviour or her medicine to Da, not that she wanted to worry him, but he'd need to know eventually.

As she flitted from table to trestle to table, the talk among the customers was mostly about the public hanging last month of William Palmer for murdering his friend. In the past, she'd not paid much attention to the talk. She never understood people who found pleasure in watching such a thing. She knew it was meant as a deterrent to warn others not to break the law or they too would end up on the gallows, but to go and watch someone die like that sent shivers up her spine.

What caught her interest this time was that the man was a doctor who knew about poisons, but that wasn't what got him into trouble.

"Not a surprise really. It's what 'appens when ya gamble."

"He were on 'is way to debtors' prison, they said."

"But how did 'e get to sabotage the autopsy?"

"He were a doctor, numbskull. And were allowed in the 'ospital. They say he threw away the guts so they couldn't find the poison."

"He was probably on the poppy. Ya know what that stuff does to ya head."

Although a lot of gossip circled from all sides after his trial the previous year, rumours had spread in the interim about the deaths of several other people surrounding this so-called Dr Palmer.

"They reckon he done away with his missus and the kiddies 'n all."

Shocked by what she'd heard, Sarah felt sorry for the woman and her children who had been pushed into penury by the evil man, and who died in unusual circumstances, but there was nothing she could do. What she wanted to know about was the opium and what it did to people. And she had an inkling as to who she could ask, if she could avoid arousing suspicion.

The chemist's wife was known to mind the shop alone while the doctor and the apothecary took lunch together at noon on a Friday. Sarah decided she would go then to talk with the woman, as soon as she could find someone to fill in and help her da with the lunchtime trade while she was away.

Two weeks later, her nephew Ted popped in unexpectedly, giving Sarah an opening.

"Hey, Ted lad. Nice to see ya," said Jacob. "What brings you in this day?"

"Nothing special, Grandpa. I've an hour off, and Ma said I should see how things were doing."

Sarah saw an opportunity and started to cough; she rubbed her eyes vigorously until they were red and looked sore.

"Oh, Ted, am I glad to see you. Can you hold the fort for me while I race up to the apothecary and get summat for this cough?"

"When did this start, lass?" asked Jacob, concerned. "Are you feeling al'right?"

"I'm fine, Da," she said between forced coughs. "I just need some cordial to soothe me throat some."

"Of course, I can," said Ted, stripping off his jacket and rolling up his sleeves. "Be a pleasure to do something different."

"I won't be long. Promise." Sarah threw her cloak around her shoulders, tied on a bonnet and dashed out the door before he could change his mind.

While Mrs Spence was above Sarah's class and they would be unlikely to ever share tea together, she was a chatterer and liked to talk to anyone who came into the shop. The bell behind the door tinkled as Sarah entered.

Mrs Spence immediately looked up to see who it was. "Hello. Mrs Clements, i'nit? How can I help you?"

Before she forgot what she said she'd come for, Sarah said, "I need some cordial or tonic for my cough," and proceeded to demonstrate.

"Sounds like an irritation rather than a chesty cough," said Mrs Spence. "I have just the thing."

She reached for a bottle and placed it on the counter, while Sarah pushed a few small coins towards her.

"I wondered," Sarah mused, pretending more ignorance than was real, "can you tell me anything about this medicine I've heard of, called lord-y-mun, or summat like that? Is it any good?"

"Do you perhaps mean laudanum? Oh, I can tell you it's a wonder drug. We've had so much success with it. Ladies who – you know," she whispered, "– suffer during their courses," before continuing in a louder and more enthusiastic voice. "And it's a great help for those with the vapours or fainting. It's perfectly safe for babies and young children with teething problems, and it's the perfect answer for anyone who has a headache or stomach ache. It's a very good painkiller. I could highly recommend it. Why, do you want some, dear?"

"No, I don't think so, I just wondered what was in it." She lowered her voice to a murmur. "I've heard there's opium." Sarah glanced about, pretending to make sure they were alone and not overheard. "And people go all funny in the head and can't get enough of it."

"Oh, Mrs Clements, you mustn't listen to gossip. Yes, I'm sure those who partake of pure opium do indeed get addicted and go 'funny in the head' as you put it. But it's because they smoke it, rather than taking the recommended dose. It's a vice then, not a tonic, mind. Nothing like we suggest. It can make them very disoriented and overly tired when taken that way. And those places you hear about that supply it are not to be recommended; full of vagabonds and militants, so I'm told. But laudanum is harmless in its diluted form and is purely a medicinal aid. It's very good for you, I can assure you of that."

"So, do you think some of our sailors take it? The opium, I mean. Do they perhaps get ... how can I explain it?" Sarah hesitated, trying to find the right words. "Um, quarrelsome or perhaps sullen? I sometimes worry for our safety, with some of the people I see around the streets."

Mrs Spence pursed her lips. "Well, I have heard of some, I admit, especially the long haulers. They get a taste of it in those foreign places and can't do without when they get back, but I'm told they are harmless, even if they do appear to be not quite their usual selves."

Sarah nodded. "Ta to ya, missus." She took her bottle of cough cordial and left. She'd got the answer she needed.

9
Nothing but heartbreak

December 1858

Over the last two years, Sarah had heard more about war than she'd ever wanted. First, there was the seizure of the cargo ship *Arrow* in Canton in 1856, with the crew arrested on suspicion of piracy, and before she could grasp the consequences of that event, less than a year later, there was a rebellion in India against British rule.

Neither skirmish made a lot of sense to Sarah, but she was glad she was safe on home soil. Deep down she could understand why those foreigners would fight back against being told what to do in their own land. She couldn't imagine what it would be like if invaders tried to take away her way of life, uneventful as it was.

Back in her world, little had changed. The inn was as full of regulars and incoming sailors as always. Molly and Ma still churned out meal after meal to feed the hungry, and Mary Jane continued to delight.

One day, Sarah finally found a chance to talk to Aunt Nettie. "I'm worrit about Ma," she said. "Have been for some time. She takes an awful lot of laudanum. I didn't realise it were so much. I thought it were a simple tonic the doctor had given her, but it's got opium in it. Didya know? Should I do summat?"

Copious and obliging as always, Nettie agreed. "I know dear, I did wonder myself when she had those nasty turns backalong but decided she were better with it than without. I did have a talk to her, mind, and she's reduced the amount she takes a little. It's so common these days, I'm sure there's nothing to worry about. I'd leave well alone."

Sarah wasn't as convinced, but Nettie was right. Ma was in a far better frame of mind most days and less prone to melancholy when she took it. And since Ma in a better mood made her life easier, Sarah said no more.

Over the ensuing months, she became increasingly aware of how many British soldiers and seamen were being sent to fight and never coming home. Some of their regular customers fitted that bill. She just hoped it wouldn't include John, but she would have no way of knowing until he either turned up or the authorities told her he was missing, or dead. Often, she didn't know where her husband was, what route he was sailing or what ship he was on.

You can't worry about what you don't know, was his repeated philosophy, but she worried anyway.

Months would pass without word, then more months.

'Get used to it,' he'd told her one time when she asked. 'There's nuffin' I can do about it when the ship don't go to port.'

But she sometimes wondered if that was an excuse. She knew he didn't like writing and sensed he had better things on his mind. She often pondered if it was other women or the poppy that drew him most. On one occasion, he arrived home before the mail telling her he was on his way. But as usual, his stopover was short, and he was soon back at sea again.

Sarah tried asking, "You're not leavin' so soon, are ya? Can't you stay a while longer? 'Twould be good to have ya home for a bit."

"Stop harpin' on all the time, will ya? You knows how it works. Now leave me be," came his churlish response.

Sarah felt terribly lonely a great deal of the time, despite having Mary Jane and her family around her.

On the rare occasions John was home, she began to wonder what difference he made to her life. Often distracted, he seemed excessively tired and cross more times than not. He still refused to talk to her about what he'd seen that was so terrible it had eaten into his soul, or what life was like aboard his ship. She'd learnt more from the sailors in the barroom about the harsh conditions on board an ocean-going ship than from anything John said. What upset her most was that he spent such little time with their child, but more importantly, she realised her spirit no longer lifted the way it used to when he was around.

He was gentle enough during intimacy, with no repeat of the aggressive mating she'd once endured, but nothing like the way she remembered of their early days. To her mind, they didn't make love any more, he simply took her as if it was a duty before he went to sleep.

Still hoping to hold her marriage together and

recapture some of their earlier closeness, Sarah tried to engage him in conversation. She asked about the things she hoped he might talk about, like places or anything that had taken his fancy, or what he knew about the things she'd heard talk about. She wanted to understand how the impounding of the *Arrow* had caused an incident big enough to start a second war with China, and why both sides accused the other of disrespect and disputed ownership of the vessel.

"Whadya wanna know?" he growled.

"I'm betwaddled by all the names. They sound so strange I can't get me tongue around them, and get 'em mixed up. But I think I've worked out that we, the British, want to anchor in certain ports, and for traders to live and work there, but the Chinese won't let us."

"More or less. Tis the opium. It's against the law to trade the stuff, but it don't stop the trade none. Or the smuggling. Tis a cut-throat business. If we shared, 'twould be better for all."

Sarah didn't think she liked that idea. If what she'd been hearing – and seeing – was right, then opium did a lot of damage. Too many men were coming home with that glazed look, dull grey skin and utterly morose frame of mind she saw in John. If people weren't killing each other over the stuff, they were likely killing themselves using it.

"So, are ya telling me the *Arrow* incident was an excuse for the British to start another war to get what they wanted?"

"Pretty much," he shrugged, no longer interested. "But why d'ya care? It ain't nuffin' to you nor's it gonna affect ya."

Sarah couldn't agree. She knew it already had. Both her husband and mother were addicted to the poppy, each in their own way, but John's addiction was greater and would be the death of him.

* * * * *

In the twenty-one years since Queen Victoria had been on the throne, Christmas had become a celebration for everyone to enjoy. Sarah had grown up with cards and decorations and gifts. Her joy with it all, lost after losing her first baby, had returned now she had Mary Jane.

And John was home. Could this be a turning point?

"Whadya think?" she asked of the two-year-old at her feet with a tinkle in her voice. Mary Jane, playing with the brightly coloured pieces of paper and strips from magazines in the basket on the floor, uttered some indistinguishable sounds that delighted her mother.

"Clever girl. So do I."

With no space for the sort of Christmas tree that Sarah had seen on the front of greeting cards in the shops, Sarah had gathered sprigs of holly and mistletoe, branches of catkins and swathes of ivy. She hung them around the walls, held in place by ribbons pinned to the picture rail then, using a mixture of flour and water, she had glued the strips into loops and strung them together to make paper chains and was now hanging them around the room.

"I'd better hurry before the doors open, or your grandma will be onto me," Sarah told Mary Jane as she gathered up the child and what was remaining in the basket. "I'll finish it tomorrow morning."

The child giggled in her arms as Sarah blew raspberries on her neck. At times like this she felt like a child herself, but before the year was out she'd be twenty-four, and certainly no longer a child. She wondered what her life ahead would look like, and hoped her heart would not be as heavy as it had been these last few years.

Early in the new year, while England was still in the depths of winter, she and Mary Jane waved goodbye to John as he headed overseas on another journey.

As she stood in the doorway watching his figure fade into the distance, she realised she no longer cared.

Part Two

Joy and Sorrow

10
A new era

March 1861

Nonplussed, Sarah sat staring at the enumerator, trying to take in what he was saying.

"I need to list the details of everyone who resides in this dwelling on this day: their names, age, gender, marital status, occupation and where born, starting with the Head of the Household. Who is the head?"

She struggled to know how to answer, not the actual questions, although she sometimes wondered who the head was, but the intent. According to law, ostensibly her father was the head because he was the oldest male, but in fact, she now ran the business, even if someone else held the licence. Incensed the brewery had taken away their licence, she struggled with how overlooked she'd become in the process.

"My name is Sarah, I'm 26, I live with my parents, Jacob and Elizabeth, at The White Hart Inn, and I'm a ..." She hesitated. What else could she say? The facts were so cold and didn't remotely tell the story of her life.

"I'm a widow. No, no children living here." Not that day. Not the day he was asking about.

The man wrote down everything she told him and left, moving on to the next house, the next family, the next set of records.

After he'd gone, she thought the details she'd provided of the transient sailors who currently lodged upstairs would tell a greater story of their comings and goings than that same information would act as a witness of her life.

What none of it said was how her life had disintegrated, and she had no idea how to put it back together.

When John left on that cold winter's day over two years ago, she'd known – or rather suspected – she was pregnant again. As she watched him walk away, she chose not to tell him. Deep in her heart, an instinct, an unsettling gut feeling, told her it would be the last time she would see him.

From then on, she'd never heard from him again. No one had heard of him. No one knew where he was. Eventually, two ships from the same line were declared wrecked at sea – a storm had claimed both vessels, the cargo and all lives were lost, or so they said. But was one of them John's ship? She didn't know. She'd received nothing from the authorities to confirm the reports. Nothing to say John was actually dead.

Was she a widow? Or an abandoned wife? Would she ever know for certain? She knew there was no hope he would return, but the thought lingered. Without a body, without someone verifying they'd seen him dead, without proof, she would have to wait seven years before he would be declared officially deceased. With each passing year, loneliness and despair ate deeper into her soul.

The only good that had come from their relationship was the children; or specifically, her son John Jacob, whom she had promptly nicknamed JJ. He'd gone his full term and was a big, hearty boy when he arrived in the autumn of '59. He immediately brought joy to the household, but less than three months later, she clutched Mary Jane tightly in her arms and mourned. 'Oh, please no. Not my baby girl. Not so soon. I promise I will never forget you.' Sarah keened as she'd heard her mother keen, as other women had keened for children taken too young. Heart-wrenching sobs racked her body.

Two weeks before Christmas, Mary Jane succumbed to the terrible whooping cough killing children throughout the city. Sarah rocked the girl to and fro, murmuring sweet nothings in her ear, words she would never hear. Sarah remembered the Christmases when she had happily decorated The White Hart with garlands and swathes of greenery, Mary Jane at her feet playing with the coloured pieces of paper. She doubted she would ever feel that euphoria over Christmas again, not without her daughter.

Sarah swore it was one of the mariners who brought the illness to her door, and the poor child suffered because of it. Coughing and coughing until she couldn't breathe. Sarah would never forget the frightening sound of the horrible whoop as the girl gasped for breath. The three-year-old's nights were fraught with coughing, followed by vomiting. Her eyes rolled into her head with exhaustion. Nothing Sarah did helped. The girl couldn't even swallow to drink enough to sustain her.

Night after night, Sarah sat with her, unable to leave her side, unable to rest and unaware of anything going on around her. She assumed Ma and Da were managing the pub downstairs, but she'd not set foot in the taproom for weeks, deliberately. It wouldn't be good for custom if she gave the cough to everyone else. Nor did she want to. She was bereft – and alone.

Long after the census keeper had left, she still sat vividly recalling the moment she gave her son up. 'Mary, please, I beg you.' Tears flowing unhindered down Sarah's cheeks. She wiped her nose on the sleeve of her blouse. 'You have to take 'im. He can't stay here.'

'But Sarah, JJ needs his mother. He needs your milk.'

'I've nothing to give 'im, Mary. Nothing. I've no energy. No milk. I'm so scared of giving him this disease and losing him too, that I've not been near 'im.'

'Tis true that,' said Aunty Nettie, nursing the wee babe in her arms at the other side of the room. 'We've been managing but …' She let the sentence drift. Her meaning clear.

Sarah knew it was a lot to ask. Mary was grieving, still in official mourning, having been widowed less than a year before. On top of everything, she now had to earn her own living as a seamstress. She'd lost weight and seemed taller and thinner than ever. But Ted was home again. Ted would help. Sarah was desperate.

Mary looked at her distraught sister, at JJ in Nettie's arms and, after a pause, nodded.

'Oh. Ta, Mary. Ta ever so much.' Sarah sobbed, keeping her distance, although desperate to hug her sister in gratitude. She didn't know how the cough was passed on but she was taking no chances. 'I'll come get him back as soon as Mary Jane is well, and I'm back on my feet,' Sarah promised. Except that had been 16 months ago. Mary Jane had never recovered, and her precious boy was still with Mary …

Sarah pulled herself out of her reverie. She had work to do. She would gain nothing by looking back. What was past was past, but she felt like a lost soul looking for something, anything, that would lighten her spirit.

She had donned black the day of Mary Jane's passing and had worn it ever since. She mourned her daughter, and appearances suggested she also mourned her missing husband. If society wanted to believe that to be the case, she wouldn't disappoint them. She no longer went to church, no longer found enjoyment in reading Dickens's stories, no longer bantered and laughed.

Her life had shattered as surely as the panes of glass at the Crystal Palace during a storm last February, which had also brought down the enormous spire on Chichester Cathedral. She'd never been to Chichester or seen the cathedral, but if it were anything like the spires of churches hereabouts, then it was big. If edifices such as those could succumb to the will of nature and be rebuilt and survive, then so could she.

She rose from the table and went to find her father. "Hello, Da. What's to be done this day?"

"Aye, Sarah lass, not much I'm afraid to say. Tis quiet, too quiet if I'm honest. Has that gov'ment man gone yet?"

"Aye. I told 'im the facts he asked for and he left. But I told him you and Ma were a good twenty years younger. I don't want no officials telling us you're too old or summat."

In truth, Da was seventy-three and had aged a lot in subtle ways. He appeared more bent, not because his bones couldn't hold him up, but because he carried such weight on his shoulders. Both he and her mother missed little Mary Jane almost as greatly as she did. But where her da carried his grief inside, Ma had added Mary Jane's death to the list of her own children to mourn and had become more querulous and pettish as time had passed.

As if reading her thoughts, Da asked, "How's your Ma?" nodding to himself, but not reprimanding Sarah for lying on the census forms.

"She's as good as she'll be for today," Sarah answered carefully.

Over time, she and Aunt Nettie had persuaded Ma to be more mindful with the laudanum. Coming off the drug had caused endless problems and exacerbated her melancholy to the point she'd taken to her bed and hadn't risen for days. But two years on, with small, careful doses, her ma could keep the kitchen operating and keep the place running. She had to.

They'd been forced to let Molly go when the brewery decided to award the licence to another man without any warning; a man who'd walked in and thrown his weight about but never hung around to do any work. She and Da became the drudges while the man did the ordering and paid the bills. He usually ordered the wrong type of scrumpy and beer to the ones their regulars were used to. That alone, she believed, was to do with the slower trade. That, and maybe the fact she wasn't their favourite barmaid any longer since she'd lost her spirit.

Something about not being the licence holder ate at Sarah until she decided it was time to take matters into her own hands. She was determined to take charge of her life for a change. It would take effort. She had closed her heart and mind to so much for so long, and they'd have to fight the brewery and the manager, but she'd win them over, somehow.

"Time to step up, Sarah," she said to herself, "and your first step is to get JJ back."

Three weeks later, on a fine spring day, Mary came up on the train from Bath bringing JJ with her. Ted accompanied her to help with all the paraphernalia an eighteen-month-old boy needed.

"Can you take those things upstairs to my room, please, Ted?" said Sarah with her eyes glued on the child Mary held by the hand. "And put ya ma's bag in the room you used to use. You staying too?"

"Not this time. I'm aways off after I see Grandad. I'll see ya dreckly."

"Righto, lad," she said absently, her whole focus on JJ as she sat on a chair leaning towards him.

"Say hello to your mam, John," said Mary, crouching down beside the toddler as he stared suspiciously. Sarah eagerly held her arms out to him, inviting him to sit on her knee.

"Tis wonderful to see you again, my darling boy," she murmured, hoping that something about her voice might stir a memory, but she was disappointed.

The boy buried his head into Mary's shoulder, threw his arms around her neck and refused to let go.

Almost unbalanced by his unexpected movement, Mary reached out a hand to steady herself, but then placed her arm underneath his legs and stood up. "Come on, silly boy," she cooed, chucking him under the chin. "What's the matter, then? Eh? You know who this is. We've talked about your mam a lot. I've told ya all about her. She's a special lady and we all love her and we want you to love her too."

Gradually, the boy lowered his arms and turned his head enough to peer out with one eye only. Mary nodded to Sarah as she felt the boy relax.

Sarah approached, looking over Mary's shoulder with a grin, and whispered a quiet boo. The boy giggled, shrinking his head down between his shoulders.

"See what I've got for you," offered Sarah, holding out a biscuit. "Would you like it?"

JJ nodded. From within the safety of Mary's arms, he stretched out his hand to take it from Sarah.

Keeping her voice smooth Mary said, "How about you sit on Sarah's knee and eat the biscuit, while I take my off my gloves and coat? That's a good boy."

Sarah swiftly sat down on the rocker, and Mary lowered the boy onto her knee. His skin smelling of soap gave Sarah gooseflesh as she tried not to hug him too tightly and scare him.

"There's a nice biscuit, i'nit? See how Aunt Mary has taken off her coat and is going to make a nice cuppa for us both. We're all family here and you are my precious, precious boy."

Her heart hammered in her ears. It was a wonder he couldn't hear it too, since it felt so loud, but she couldn't control her emotions. She had her child in her arms and all seemed right in the world again. She closed her eyes to force back the tears threatening to let her down and maybe frighten the youngster. She couldn't let that happen.

A few minutes later, as Sarah rocked back and forth, his half-eaten biscuit still in his grasp, the toddler sank deeper into her arms and fell asleep. Sarah sighed with relief. Maybe the transition wouldn't be so bad after all.

"That's gert, i'nit?" whispered Mary, quietly putting the tea things together. "He were so 'cited on the train, making sounds like the clack of the wheels and the hiss of the steam, he used up all 'is energy."

"Tis almost too good to be true," Sarah breathed. "To have him with me again. For a long time, I didn't think I'd ever find the strength to open me heart again, and I began to think he'd be better off staying with you forever. You must have read my mind when ya wrote to me that day."

Sarah remembered, the day she decided she needed to take hold of her life and turn it around was the same day she received a letter from Mary suggesting they come up to visit. "The timing was perfect."

"And for me, Sarah," said Mary hesitantly.

"Why? Whatcha mean? Is there anything wrong?"

"No," Mary assured her hurriedly. "Not wrong exactly, but I've the need to take in a boarder. With Ted home, and Amey workin' as a nursemaid and Ann still needing my attention, there don't seem to be the time or the money to properly care for this beautiful young man. And he should be with his mam. He'll soon forget me, and that's the way it should be. But any longer and he'd never accept you as 'is mam anyway. Tis best this way."

"What way? Whatcha saying?" asked Sarah suspiciously.

"I'll be leaving now, while he's asleep. I won't stay like I said. I think you need time alone together."

Sarah suddenly wasn't so sure.

At that moment, Betsey wobbled into the kitchen.

"What's all this going on?" Her eyes narrowed, she looked from Mary to Sarah and JJ. "What's he doing here?"

"He's me son, Ma. You know that. It's time he came home to me. Mary's done enough."

"Humph!" Betsey plopped down into her armchair that no one else dared use. "Well, you'd better make sure he behaves. I'm too old to have little 'uns under me feet and by all the saints that be, if he makes any noise he'll hear about it from me."

"Ma, that's unreasonable," intervened Mary before Sarah could say anything she'd regret. "He's only a babber still. He's bound to cry from time to time, but the gentler ya be with 'im, the more ya talk with 'im and help 'im learn, the better he be."

"Ere, I've done me time with all that after Mary Jane. And a waste of time tis when they go too soon," grumbled Betsey, the patience she'd shown with her granddaughter no longer evident. "Some'un else can do it all."

"Exactly," chipped in Sarah. "It's my turn. He belongs with me. And I'll look after 'im and teach 'im 'n he'll bring the joy back into this place."

Betsey glared at Sarah, grunted and settled back into her chair. "Now, Mary, you'll be staying awhile then? Haven't seen you in months, mind. Time we had a proper chat. Sit down, girl, sit down."

Mary shrugged. "I've just made a pot o' tea. Let me refresh it and I'll stay a bit, but I must be on me way soon. We don't want JJ to see me leave, and I must get the last train. The girls are at 'ome, waitin' for me."

Sarah took the hint. She eased her way to the edge of her seat and stood, carrying the sleeping JJ in her arms up to her room. She lay him in the crib that had awaited his return and watched him sleep, filling her mind and heart with precious memories.

October 1861

In an attempt to cheer her mother up, Sarah bought one of the newly released editions of *Mrs Beeton's Book on Household Management*. Sarah had heard of Mrs Beeton for a couple of years because of the serialised instalments, but having all the advice and information in one book had prompted her to purchase it. "Whadya think, Ma?"

"Some good suggestions, I'll admit, even if she is a whippersnapper. She's even younger than you, I hear," nodded Betsey sagely while turning the pages. "But I'll agree with a lot of what she says. But some of it's so easy it's hard to believe it needed writing down."

"Maybe, but not everyone is as clever as you at cookin' and managin' a kitchen," praised Sarah. "Some women might need it."

"Aye. Tis true that. I been doing it since I were a young 'un and it comes natural now."

"And ya taught me well, and all the kitchen maids we've had. Ya should be proud, Ma."

From then on, Sarah noticed the book always sat open on the dresser. Frequently, Ma complained about a recipe not being to her liking, or not working out the way she expected, even though the book promised that all recipes had been tested and proven. After a time, Sarah realised Ma had chosen to work her way through the book to show she knew as much, or more.

And since then, there'd been a change in her mother. Progressing through the recipes page by page meant she tackled fare she wouldn't normally make, including desserts and biscuits. Two things happened. Business picked up as word got around *The Mistress* was cooking tasty meals that were different to the norm and, bit by bit, JJ wormed his way into her affections.

Fascinated by the biscuits and sweet treats his grandma made, JJ hovered in the kitchen, keeping well out of the way, but his eyes watched her every move. Many a time, Ma used to try to shoo him away, but he'd simply smile coyly and point to whatever she was cooking and say, "I try?"

Making sure to say 'fank u' every time she handed him a morsel, he'd lick it carefully first, then bite off a small piece and roll it around his mouth. He'd nod, never talking with his mouth full, and then say 'e-um' or 'i-ce', another of his words that meant he liked what he'd tasted.

For his second birthday last month she had baked a cake and made a variety of jellies to please him. He was even allowed to stir the bowl on occasions, just like Mary Jane had. As she talked to him, the more words he learned; and the more he talked, the more Grandma Betsey taught him, just as Mary had predicted.

Sarah was forever grateful that the day she had been in the bookshop buying the cookbook, her eye had been caught by another set of books. She'd known for some time that Charles Dickens's latest novel, *Great Expectations*, was out in serial form, but this was the first time she'd seen it produced in softcover form. Three beautifully cloth-bound books, with the gold-embossed title and volume number impressed on the spines, appealed to her.

She'd fingered them longingly, her love of reading rekindled, and she'd opened the first volume to the front page.

"Do you also wish to purchase these remarkable books?" asked the bookshop owner, watching intently to gauge if another sale was in the offing.

"I'd love to, sir, but I fear they're beyond my pocket at the time. Thank you for letting me look, but I'll just take Mrs Beeton's book for Ma."

"What if I put them aside for you and you only pay me half for the first book now, and you can collect the other volumes when you have recouped your finances?"

Sarah's heart did a little thump and her eyes strayed back to the three volumes where the weak sun shining through the plate glass window accented the covers. She looked between the shopkeeper and the books and saw a gentle smile light up the man's face. "You'd do that for me?" she asked cautiously.

"Yes, my dear Mrs Clements. I would. You have been a loyal customer for several years, and I admire your delight in the written word, and your tenacity in life."

"Thank you, sir. Then I will," she blushingly agreed, wondering how much of Bristol knew of her life and all she'd struggled with.

Sarah carried her parcel, containing her ma's cookbook and her first volume of Dickens's novel, clutched to her chest all the way home. Dreams of sinking into another world drew her into fanciful thoughts of what else was possible in life. The reality was she had little time for reading at all, but the opportunity to have a set of such beautiful books on the shelf in her room was too much to pass up.

Watched over by young John Jacob as she placed the volume in pride of place, she had another thought. She could make the most of their time together by reading to him, like she had at the church to all those other children who couldn't read. She would instil in him her joy of reading and stories and the other worlds that words could take them to.

"Whadya think, JJ?" she said, lifting the two-year-old into her arms. "Would ya like that, me boy?"

JJ laughed, which Sarah took as agreement.

December 1861

Sarah's daily routine gave her little free time and even less opportunity to dream about the possibilities she'd once thought about, before John had stolen her heart, and long before he'd broken it. What she was grateful for was the increased business. Ma's cooking had generated a lot of new custom and armed with that uptake, she and Jacob had tackled the brewery about who should do the ordering and what they needed.

There'd been a right set-to, with voices raised, but finally the manager had agreed. 'Al'right, al'right,' he said. 'Didn't work the way I fought it would. Have it your way and send me a list.'

Sarah suppressed a grin. Getting him to admit he'd blundered and would allow Jacob to decide what he wanted from now on was all Sarah cared about.

"It might only be a small win, Da," she reminded him later, "but it was a win."

At least, with more money coming in, they'd been able to re-employ Molly to help Ma, and engage Ada to do the more menial tasks.

Life was looking up.

* * * * *

News that the Prince Consort, Prince Albert was ill gathered momentum, but even so, the news of his death came as a great shock.

"Oh my, have ya heard the news?" gasped Sarah, reading the headlines.

Monday, 16th December 1861, would be a date that would be remembered throughout history. Every column in every newspaper was filled with stories about the prince and what he had achieved in the twenty-one years he had been married to the Queen, and how respected he had become.

Before long, the inn filled up. As she went about her tasks, the gossip around the taproom seemed genuinely heartfelt, even though most people had been suspicious of the foreign prince to start with. But all that had changed with the passing of time.

"He was only forty-two, 'n all."

"Too young. Too young by far," she heard, which was

saying a lot, since life expectancy was close to forty for the average person. But Prince Albert wasn't average. He was privileged and had the best of everything at his fingertips, but he still thought of those who didn't have the same options.

"He did his best, 'e did."

Through his humanitarianism, speaking out against slavery and child labour; his interest in all things new, manifesting itself in science, the arts, and music; and his determination to modernise the monarchy, the military and the universities, he endeared himself to the many.

He might not have lived in any of the ramshackle houses with fetid water running in the streets that many did, but he knew about them.

"He tried to get the officials to improve living conditions. I'll give 'im that."

And unlike those in such impoverished states, and even though he would never lack food, or money to buy medicines, or bury any of his nine children due to squalid and polluted conditions, he challenged the authorities, time and again, to make improvements and raise the living conditions of the poorest.

The chatter continued as she moved around the barroom.

"Why him? Why was 'e taken when 'e did such good?"

"Death comes to all of us, never mind 'ow well off."

"And the Queen, poor woman. They say she's distraught."

"Course she is, mate. And it be a bare nine months since she lost her mother 'n all."

Sarah felt her skin creep and a shudder slither its way down her body. She remembered all too clearly when the Duchess of Kent passed. She couldn't imagine the pain the Queen must be experiencing. Sarah still mourned the loss of Mary Jane, and John at times, both emotionally and physically, even though he'd essentially left her long before he'd died, but to bury her ma or da would be more than she knew how to cope with.

As the days went on and more stories of Albert's deeds emerged, Sarah thought back a decade, to the time she'd attended the Crystal Palace and how wonderful it had all been. The prince was credited with doing so much good, pundits began to question how well the Queen would manage without her beloved Albert at her side.

At another table, she overheard more toing and froing of comments.

"Let up, will ya? She's gone into mourning. We can hardly expect anything from her for some time," argued those who sympathised with her.

"But we can't let those vagabonds in parliament loose. It were 'im that mostly kept 'em under control," raged those who hated the government.

"Don't you believe it. She's her own woman, that one. She's as tough as can be."

"Are you daft or summat? He never said a word publicly about politics. It's she who is our Queen and don't you forget it."

"He were a grand bloke in the end."

The country mourned as tributes to his memory continued. Funeral arrangements were outlined in detail by the newspapers. Sarah read about who would be in which of the coaches, how many horses would draw them, who would accompany the hearse drawn by six matching horses, and which guards would do what, but Victoria, too overwrought to attend, withdrew to Osborne House, their family home on the Isle of Wight.

On 23rd December 1861, Albert was taken from Windsor Castle, along a prescribed route that Sarah could not picture as she'd never seen the places mentioned, to his resting place at St George's Chapel. Every shop was closed and every blind drawn. The streets lay silent. The route was lined by the public dressed in deepest mourning.

Sarah's heart went out to her Queen. "God bless ya, Your Majesty," she whispered, understanding how sorely she grieved. Sarah still mourned her two children, her marriage, her loss, in the same way that thousands of women across the land grieved.

If they could persevere, then so could she.

11

The passing years

July 1863

Sarah sat beside her father's bed knowing he wouldn't remain long in this world. Much as she would have wished the whole family could be sat beside him, she knew that was impossible. There was a great deal to do still downstairs. They'd secured their victualler's licence back from the idiot manager and had been in full force trying to restore The White Hart to its past glory. So far, they'd been successful, but it had taken its toll on Jacob.

His raspy voice broke into her thoughts.

"What's that, Da? Are ya in pain?" Sarah quickly looked around for the laudanum she'd taken to giving him. It couldn't do any harm; the harm was already done. Years of being on his feet, years of lifting heavy barrels, and years of drinking had left him in severe pain.

His head moved from side to side. "No, my girl, wanna say ta," he forced out between laboured breathing. "You've been a blessing."

"Shush now, Da. Save your breath. Tain't nothing I've done that no one else could've. Rest now."

Her heart went out to him in his anguish. The gout had worsened over the years, and now his nights were filled with tossing and turning as he tried to find a comfortable place to lie. He complained his feet felt like heavy blocks of ice, and a burning pain throbbed through his big toes and up his legs. He'd reached the stage he could hardly stand. He deserved a better end, a more fitting reward for his life, but life was never kind, in her view.

Mary crept into the room. "Do you want a break, Sarah?"

Sarah shook her head. "Not unless you need me. I'd like to stay, if I can."

Mary had been a godsend the last couple of years. For several reasons, after JJ returned to live with his mother, Mary had decided to move back to Bristol. It allowed her to be closer to her parents and help her sister. Her son Ted had come back to live with her, which helped with the finances, and by being in a larger town, she had picked up more work as a seamstress.

"We'll manage. JJ's a good little fellow, i'nit? You've done well with him, Sarah."

"He likes his learning, that one, he do," Sarah commented, thinking of all the moments when she read to him, or he practised using a crayon. "How's Ma?"

Mary chuckled quietly. "She's in fine fettle. She and Aunt Nettie are happy lording it over the kitchen while Molly and Ada do all the work, but my Ted's never going to be a landlord. He spends too much time laughing with the clients and drinking the product."

Sarah tried to smile, she couldn't raise a laugh, even though she could imagine the scene. Ted was good at the books, a great accountant, but too friendly for his own good sometimes.

"I'll be down dreckly to give him a hand. Any news on Harriet?" Sarah could barely remember when she'd last seen her other sister.

Mary pulled a face. "It doesn't look like she'll be here anytime soon. I got a message to say she was unwell herself."

Sarah bit back a retort. Maybe she was. Harriet's life had been a difficult one too. Like Sarah, Harriet had lost one husband and buried two of her children, the most recent being ten-year-old Alex, less than twelve months since. She would still be in mourning. Even so, Sarah thought her lucky. Harriet had a new husband, a second chance, and nine other children to love and nurture and work beside her in the confectionery business. Sarah only had JJ, and she had so wanted a big family, but that didn't seem likely any longer.

Who would marry her, with her encumbrances?

Her mind skipped back a few months to the lavish March wedding for Edward, Prince of Wales and the Princess Alexandra of Denmark. She'd devoured the newspaper reports and wished she could have at least seen it, with all its pomp and glory and glitter. But like the wistful child she'd been a decade ago, wanting something that could never be hers, all Sarah could do was read about it. Not that she wanted such glamour, but she did yearn to be loved, and who would do that once Da was gone?

Her father suddenly grabbed her wrist, making

her jump. "Take the licence, Sarah. You promised. The White Hart is yours now."

"All will be right, Da. Don't upset yourself. I told you I'd never let ya down, and I won't."

"I know, I know, but you've been low for such a long time, I feared you'd give up. But think of it as your future, and for that lad of yours. I've got faith in you, I have. And promise me to look after your ma." He grimaced as he tried to move to a more comfortable position and bit his lip to stifle the groan.

"Be still, Da. Rest easy."

"I can't. Not till I know you're all set. Your ma. She won't manage on 'er own, she won't. She been a good woman, she has. A good woman …"

His voice faded and he seemed to drift into an uneasy sleep again.

Sarah picked up her book and started reading out loud. She'd started reading to her da a while back, just like she did with JJ, trying to take his mind off the numerous things bothering him. She kept the tone of her voice even and calm as she reread some of her favourite stories, and she sensed him slipping into a deeper sleep.

Quietly she tiptoed from the room, her mind already shifting to the chores that needed doing and the paperwork that would soon consume her.

Sarah walked into the taproom and felt her spirits lift immediately. This was her home, her comfy place, and she loved it best when it was full, bustling and noisy, like now. The only thing missing was the heat and smoky aroma from the fireplace, thanks to the warm July weather, in contrast to the previous unseasonably cold start to summer.

Behind the bar Ted looked frazzled. Spilt ale from overflowing tankards ran over the floor while customers hassled him for service.

"Ere, lad, fancy a hand?" She winked at him with a grin, picked up some of the filled pots and started to hand them out.

"Here y'are, lads. A pot or two to wet your whistle."

"Ere, Sarah, good to see ya smiling again."

"Just for you, me fellas. S'long as ya drink up and eat well, you'll always get a smile from me."

Sarah beamed inwardly, happy to be back to her old bantering self. Quite why the change she didn't immediately understand, since a lump sat in her chest and her stomach churned every time she thought of her da. But she'd promised to never let him down, and keeping the business going was her gift to him.

"Ta, Sarah," said Ted, wiping his brow and swallowing a slug of ale. "It's been right manic by meself."

Sarah swished a mop around to reduce the slops on the floor. "It's not what you're used to lad, that's all. This is normal for Da and me. Now keep filling 'n I'll do the serving."

As she dashed in and out between tables, she picked up snippets of conversation about the usual bankruptcies, petty crimes, and who felt hard done by. On the larger scale, she heard the gist of the political rumblings to do with whether there should be better port facilities at Avonmouth or Portishead some ten miles down river – and how much impact it would have on the local wharves and trade. So much had happened she really didn't understand, but if the mariners were worried about the increasing trend to use east coast ports instead of west coast, like theirs, then so was she.

"Raise a glass to those big wigs who did summat right for a change and gained gov'ment approval for the proposal."

"I'll drink to that. A rail line to Portishead can only mean more business."

"But not wi'out proper docks," argued one surly customer.

"They'll come. They'll be building a proper pier, 'twill be enough for now."

This was all news to Sarah, but if a rail link between the city and the coast was going ahead, even she knew that had to be a big benefit.

"As long as they don't take forever to build the damn thing, it'll be al'right, I guess, but if'n they take as long as this 'ere sur-spen-shun bridge near Clifton, it'll be generations afore 'twill be of use."

The building of the bridge, just a few miles from where she stood, suspended high above the Avon River across the gorge, had been the target of disgruntlement for thirty years. Some work was done, then it got held up due to rising costs while the design was revamped. Bankruptcy and a lack of funding stopped it completely for a time while they argued over the costs and whether it was still the best idea and in the best place. For many years, the two stone pillars on either side were the only indication a bridge would be built one day. After the death of the original designer, Isambard Kingdom Brunel, back in

'58, everyone believed it would never get finished, but it now looked imminent.

Sarah didn't pay attention to the detail because she didn't think it would make much difference to her life. She had far more immediate worries on her mind.

* * * * *

Even though she was expecting it, and – she thought – prepared herself for the inevitable, she hadn't expected the intensity of the sorrow that surged through her. Neither could she hold back the wail that escaped as she tried to push air into her lungs to release the pain. "Daaaa! Oh, Da. Nooooo!"

Mary held her sister close while Sarah's shoulders shook, and her hands covered her face hoping to block out the image of her ashen-faced father lying on his bed, his skin the colour of the freshly laundered pillowslip under his head.

"Shh. Sarah, my love. Don't weep," murmured Mary. "He's gone to a better place, where there'll be no more pain."

Sarah rested her tear-soaked face and red-rimmed eyes on her sister's breast, trying to regain control of her breathing. "I know. I do know, but oh, Mary, I'm gonna miss 'im so much," she said between hiccoughs.

"We can't be selfish about these things. He were ready, and we have to carry on with his memory lookin' over our shoulders."

Sarah nodded as Mary continued talking. Suddenly feeling more like a child than a woman approaching thirty, she let her big sister take charge.

"I've given Ma some extra laudanum. It'll help her sleep, but she'll be in a dark place when she wakes up, between the effects of that stuff and the realisation that Da's gone. It's funny, I never really thought of them much as a couple. They were just Ma and Da, but they've been together for well over fifty years. They shared in the loss of four of their children and kept home and hearth together for the rest of us. Makes ya think differently somehow."

"Aye, it does, I suppose. Never thought of it that way."

She listened to Mary as she moved around the room, closing the curtains and covering the mirrors. "I've arranged for a wreath to be hung at the door. I'm sure all Da's customers will want to know of his passing and to raise a toast to him."

"Will Ma want to wash the body alone or should we do it together?" asked Sarah dolefully, thinking she should have stopped the grandfather clock downstairs before she came up. "And we'll need to move him into the parlour for those who wish to say their farewells."

Sarah would regret not being beside her father, holding his hand, at the moment of his death, but that wasn't her destiny. That moment had belonged to her ma.

"Once the doctor's been, Sarah, we shall, but for now can ya get me as much black crape as ya can find to hang over the mirrors and swags for the doors? Since the three of us wear black anyway, there's little immediate need for more suitable clothes. I'll need lots of ostrich feathers. Are you listening, Sarah?"

Sarah pulled her eyes from her father's body. "What? Oh, yes, Mary, I heard ya. Are we sure he's gone? I wouldn't want him waking up in the coffin like we've heard of happening afore?"

Mary slipped her arm around Sarah once more. "I'm sure. And the doctor will confirm it. I promise. Unfortunately, Da won't be one to be saved by the bell."

Sarah offered Mary a weak smile, remembering how some of the more superstitious families tied a rope around the deceased's hand and attached it to a bell sitting above ground in case the person woke up and needed to alert someone.

"Can you also arrange for the notice in the newspaper? It doesn't have to be much, but it's important these days; oh, and Ma wants to have black-edged handkerchiefs made, but I might be able to sew some up."

"I can help with those," said Sarah.

Over the following three days, Da's body lay under the constant eye of Ma and Aunt Nettie, who came for her sister's sake, or Mary, herself and Ted, depending on the demands of the taproom and kitchen. Their sister Harriet remained in the valleys of Wales, with her new husband and brood of youngsters, still in mourning for her ten-year-old son.

Streams of people paid their respects to Jacob, some pithy, some eloquent, some meaningful. Nearly all brought tears to the mourners' eyes, despite the Victorian traditional of silent, respectful mourning.

"Will you hire mutes?" asked Sarah of her mother who was being anything but stoic. She shuddered while waiting for her mother's response and took deeper breathes to calm her nerves. She hated the mutes, who always made her feel inadequate with their soundless scrutiny.

"I don't want them silent, solemn-faced numpties anywhere near my Jacob," said Betsey close to anger. "They'll do no good."

Eventually, the wake was over. The undertaker called to remove the body, feet first through the door, so the spirits wouldn't call anyone else to death. The hearse, pulled by two bay horses and adorned with the almost regulatory ostrich feathers, made its way to the Holy Trinity of St Philip church on the hill above, where her father was laid to rest.

A memory seared on her brain forevermore.

"Goodbye, Da. I don't know what I'll do without ya."

12
Disaster looms

August 1863

"What's going on, Ma?" asked Sarah, rushing into the kitchen at her mother's raised voice, where she was met with smoke billowing from the firebox.

"This chit of a girl knows nothing," she snarled, pointing the stirring spoon in her hand towards Molly. "She nearly set the place afire, she did."

Sarah glanced at Molly's distraught face and saw the slight shake of her head and knew she was being unfairly blamed, again. If anything, Molly knew more about the vagaries of that range than anyone, having learnt to cook on it since it was new over a decade or more ago. She continued her attempts to clear the smoke and keep out of the way of the mistress's temper.

"Let me help," said Sarah, aiding Molly's attempts to pull open the two flues and, finding suitable cloths, she reached into the oven to rescue the food.

"Whadya know about it? You're never in the kitchen," grizzled Ma.

Sarah bit her lip. When Ma was in one of these moods, there was no arguing with her. She knew Sarah now managed the inn completely and had little time to spare. Reluctantly, she'd employed a man to help. She simply couldn't be in the taproom pulling handles, and serve them, as well as clean up and deliver food at the same time. Like now. If Mr Davidson hadn't been in today, Sarah could not have left the customers unattended.

She sighed. "Molly, open the outside door, then will you do whatever tis ya do to this thing to make it behave."

Molly needed no second bidding and quickly readjusted the fire and watched over it until it settled to a gentle heat.

"Well, I'm here now, Ma. Shall we have a cuppa?" offered Sarah.

"Miss Sarah," said Molly quietly, "I'll put the kettle on right away, I will, but see here?"

Sarah peered over Molly's shoulder. Lowering her voice to a bare murmur, the girl said, "See these bolts keepin' up the grate. They're right worn. They won't hold if any pressure is put upon 'em, but the mistress won't let me put the fire out to get 'em repaired."

"Hmm. Thanks, Molly. Good girl. I'll see what I can do."

Ma bustled around the table towards her favourite chair, her wide bombazine skirts rustling as she moved. At times, Sarah was convinced Ma made the most of her widow weeds, including the new widow's cap with a long black streamer at the back. She had no doubt her mother's grief was genuine and deeply felt, but Ma also liked to make sure people knew she was mourning.

"Very well, but it stinks of smoke in here. I don't know what this place is coming to since your da went."

"It'll clear soon, now we've got the door open, and whatever's cooking smells delicious." Flattery always put Ma in a better mood, and Sarah was willing to balance what she really wanted to say against what she knew would bring about a better outcome. "I've been telling customers you're back in the kitchen and cooking up Mrs Beeton's recipes again. They're lookin' forward to it."

"Is that right?" Ma said with a smile in her voice. "Well, then I suppose I better had. Molly, do you hear that girl? We've got more cooking to do."

Molly glanced at Sarah, her eyes speaking louder than her words. "Of course, ma'am." Since she did all the preparation, sauces, and pastry making, and whatever else the mistress asked of her, there was little respite anyway. Thankfully Ada, the new scullery maid, did all the scrubbing and cleaning these days.

Sarah studied the girl, well, woman now, since she was only about three years younger than Sarah herself. Dressed in black, as Ma had insisted, with a clean white mob cap, and now one very sooty grey apron, her small stature always belied her stamina. The whole household was in deep mourning, and would be for an entire year, but Sarah had a business to run, and while she wore black herself, she had to remain jolly with a happy smile on her face. Molly, on the other hand, had been with them since barely more than a child, except for that hiccough with the idiot manager a couple of years back, and knew more about the kitchen and that blasted range than anyone. And how to manage Ma and her moods.

Sarah would give the girl an extra coin when she could.

"Thank you, Molly," she said, as the woman delivered their tea. "You're an angel, ya know. I don't know what we'd do without ya."

"Ta for saying so, Miss Sarah." Molly blushed, never one who liked to be noticed.

"There, Ma, a nice cuppa. Now tell me about your day."

Sarah let her mind drift while Ma moaned about the price of vegetables, the difficulty getting the ingredients she wanted, the fact that Nettie hadn't been to see her this day, and how she would stay in deep mourning like the Queen.

"What's that ya said about the Queen?" asked Sarah, taken by surprise.

"I said it's been two years nearly since Prince Albert died and our Queen, bless her soul, is still wearing deep mourning. If it's good nuff for her not to enter half-mourning, then it's good nuff for me."

Until now Sarah hadn't thought about it. Da had been gone less than three months; it was rather too soon to make those decisions. Her mother had always worn black, or dark grey at best, saying she was still mourning the loss of her children. Mary had come out of deep mourning for her husband and mostly wore the lilacs and greys of half-mourning, until Da passed. As for herself, she shrugged, she too, had espoused full mourning for Mary Jane.

She stopped her train of thought and let the memories form. Four years had passed, and she could still hear the child's laughter and her voice as they read stories together. Sarah had stayed in mourning as the years slipped by and John didn't return. She still didn't know whether she was truly a widow or if he'd deserted her. Logic said he was dead. Not that it mattered any longer, wearing black had become an easy habit rather than a deliberate thought.

"Well, I'd better be getting back to it. The place will be full o' customers soon. And take care with that firebox, Ma. We don't want to be setting the place alight, now do we?"

Within a short time, the busyness of the taproom took her mind off her worries and allowed her to at least smile and chat and feel part of life. While the customers didn't chatter with her in quite the same way as they used to, especially since Da died, she was quietly pleased they kept coming. She must be doing something right. As long as she had customers, everything else would sort itself out.

Or so she promised herself.

* * * * *

Early one morning, a few weeks later, while readying for the breakfast crew but before she'd unbolted the main doors, she heard screams like nothing she'd heard before.

Terror-struck, she ran towards the kitchen. She could smell burning as smoke wafted into the corridor, and knew they were in serious trouble. As she ran through the kitchen door, she was met by a wall of fog. She raised her arm instinctively to protect her eyes, trying to see what had happened. Embers from the cooker lay on the stone floor and flames were starting to eat at the wooden table.

"Ma? Molly? Where are you?" she shrieked at the top of her voice.

From a distance, somewhere towards the outside door, she heard Molly shouting. "Outside. Out back."

"Stay there!" ordered Sarah.

"Oh, whatever shall we do?" Molly wailed.

Overtaken with black smoke, Sarah began to cough. She backed out of the room, shutting the door firmly behind her. She reached for the leather fire bucket they kept by the stairs and threw water at the door to damp it down. Then she rolled up the floor rug and stuffed it into the gap to prevent the smoke escaping.

Muttering to herself, her thoughts raced ahead. "Hope that holds. For now. Must call the brigade. I can't lose this place. Not now. I've got to save it. I just have to."

Bucket in hand, she raced into the taproom, gathered up a second pail, and tried to unbolt the door.

"Come on, you stupid thing!" she cried, frustrated that it hadn't slid easily the first time. Wasting precious seconds, she put the buckets down and used two hands. Finally, the bolt freed, she again grabbed the buckets and ran around into the alley that took her to the rear of the building. Breathless, she was glad to see Ma safely sitting on a stool well away from the kitchen wall. Molly was throwing water ineffectually from the trough into the doorway.

"We need a chain of people, Molly. Go sound the alarm. Make sure the brigade's been called and send people this way."

"I sent Ada. They should be on their way."

Sarah nodded as she repeatedly filled the bucket

and tossed water as far into the kitchen as possible. She doused the door and frame. Somewhere in the back of her mind she could hear Ma shouting, and in that moment an extra jolt of panic surged through her. Where was JJ? He should have been with Ma.

Shortly after, people arrived, and men took over the front position. Bucket after bucket was passed from hand to hand, but from her now safe position at the back she feared they wouldn't save much, but hoped they might save the upstairs. She prayed the door in the stone wall held, between the main part of the building and the kitchen.

The clanging of bells and the clop of hooves announced the arrival of the fire engine.

"Step out of the way, lady," said one of the uniformed firemen, pushing her aside. "Let the professionals do their job."

The adrenaline that had kept Sarah going drained away as soon as the pump was going and the hose began to make short work of the fire. Smoke billowed everywhere, irritating eyes and throats, and visibility was minimal. Suddenly, Sarah's earlier sense of panic returned as she realised she had no idea who had JJ.

"Ma," she called croakily, breaking into a spasm of coughing. "Ma?" She tried again, her throat burning with the effort. She felt her way along the wall to where she remembered seeing her mother last. "Ma?" she sobbed.

"I'm here," Betsey finally answered, sounding a lot further away than Sarah thought. "Where are ya, girl? I need ya to help me. I can't see for all this smoke, and it's hurting my lungs."

"I'm here, Ma," Sarah said, finally reaching Ma, her eyes red with weeping as she struggled for breath.

"Give me an 'and and 'elp me up."

Taking hold of Betsey's arm, Sarah helped her mother to her feet. "But Ma, where's JJ? I can't see him. I must find him!"

"He's fine. I sent him round to Mary's."

Sarah sucked as much air into her lungs as she could, almost sobbing with the pain. "On his own? Why? He's not safe on his own. He's only four."

"Phht! He'll be fine. It's only round a corner or two. He knows the way and he's much better there than here."

Sarah had to agree he was safe at Mary's – if he got there.

"I have to go check, Ma. I have to see him."

"What for?" she snapped but, after seeing her daughter's face, capitulated. "Al'right. Off with ya then. Molly'll help me."

Sarah picked up her skirts and began to run, but within moments was forced to stop. Bent over nearly double, she struggled to breathe as a coughing fit took hold. Using the walls of the houses for support, she made her way to her sister, her mind arguing with her instinct. She needed to see for herself that her boy was safe.

Shortly, Mary's door opened before her. Sarah stepped into the gloomy hall searching everywhere for JJ.

"He's in the kitchen, sis. And perfectly well," said Mary.

Sarah hurried down the corridor and, seeing the child sitting on a stool at the table, swept him up into her arms. "Mama's here now, JJ. You're safe, my boy. You're safe. Thank God."

JJ started squirming and wriggling but Sarah didn't care. She clung on tightly, even while scenes of the devastation at The White Hart, awaiting her return, played on her mind. "I can't lose you. I can't. I wouldn't survive if anything happened to you."

The insurance assessor was due at eight o'clock the following morning. Sarah had spent most of the night tossing and turning. She'd been told not to touch anything until the engineer had been, but she fretted about the mess, and the damage, and the extra workload, and the cost ... and in the back of her mind lurked Molly's remarks about the fire grate. She hadn't had the time to work out how to manage with the fire out for a couple of days or tackle Ma about the accident waiting to happen ... oh, what was she going to do?

She rose early and dressed carefully in her best mourning dress, which was hardly fashionable, but she didn't think the man would care. She had never adopted the heavily petticoated or crinolined dresses popular a few years before as they got in the way in the bar. She'd always kept her skirts narrow and gathered towards the back. At least the newest trend fitted with her usual silhouette, but she hadn't yet added any trims or ribbons to soften the look. Donning a small black hat and tying the ribbons at the back of her head under her bun, and pulling on her gloves, she was ready.

"Mrs Clements? Good morning. My name is Hunt. Richard Hunt." He reached out to shake Sarah's hand, which she tentatively accepted. Initially daunting and looking very professional in his smart navy uniform and silver badges, his soft grey eyes expressed compassion and respect. "I'm sorry to hear about your misfortune. You must feel quite unsettled." Sarah felt some of her nervousness slip away at his warm and gentle tone. "Would you care to show me the seat of the fire and tell me what happened?"

Sarah thought it was fairly obvious where the fire had been, but she did need to explain how it really wasn't her mother's fault. "This way, please."

She led him along the corridor to the kitchen door, which was still shut. The smell of char and smoke was overpowering, and bile churned in her stomach.

She coughed rather inelegantly. "Forgive me," she said as she cleared her throat. "It was in here. I did my best to stop it spreading. I doused this side of the door with water from the fire bucket kept here by the stairs." She pointed to where the bucket once again sat where it always had. "And I rolled up that rug to fill the gap under the door," indicating the carpet that had been pushed to one side.

"Very quick-thinking of you in the circumstances, I must say. Allow me," he said, reaching past her to open the door. The vile stench engulfed her, and in the light of day, the room looked worse than she had expected. Water still dripped from the ceiling beams, but at least they held, and the roof looked intact. Black soot stained the walls and clung to every surface. Remarkably, the Welsh dresser on the internal wall still stood and appeared undamaged, even if it was covered with the detritus of cracked and broken china, and dripping water. The central worktable lay lopsided on the floor, one of its legs completely burnt. But, she thought, the top, or part of it, could be reused if she was lucky. Buckled and melted pots and pans were scattered across the flagstones and as she stepped further into the room, she saw the cause of the blaze.

Staring at the distorted range she wondered how it still stood. The chimney piece had collapsed, oven doors hung twisted from their hinges, and the grate to the firebox was upside down on the stone floor – its bolts sheared away.

"I guess logs fell from the firebox and in a panic Ma and our kitchen maid, Molly, tried to move them and made it worse. They only just escaped before being overtaken by smoke."

Sarah gulped down the sobs threatening to break. She didn't want to appear weak before this man, who was here to help her, she hoped. He was meant to assess the damage and costs, and report back. His opinion was vital. If he didn't accept the claim, then she really had lost everything.

13

The very nice man

August 1863

"Permit me," said Mr Hunt, handing her a clean white handkerchief, which appeared incongruous in the blackened kitchen. "I realise how upsetting this must be for you."

Sarah nodded as she took the cloth and dabbed her eyes. She took a deep, shuddering breath and when she felt able to speak, murmured, "Thank you. You are most kind."

Again, noting his soft grey eyes and solicitous expression, she smiled tentatively and was rewarded with a generous smile.

"My pleasure, Mrs Clements, my pleasure." Mr Hunt put his fist to his mouth and cleared his throat. "But we must return to business now, I fear. Once I have gathered all the information, I will complete the paperwork, get you to sign it and advise you of the outcome. Is now a convenient time to discuss the events of yesterday morning?"

"Aye, sir, it is." Sarah shuddered as the memories returned.

Mr Hunt noticed her discomfort. "During the process, I'd be willing to answer any questions you have. Any time. You just have to send a message, and I will do what I can to assist."

"That is very kind of you, Mr Hunt." Sarah paused. "I do, in fact, have some worrisome questions on my mind."

"Is that so?" He stroked his clean-shaven chin, unusual for the times. "Then let us repair to a somewhat more convivial space to complete our business."

Surprised at her sudden attraction to the man, Sarah wondered, should he ever sport a moustache or goatee, if it would be as dark as his fashionably styled hair.

Interrupting her thoughts, he said, "Do you, perhaps, have time for a cuppa? There is a delightful little tea shop I know of not far from here."

"But I could …" began Sarah, gathering herself from surveying the broad-shouldered gent before her. *How could she forget her manners like that and not offer him refreshment.*

Momentarily, Sarah looked around at what remained of the kitchen, and realised even making a cup of tea would be impractical.

As if reading her thoughts, he said, "I wouldn't dream of putting you to the trouble, given the current state of your premises, and your obvious distress. No. I insist."

He extended his arm so she could link her hand through and escorted her from the premises. Sarah suddenly wished she had dressed better this morning, but to be fair, she was sure one black dress was much the same as any other.

As they walked along the Back, he chatted easily about the workings of the port, and how valuable the trade was. They traversed the lane leading to Queen's Park and commented on the surrounding trees as he led her to a tea shop she had never visited before. After placing the order, and adding a teacake each to the list, he returned his attention to her. "Forgive me for saying so, but it strikes me you are very young to be carrying such burdens as running an inn, caring for your mother and managing the servants, while still in mourning for your dear papa."

Sarah gulped. How did he know so much about her?

"I'm not that young, sir. I'm both a widow and a mother, and I've been helping my father manage The White Hart since I were fifteen. It's second nature."

"You are still young to me."

They were interrupted at that moment by the delivery of the tea. Cushioned from embarrassment and wanting to learn the proper ways of serving, Sarah carefully watched the maid unload the tray. She put matched flowery teacups and saucers with a teaspoon to each right hand, a cake plate in front of them, with a neatly folded napkin beside. The milk jug and sugar basin positioned off to one side, and a silver teapot placed ready for pouring. The young maid quickly returned with a plate holding two sugar-coated teacakes.

"Shall I, sir?" asked Sarah as she lifted the milk jug to pour into the cup first.

He smiled again, and she could see lines at the side of his eyes and around his mouth she hadn't noticed before. He was a good-looking man, cultivated and courteous, and nothing like the people she came across every day in the inn. Why was he paying attention to her?

"And you mustn't call me sir. I am not that important."

The tea-pouring ritual paused while she looked at him. "Oh, but you are." Her eyes flared with respect. "You've an important job."

He squinched up his face. "To some, but I'm not the one who has to suffer the consequences of a fire, nor do the work to repair the damage. I only determine the what and why."

"And the cost," she murmured fearfully, continuing to pour the tea.

For a moment neither said anything more while a sip of tea was taken and the teacake broken into pieces and tasted.

Richard dusted his hands on the napkin before speaking. "To help me with the paperwork, can you tell me in your own words how the fire unfolded. I've seen for myself the resultant damage, but I'd like to hear your version of the events."

Sarah quickly told him what she'd seen and heard, and how frightening it had all been, repeating her anxiety over the cost of rebuilding.

"Do not worry for one moment about that. I will be certain to make a favourable mention of your quick thinking. I am sure you will receive the full amount insured to make amends as necessary."

Pausing briefly to dab her lips, Sarah gathered control of her wits. "I cannot thank you enough. You've been more than kind, and generous."

"You said you had questions," he prompted.

"Ah, yes, but if you've already decided the outcome,

and I am to receive the insurance, then they don't seem so important."

"Surely, if you are curious, then any question is worthwhile, is it not?"

Sarah felt a little flustered by his consideration. Nobody had considered her worthy before. "Well, yes. Put like that, I suppose it is."

"Go ahead, then, ask," he encouraged.

"Oh, goodness me. Where to start? Do I have to report what I spend the money on?"

She instantly cursed herself for such a brash question and for missing the chance to ask something about him.

Richard sat back in his chair, looking quite relaxed while he watched her intently. "No," he replied. "That is entirely your decision, based on your most pressing need, but I would suggest two things. Get help to clean the soot off the walls and whitewash them, and update that cooking range. It's lucky no one was hurt. The fire could have been much worse."

Her shoulders sagged a little, and her posture relaxed from the stiff upright position she'd been holding as relief flooded through her. "That's very good advice, Mr Hunt. I shall do that."

Seconds passed and she began to get nervous. She'd been away from the inn far too long and while she was enjoying the respite – and the company, very much – she knew their time was over.

"I'd better be getting back," she said, hoping that Mr Davidson was up to the task alone. He could be a bit of a mischief-maker, and she had already considered she might need to replace him. "There's so much work to be done. How long do you think, um … well, before …"

"You get the money?" he finished for her.

"I'm beginning to think you are a mind reader, Mr Hunt. That is most disconcerting to a woman, to think her thoughts can be so easily guessed."

He rose and held her chair as she stood up. "Not at all, Mrs Clements. Not at all. The process is well known to me and not at all to you, so it's simply a matter of deduction. Your thoughts are safe."

His face again shone with that disarming smile of his, and she briefly wondered if he was being totally honest with her.

Flustered, she said, "Thank you for the tea. I'll be on my way. Good day."

"I'll walk you back."

"That's not necessary. You must be a very busy man. I can walk by meself."

"I'm sure you can, but I consider it my duty to escort you safely back." He smiled warmly.

Every day for the rest of that week, Richard Hunt paid a visit to the pub. On the third day, he once more invited her to take tea with him, so they could discuss the work privately without the constant presence of Mr Davidson or, for that matter, Ma.

"I like to keep abreast of progress," he said, in answer to Sarah's surprised enquiry.

"Well, you're more'n welcome, sir …"

"Didn't I say there was no need to call me sir? My name is Richard."

Sarah blushed at the intimacy indicated by the casual reference to his first name, even though she was finding herself increasingly intrigued by – and attracted to – this man.

"Surely, we're not well-enough acquainted to be using first names. After all, Mr Hunt, I've only just met you."

"My apologies, Mrs Clements. I didn't mean to offend. It's just …"

"Yes?" Sarah urged. "Just what …?"

"I hope I do not speak out of turn, but may I say I find you surprisingly cordial, despite the circumstances that brought us together. You are refreshing, but I forgot myself. Do forgive me."

At a loss for words, Sarah merely nodded. "The lads we hired have scrubbed the walls clean and started on the whitewash, and the new cooker is to be fitted as soon as they're clear of that wall."

"I'm pleased to hear of such progress so fast."

"Tain't fast t' me, Mr Hunt," said Sarah, stress accentuating her accent. "I'm near out on me pins tryin' to keep the place goin'. That I am."

"Hire more men if you want to. Send their accounts to me and I'll see they are paid. We can't have you wearing yourself out."

Sarah looked sceptically at her professed saviour, wondering why he had picked her out in particular. She'd made enquiries and discovered the man had a good reputation for being fair and honest in his dealings. But that still didn't explain his unusual attention to the details of this case, or to her. He was far more important than that, but she felt drawn to him despite her reticence.

"I'd be grateful. I would, but they're tripping over one another in there as it is. And the regulars have been that understanding and patient with me. There's been no clamour for hot food. As long as I can serve 'em bread and cheese or pickles, and cold meats, there's been customers."

"I'm pleased to hear it, Mrs Clements, pleased indeed."

If the uniformed gent before her found her delightful, his sentiment was returned tenfold. Sarah grew to like him more each day. She made an extra effort to dress in something other than her work-a-day dress and, when she wasn't feeling quite so agitated, she minded her manners and her speech. His demeanour, his elegance and his eloquence entranced her, and she tried to emulate his standards when they were together.

Some of her customers might think she'd gone all uppity, but she didn't care. Being working class didn't mean she had to be uneducated. Sarah's love of learning had never wavered, and Mr Hunt gave her a chance to learn from someone better educated and qualified than her, but still of her social class insofar as he too worked for a living.

She said as much to him one day, several weeks later when he returned to finally sign off the finished kitchen.

"I shall miss our conversations," she admitted, as they took tea together, which she assumed would be the last time. "I have taken particular pleasure in listening to you and have tried to improve my manner of speech. It's hard being in the taproom all day, surrounded by coarse language. The accent around these parts, while honest, is not soft on the ear."

"I'm honoured. I completely understand your sentiments, my dear. Believe it or not, my speech was, as you put it, coarse and local, and I had to learn by listening to those who spoke better."

His disarming smile stirred butterflies in her stomach.

"You did?" she queried, astonished. "I was sure you'd been better educated."

"No more or no less than you, I suspect. I was born here and learnt words through reading, and how to speak by listening."

Suddenly feeling on a much better footing than she expected, and more like an equal, knowing he liked reading as much as she did, her opinion of him wrenched up a notch. She knew she'd slide into the local dialect when others used it, and words unique to this area would continue to slip off her tongue, but at least she could speak properly when she chose to.

She looked at him over the rim of her teacup, as a thought jumped into her head. Did she dare? She wanted to know more about him and if she didn't ask, she might never find out. *It's now or never*, she thought.

Putting the cup back in its saucer, she cleared her throat. "How long have you been working for the Sun Fire Insurance Company?"

"A few years."

His unelaborated response threw her briefly. "I didn't see you when the fire engine came. Do you go out with the brigade?"

"On occasions. I am responsible for keeping the engine in full working order." He scrunched his face. "And I do the paperwork. I try to leave the hard work to others. But it is up to me to decide if a fire is genuine or not."

"Do all those men work for you, then?"

"In a manner of speaking, yes. At least, I supervise seven men and pay their wages, such as they are."

"That is quite an important position you have. You have been too modest, I feel."

"I have been fortunate, let us say. I remember all too well my younger days labouring at whatever I could get and appreciate what I now have. I just don't talk about it."

Feeling reprimanded, but not ready to give up just yet, Sarah changed the subject. "Do you have family? Anyone you like to talk about? If I get started up about my son, John Jacob, you won't stop me twittering for hours." She laughed to soften the brazen question, hoping he might ... Might what?

He was much older than her. At least in his forties, she'd say. Did he have a wife and family, and if so, how would that affect their friendship? Because she truly believed there was a friendship developing between them, and not just because of their business dealings.

Fleetingly, she wondered, if the boot was on the other foot, how she would like it, knowing her husband had a female friend. She dismissed the thought before it grew. Instinctively, she'd known that John had had many women. Whether they could be called friends was a moot point, but why was it acceptable for men to have friendships of any form, but women associating with men were frowned upon. *Oh, well*, she mulled. *The reputation of barmaids and licensed women victuallers is pretty low anyway, so I might as well add another nail to my coffin.*

After several moments of silence when Sarah wondered if he would answer, his face turned melancholy. His eyes gazed into the distance as he spoke.

"My wife is unwell, and my eldest daughter, a Sarah like you," he mused, before pulling himself up. "Regrettably, sadness overwhelms my wife after the loss of our daughter last year, as well as the other five children she has lost. I'm sorry to say she is quite unsound these days."

An emotion Sarah couldn't quite place creased his face. Grief, regret, despair all mixed up. A half-smile banished his expression.

"Yes, well, um, my daughter manages the home and her two younger siblings."

Sarah gasped and put her fingers to her lips. "Oh, golly. I'm so sorry. I didn't know. How wrong of me to ask." Poor man. Her heart went out to him as much as his wife for a child lost, but to lose six was beyond contemplation.

"Not at all, my dear. If we are to become friends, then we need to know these things about each other, don't you think?"

14

A friendship matures

November 1863

Throughout a mild autumn, Sarah continued to enjoy Richard's company. He would drop into The White Hart unannounced on the pretext of checking the repairs had been done properly and the new cooking range was performing as it should.

She began to look forward to seeing him the more time passed. She felt more mature, more worldly in his company, and keen to broaden her thinking and conversation. Sometimes they would walk out and take tea, leaving Mr Davidson in the bar. They began to spread their custom among several tea rooms to avoid speculation at being seen together. As winter set in, they would visit his office situated an easy walk from the Back, in an area Sarah did not know well. She clearly remembered one occasion.

Climbing the stairs from a side door, Richard escorted her into the rooms of Sun Fire Insurance. Sarah had been surprised to see how lavish they were.

Polished wood panelling in a warm golden shade lined the walls below the windows that looked out over the town. Bookcases filled with huge tomes took up two of the walls, filing cabinets lined the internal wall, and a large desk in the centre for the clerk. A sideboard and several comfortable, well-upholstered chairs placed around the room completed the furnishings.

"I'm impressed, Mr Hunt. This is far more stylish than I expected."

Richard laughed. "So what did you expect, Mrs Clements? A rough, draughty stone building with barely adequate quarters?"

"No, not at all. I'm really not sure …" Sarah drifted off, unable to say what she expected. Clearly, he didn't live there, or at least he didn't sleep there, but numerous personal items, and a whisky decanter and glasses on the sideboard, suggested he spent a great deal of time there.

"Well, such a draughty building is below us, open on the other side. It's where you will find the horses and the fire engine. The men on duty find shelter there too, but I assure you they are all well served. But come, there is more to see."

He opened a door into a smaller room, which was patently his private domain. A long, buttoned velvet sofa sat against the far wall paired with matching armchairs, while a well-padded leather swivel chair sat in front of a large roll-top writing desk, currently covered in paperwork.

"And through here," he said, returning to the reception room and passing through another door she hadn't seen earlier, "is my changing room. I can get very grubby being in a building after a fire. Fortunately, there's a water standpipe outside."

Sarah noticed the jug and ewer and a few clothes but didn't linger. The personal nature of the room made her feel uncomfortable, and she quickly returned to the reception area.

"Thank you for showing me where you work, but I should be going."

"Please stay a while now we have a chance to talk freely without being disturbed," he insisted, ushering her into his smaller office space.

"What do you wish to talk about?" Sarah's nerves were beginning to get the better of her as she perched on the edge of a chair. She folded her hands on her lap to stop them shaking while her eyes continued to scan the room, taking in more detail. This man gave rise to sensations she'd almost forgotten about, but were quite different to the youthful flutters John once created.

She jerked her head up at the sound of his voice. "We could get out your file, discuss the fire, and you could sign the papers I have, or ..." His warm smile disarmed her even further. "Or that's what you can say brought you here, should anyone ask, but in truth, I just want to get to know you better."

His solicitude was so out of the ordinary, she could feel her cheeks burning with embarrassment. "Ere ... you're such a riddle, I can't make you out sometimes. You say you come from working stock like me, and yet you speak so well, and nothing at all like the men I know."

"But you, yourself, speak well. What is your secret?"

She couldn't blush any more than she already was, so she decided to throw aside her caution. "I were lucky.

My da wanted me to be able to read and write. He said I needed it, and to know my numbers to run an alehouse and he wouldn't be around forever."

Sarah drew a breath at the mention of her father, striving to clear the burning sensation at the back of her throat. She still missed him so, even though she had more help these days. "And I like reading. I started when I were not much more than a nipper and I've got several of Mr Dickens's books. I used to read to the young 'uns after church on Sundays, but I stopped when I were …" Sarah paused. She didn't want to talk about John or the children he'd left her with.

How long would she go on wondering if he really was dead?

Richard filled the lull. "See, your father saw your potential and encouraged you. He thought you were special too."

"That's as maybe, but he didn't have no son to follow him, so it was me or nobody," answered Sarah honestly, willing her eyes not to let go of the tears welling up.

Richard rose from his chair and taking his ever-present white handkerchief from his pocket offered it to her. "I'm sorry to have upset you. That wasn't my intention."

She took it from him and lowered her eyes while she dried them. He rested one hand on her shoulder, extending his thumb a little closer, caressing her cheek.

His touch set off fireworks in her veins. Startled, she turned her gaze to meet his and revealed the longing that echoed in her being. Seconds later he had bent down, taken her face in his hands and kissed her.

Stepping back to allow her space, he cleared his throat. "Forgive me. I, um, was out of order."

Sarah sat assessing him, her head full of thoughts, her body full of emotion. She should be shocked. She should be offended and walk out right now, but something pivotal had just happened, and every ounce of her wanted more.

"Maybe you was," she answered softly, "but it's nice to know someone like you is partial to the likes of me, all the same."

"You are quite beautiful, you know, and have charmed me from the start. But I'm a married man and have no right to …" He ran his hand through his hair in frustration; pain and misery ruckled his face.

Sarah stood and took two steps towards him. She wanted him to kiss her a second time. She wanted to feel something again after so long. To feel alive again. For years she had bottled up her craving, her heartache, her desperation.

"Did I?" she croaked; her eyes settled on his. She yearned to be desired once more. She needed love, easement, a shoulder. Overwhelmed by her sudden ardour, she threw propriety to the wind. "Will you kiss me again?"

She didn't care what anyone else thought, she wanted this man, desperately.

"Mrs Clements. Sarah. Are you sure?" He sounded surprised.

"Yes, Mr Hunt. I am," she sighed.

"I can only offer you my deepest affection." He held back, still unsure, knowing the risks.

"That is all I need."

Richard required no further encouragement. He began to kiss her fervently, inching his way down and around her neck, his hands exploring her back, her face, her throat. Tentatively, he rested his fingers on her breastbone, their warmth burning her skin through the fabric of her dress. His other hand pressed against her back as he sought her eyes once more, seeking a signal that would take them down the path of no return.

She placed her hand over his and pushed it a little lower and held it to her breast. He started to fondle her gently, while kissing her throat. With a small moan of pleasure she tilted her head back and was lost to his loving embrace.

"What's that man after, I'd like to know," muttered Betsey, after another visit.

"He's just being friendly, is all, Ma," said Sarah, clearing away the tea things. While she preferred it when she and Richard went out and had tea privately, that wasn't always practical.

"A man of his age has no right bein' friendly to a young widow like yourself, unless he has proper intentions." Betsey continued her grumblings, keeping a beady eye on her daughter.

Sarah busied herself washing the few dishes in the scullery, keeping out of sight until she could get thoughts in order, hoping her face would not betray her. Richard, or Rick as she'd chosen to call him since his wife called him Richard, could not have any intentions, proper or otherwise, while his situation remained as it was, but she couldn't deny her attraction. Neither of them could stay away from the other.

*****

As the weeks and months passed, they took every opportunity to be together. She either visited his rooms, or she would stroll into one of the less-popular parks after church on Sunday where he'd meet her with a pony and trap, and they'd head into the countryside.

On a cold but sunny winter's day, they sat side by side on the blanket Rick had spread on the grass and partook of the picnic fare she'd packed in her basket.

"Sarah, dearest," began Richard after a time. "I want to tell you something …"

He sounded nervous, and Sarah reached out a hand to touch his arm. "You can tell me anything. What is distressing you so?"

He sighed and began again. "I don't want to sound like I'm complaining, I'm not. And I don't want you thinking I'm in need of pity."

Sarah turned her head, surprised. "Now why would I ever think that? You with your fine family, your fine house and your fine job."

He grinned but his tone was serious. "Because … Sarah you've made me the happiest of men since you asked me to kiss you, when you could have deservedly slapped my face and turned tail."

"Not likely. Not after the spark you set off."

Richard chuckled. "It was something special, wasn't it? But seriously, Sarah, you've changed me. My life had become mundane, and my home life formal and dispassionate. I will not cast blame. Circumstances drove us to become who we are, but there is little joy. While I was living, I did not feel alive. Not like now. I felt alone and inadequate. Sorry. That was bad-mannered of me. Rectifying my home life is not your role, but do you understand what I'm saying?"

"I do, dear heart, because that is exactly how I felt – only half alive – and you've changed all that for me too."

"But do you realise the risk you are taking being with me? Should anyone find out, you could be shunned. It would break my heart to lose you now. You are the other half of me, but if you say so, for your sake, I will give you up to save your reputation."

Sarah gazed at him, assessing the truth of what he was saying. She reached over and took his hand. "Knowing you love me is all I need. I'm a widowed innkeeper. I doubt my customers notice me outside the taproom."

"I will always love you, I promise. And I will see you suffer no financial hardships, but I can offer you nothing more than that. Not for a long time. I will care for you, but I have duties and responsibilities I can't ignore …"

She knelt up and leaned over to kiss him, offering him her love and her body.

After their conversation, Sarah knew she should put a stop to their relationship, but while the logical side of her presented all the very good reasons why, the passionate side argued the opposite. For the first time in her life, she was admired and loved. Genuinely loved. And she loved in return. A decade on from when she was smitten by John, she had learnt the power of true love and what it meant. And it was nothing like the mediocre affection John had offered her. She couldn't give Rick up. She just couldn't. But how were they to continue?

If her mother suspected Rick was up to no good, she would blabber about it. Sarah had to get the upper hand. She would have to talk with Mary.

"Sister, dearest," she said a few days later, removing her hat and gloves, and kissing Mary on her cheek. "How lovely to see ya. It's been an age since we've 'ad a chance to talk."

"Well, goodness me, what brings you to my door at this time of day. Sit down, sit down. I'll make us a cuppa."

Mary cleared some of her sewing off the table so she could set down the tea things.

"It's Ma," said Sarah.

"What's Ma up to this time that I haven't heard about?"

"Nothing exactly, yet. But she's got it into her head that Mr Hunt from the insurance company is up to no good. And I don't want her grizzling about him or spreading tales to other people."

Mary frowned. "And is he? Up to no good? I know you told me he'd been very helpful and kind since the fire. What does she think he's doing wrong?" Mary handed Sarah her tea and offered her a slice of cake from the tin.

Sarah's cheeks coloured and she suddenly felt guilty even though she didn't want to. She wanted to love freely. "He's being friendly, is all, but he's much older than me, and Ma thinks his intentions are wrong."

"From the look of you, so do you." Mary smiled wryly.

Taken aback, Sarah spluttered, "Oh no. Not at all. You see, well, the thing is …"

"You've fallen for him, haven't you? I can see it in your eyes."

Sarah dropped her head and fingered the edge of the tablecloth.

Mary took Sarah's silence as agreement. "There's no harm in that. Unless he's married, of course." Mary paused, as realisation clicked in. "He is, isn't he?"

Sarah nodded.

"I can see why Ma might be tetchy 'bout it. And no good will come of it, but we can't help who we fall for, can we, kid?" The softness of Mary's voice and her quick understanding brought tears to Sarah's eyes. She wiped them away, exasperated.

Mary put her arms around her sister's shoulders. "It's been a long time, hasn't it chook, since you've 'ad someone to love ya? Tis hard, I know. Especially for someone as young as you. You've got so many burdens, and few rewards."

"Oh, Mary. It has been hard, very hard, and I didn't mean for it to happen, it just did."

"Whadya think I can do?"

"Can you talk to Ma, please? Tell her he's a nice man and doesn't mean me any harm." Sarah sniffled into her handkerchief. "I can't give 'im up. I can't. He means so much to me. And he loves me. He really does."

"I hope you're right, Sarah. I hope your right. But there's nothing I can say that'll change the matter. Ma'll accept it in time. Just be careful, eh."

"I think it's too late for that," confessed Sarah.

If Mary was shocked, she didn't say so. "I'm always

here to listen if'n ya need me. Whatever you decide. We women get the rough end of the deal never mind what, and sometimes I think we should get what we deserve, and I mean that in the best way. You deserve more."

"What about you, Mary? Don't you deserve more too?"

"I'm older, my love, and I had me man for longer. I don't need another. But this path you've chosen isn't easy."

Sarah buried her head in her sister's shoulder and sobbed.

* * * * *

The question of 'what next?' continued to plague Sarah as the days turned into weeks until it became apparent her options were few. Christmas was almost upon them, which meant more work, a lot of it. And right now, she didn't know where to start.

Fortunately, the brewery had let her stay on after Da's passing. She had no idea where they would have gone or what would have happened to them if they'd had to leave. She had her mother, and her increasingly difficult ways to deal with; she had JJ who she adored but was an active four-year-old who needed to be taught all his lessons if he were going to amount to something; and she had three staff to manage. Thankfully, the ever-faithful Molly was a great help. Having been with them for so long, she did most of what Ma should have been doing, including making up the bedchambers and doing the cooking, as well as coping with some of the mistress's more outrageous behaviour. She was teaching young Ada, the scullery maid, what her duties entailed to ease Molly's own, leaving Sarah to deal with the bar. That in itself was also proving to be a problem.

Soon after hiring Owen Davidson, Sarah realised she'd made a mistake. A rather squat man with thinning hair, he'd proved himself diligent and reliable, she'd give him that, but he was a tattler who spoke out of turn. He spent far too much time talking to the patrons and giving his opinion on everything and anything, including Sarah and what she was like as a boss. She'd put up with him for a few months because he'd been useful. He'd been there to fill in for her when she needed to do the books, or be with JJ, or spend time with Rick. Thankfully, other than Ma, no one seemed to have noticed her involvement with Richard, or not that she'd seen, and she hadn't heard any gossip either. But that was about to change.

"What ya standing there for, girl?" said Betsey, flapping her arms. She rolled up her sleeves and gathered various bowls and utensils and put them on the table and began to stir something with a wooden spoon in the bowl that had no ingredients in it.

"You should be doing what your father told you. Now git out of my way."

Sarah stared at her mother thinking what she could say. Clearly, her mother had regressed several years, not just the few months since Da had gone.

"I'm about to get the Christmas ribbons and wreaths out," she answered truthfully. Although when she was going to find time to get some greenery for the garlands was another matter.

"That's a good idea. Get Mary Jane to help you. She loves all those ribbons and things. Where is she? I haven't seen her today."

Sarah held her breath and tried not to react. At each of the four Christmases since, memories of the joy her daughter gave her filled her entire being, but the pain of losing her returned with every ribbon she hung. The pain right now seemed more intense than ever. How could she tell her befuddled mother Mary Jane was no longer with them, and she was more likely thinking of John Jacob, who was now a year older than Mary Jane was when the whooping cough took her?

"Yes, Ma. That's right. Mary Jane loved ribbons," agreed Sarah in a shaky voice that cracked as she finished the sentence. She prayed her boy would not be taken from her too.

"Well, off you go, then. I'm busy. I've got dozens of mince pies to make."

If, by some miracle, Betsey did make any mince tarts, Sarah would be grateful. Food was always a drawcard for customers, and if word got around that *The Mistress* was cooking again, she'd do a roaring trade.

"Are you using Mrs Beeton's recipe then, Ma?"

"Of course. What else do you think I'd use? Really girl, you are half-witted at times. Now where's the sugar?"

Sarah watched her mother's bulk disappear into the pantry, her skirts swaying with the number of petticoats she wore. If Betsey had remembered the fire, or realised there was an almost new kitchen with a different cooking range, she gave no indication. Sarah decided that was probably for the best and slipped out of the kitchen.

Returning to the bar, Sarah once again pushed her troubles to the back of her mind. Interacting with the customers always put her in a good mood. Chatting came easily and the patrons always had tales to tell.

"How you doing, Charlie? Your look mighty glum."

"Not me, maid. Not me. Iz cock-a-hoop, but me 'n Silas were just talkin' like, about 'ow Bristol's changing. It's nuff to turn yer 'air silver, i'nit?"

"'Tis that, Charlie, but they say Bristol's gaining a gert reputation for being modern with having new ideas. That's got to be good for business."

The two men nodded sagely and took slurps of their beer and continued their discussion.

Sarah knew Bristol had lost some of its trade to other ports further north as a result of the larger ships being built, but the local trade still flourished and new industries were starting to arrive. Although she hardly thought of the Fripp & Thomas soap factory as modern. It had been around for a good long time, thank goodness, as she really liked their soap. She considered it her treat, and the numerous glass factories popping up was good for business; the glass they made was quite striking.

Sarah looked at the beautifully etched windows the brewery had paid for, wrapped around the corner frontage of the inn overlooking the harbour. They provided much needed light while keeping out prying eyes. She liked how much the place had changed over time. Polished wood lined the walls of the snug and two of the barroom walls; settles placed back to back around a table provided for groups of people to sit away from the throng standing at high tables, and the lamps had been updated again. The place certainly looked welcoming.

Raised voices caught her attention. She moved towards the counter where Owen Davidson and one of her regular customers were getting into a heated argument.

"That's no way to talk about our maid. No way at all," defended her champion. "Our lass has been good as gold since she were a little 'un. She's had it 'ard, she has, so watch your tongue. That's all I'm saying."

Owen wouldn't be silenced. "It's true I tell ya. I do more work than she does round 'ere. She's never 'ere these days. Always out and about with 'er excuses. And pays me next to nuffin'. She's no right to the licence."

Sarah pulled her shoulders back and stood in front of the man.

"If that's the way you feel, Mr Davidson, then I think 'twould be better if you scarpered. I'd hate to be accused of working ya too hard."

"You can't do that," Owen blustered, his beady eyes casting side to side.

"Oh, I think I can, Mr Davidson. I'm your employer whether you like it or not. And it seems you don't."

"Now let's not be 'asty. Let's talk about it first, eh?"

"You have talked about it, it seems. And now I want you gone." Sarah walked around the bar to the money box, withdrew a few coins and laid them on the counter. "Here's your pay, fair and square, and a ha'penny more so's you can't say I did bad by you."

Sarah glared at the man, who was now looking left and right for support, but was met with grinning faces.

"Ga on then," said her champion who was still watching. "Get goin' or do ya need an 'and?" He turned to his mates watching from the nearby table. "Whadya reckon lads? Shall we give the man an 'and? Miss Sarah wants him to leave."

Snickers followed as two more men moved to stand near the bar while Sarah held her ground.

"Al'right. Al'right. Keep yer 'air on. I'm going." Owen nervously began to untie his apron and once he'd untangled the strings, tossed it on the counter. "But don't think ya've heard the last of it. Not by a long chalk." He waved his finger in Sarah's face. "You're too uppity and deserve what's coming."

Suddenly, Owen screamed. One of the men had grabbed hold of the wagging finger and bent it back until Sarah heard it snap.

"Get out!" snarled the man who towered over Owen. "And if ya as much as poke your nose in here again, or I hear any bad mouthin', you'll be getting a good kickin'. Got it?"

Defeated, Owen nodded, scooped up the money, grabbed his coat from the peg on the wall and hightailed it out the door.

"Thank you, friends. I appreciate the help," said Sarah.

"'Twere nuffin'. Happy to oblige. He won't bother you again, missus."

Sarah certainly hoped that was true, but that man had a nasty streak in him. But she had no more time to think about what he might do next. Right now, she was without an extra barman and with Christmas around the corner, had more work to do than ever.

She unbuttoned her cuffs, rolled up her sleeves and called out to the patrons. "Who's next? What can I get ya, my friend?"

15

A growing dilemma

February 1864

Richard had become a godsend in more ways than one.

Amos Baker's appearance a week before Christmas was a turning point. Sarah took an instant liking to him and happily employed him as her assistant barman. His jovial personality endeared him to the customers from day one.

"Thank ya, Missus Clements, for the chance," he said, twisting his cap restlessly in his hands in contrast to the broad smile that lit up his face, creasing his eyes into delightful pinpricks of light above his ruddy cheeks. "Mr Hunt told me your last man was, shall we say, making life difficult, but I would'na do that to ya. That I wouldn't. I like being with people, see, and the more people I get to chatter with, the happier I be."

Sarah grinned at his enthusiasm, checking he was willing to do the heavy lifting – literally – of all the barrels, and work the hours she expected.

"While I do the book work, and manage the staff, as well as care for my family," she said pointedly. "I cannot work the barroom and every other room in this place on me own. But I don't need complaints either."

"You'll be right as rain with me, I promise ya. I won't let you down. This job will be a blessing to me, you see. I was working on me own in me last job, and I were that lonely with no one to talk to."

Sarah held back the laugh threatening to bubble over. "I promise you won't be lonely here. Quite the opposite. We've some regulars who are old sailors, well most of our customers are mariners in one way or another, but these old fellers are real characters who like to tell their stories, often more than once. As long as ya listen and agree with them, you'll do well."

"Sounds gert to me."

Sarah extended her hand. "Then welcome, Mr Baker. We should do well together."

"We will, missus. And I'll watch your back."

* * * * *

"John came back," Sarah told her mother over their morning cup of tea, praying silently that she could maintain the lie.

"What?" Betsey demanded. "When?"

"A few weeks back. Afore Christmas."

Betsey eyed her daughter suspiciously. "I never saw him."

"You wouldn't have. 'Twere late and he only popped in for an hour or so."

"Is that so?"

At Betsey's sceptical tone, Sarah's hand shook and the cup rattled as she put it down, but she had to brazen it out.

"He sent a message to say he were sneaking away from 'is ship that were tied up down river cos they were leaving again on the morrow."

"Never heard such a thing. How could that happen?" Betsey folded her arms across her ample bosom and frowned.

"How would I know, Ma? I'm not the captain," Sarah snapped. She rose to clear the cups and saucers and turned away. Over her shoulder in a quieter voice she added, "And Mr Clements weren't in no mood for explainin'. He came back for more personal reasons."

She squeezed her eyes shut and hoped Betsey wouldn't ask any more questions, because she was out of answers.

"Hmm. Not much of a man then, is he? Sneaking in and out like that without even a 'owdy, and what about JJ? Did the lad see him?"

"JJ were fast asleep, Ma, but his da watched him for a while. He said they were good memories to take with 'im."

Sarah promised herself she'd go to church every Sunday and pray for forgiveness for all the lies, but she'd need to pray a lot harder to be forgiven for the reason behind it all.

Nothing further was said, but Sarah knew Betsey would stew over this information and sooner or later she'd ask the obvious questions: Where on earth had he been the last four years? And wasn't be supposed to be dead? Which would be quickly followed by …

The thought had barely entered her head when Betsey called out. "Did 'e give ya any money?"

Sarah finished drying her hands on her apron.

"Some," she answered.

Betsey snorted and returned to rocking in her chair.

"Rick," murmured Sarah softly as she lay in his arms. "There's summat I need to talk about."

"What's that, my love," he asked between fairy kisses to her forehead, cheeks and lips.

Sarah sighed with contentment but gently pushed him away. Being together like this was a rare treat, only brought about by Richard's position, and Amos's discretion.

Rick had recently decided he should travel more – for work, he told his daughter still caring for his frail wife, and his employees – but mostly he wanted to establish a pattern of him being away at regular intervals.

Sarah wasn't so fortunate. Constantly under her mother's watchful eye, and with JJ to care for, even though Ma and Molly were the best of minders, and Aunt Nettie, when she visited, Sarah struggled to find time to get away at all. Amos was the one who had made the suggestion, which gave her more free time than she'd ever thought possible.

"Missus Sarah. I heard the local victuallers meet at the brewery premises along by the bridge down aways," he hitched his thumb, pointing. "They get together every week for tastings 'n updates 'n such like. Have ya been invited?"

"Heavens above! No. And I wouldn't expect it neither.

The men would be as mad as hell to see a woman turn up. To them it's bad nuff the brewery allows women licence holders as it is."

"That's as maybe, but that don't mean you couldn't attend, if you chose. You're a victualler. 'Twould mean being away from the premises for two or maybe three hours every week mind, but I'd be glad to keep the customers happy for ya."

Sarah looked at him, wondering what Amos was hinting at. "I'll think on the idea, Amos, and thanks for telling me. But I'm not sure I'd be brave enough to go amongst all those men and say my piece."

"I didn't say you had to go, only that you could."

The more she thought on it, the more it grew, especially after he'd shared his idea. As far as the world was concerned, Sarah was at a brewery meeting and Richard was out of town. Sometimes their worlds collided very nicely.

Releasing her from his hold, Rick sat up. "So, what is it you want to talk about?"

Suddenly feeling shy, Sarah pulled the blanket up to her throat and shrunk herself deeper into it. "Um, I'm not certain yet, but well …"

"Yes?" he urged. "Come on, Sarah, stop beating around the bush. Whatsup?"

"I'm with child."

For a brief moment, Rick took a deep breath and said nothing.

In that time, Sarah rabbited on. "I told Ma that John had come back. I made up a story about him being anchored downriver and he only had a few hours to spare because of the tide."

"Didn't you tell me he was dead?"

Sarah nodded. "I still believe he is. It's been years since I heard from 'im, let alone seen 'im, but there's no evidence. I've to wait seven years before it can be official."

Richard nodded. "It must be coming up five years now."

"Aye, it is, but tis possible he's still out there somewhere, I suppose." Despite everything, the disquiet that she'd been abandoned still lingered.

"I'm not sure that makes things any easier," sighed Rick. "I don't want to find an angry husband chasing me."

"It'd never come to that. I'd never let on who y'are, but it's a way of covering me back." Anxiety getting the better of her, Sarah started to gabble. "I couldn't think of anything else to say. No one knows 'bout us, 'cept Ma is suspicious of everything I do and, if I'm right, when I start to show, she'll want to know more. And. And … I'm sorry to bring it up and tis ever so embarrassing, but Ma asked if he'd given me any money. I didn't think clearly before I said yes. But of course, he never did, cos he never came."

Rick smiled and stroked the side of her face. "If it's only the money you're worried about, that's easily solved. I'll give you as much as you want, but you've always refused before."

Sarah softened her tone and kissed the inside of Rick's hand. "You know that's cos I don't want to think of meself as a kept woman. I need to be independent and earn me own living, and I've proved I can run a business on me own."

"That's very true and very admirable, but sometimes you make life unnecessary difficult for yourself."

Sarah giggled. "Getting meself with child is one difficulty I could probably do without, but it's 'appened, so I has to make the best of it."

"I think I played a small part in that, my lovely girl."

He lowered his lips to hers and began to caress her body, seeking knowledge of every inch, committing the contours of her still-flat belly to the touch of his fingertips.

"How was your meeting?" asked Amos as she returned.

"Excellent, ta. And thanks for suggesting it. The chance to get away and talk to others is most rewarding." She didn't add that the only person she was talking to was Richard, and what he had to say had nothing to do with the brewery or the pub.

"Anything happened while I've been away?" Sarah unpinned her hat and lifted it carefully from her head so as not to disturb the rapidly redone bun sitting softly at the nape of her neck.

"Not in 'ere, but I believe there's been a bit of ruckus in the kitchen."

Sarah sighed, pulling off her gloves. What now? she wondered.

"I'll leave you to carry on, then."

"Fine with me, Missus Sarah."

Sarah could sense the atmosphere as soon as she walked into the kitchen, and sniffed at a slight but peculiar smell. Ma was busy banging the rolling pin over an unsuspecting piece of pastry, while Molly stood by watching, her arms stiff by her side, her fists clenched and her lips held tightly together.

"Goodness, Ma, what's that bit of pastry done to ya? Be careful the table don't fall down after the thumping it's getting."

Sarah tried to keep her voice light and teasing, but her mother took her words literally.

"Ain't the pastry that's the problem, or this 'ere table. It be this incompetent imbecile that's the problem. Honestly, I don't know why we give her the time of day or the space to live."

Sarah looked at Molly, who by this time had tears welling up, and gave the woman a gentle smile and a slight sideways nod, dismissing her. Molly turned and fled out the back door while Sarah faced her mother.

Putting her hands on the table, she leant forward. "Ma. What on earth …" She paused, took a deep breath and began again. "I've not seen you this upset for a long time, Ma. Al'right, are ya? What's made ya so angry?"

Betsey looked up, her own eyes now watering and stared blankly at her daughter.

"I wanted to make the pastry for the pies, but I couldna find the butter so I used drippin' and that uppity young miss told me I couldna use it. What would she know? I've been making pastry with drippin' since before she were born."

Sarah doubted most of that story. Molly would more likely have offered butter, but Ma was being stubborn.

"She said it were better with butter, but it's not, see," continued Ma, confirming Sarah's suspicion, and pushing a bowl of dripping under her nose. Sarah immediately knew what Molly was trying to do, and why. Whatever was in the bowl was inedible. Sarah pulled her nose back in disgust.

"Ma! That's awful. Where did you get it? It stinks."

Ma looked lost suddenly, her eyes wandered around the room, from the table to the bowl to the pantry. "I don't 'member," she said pitifully and burst into tears.

Sarah guided her to her favourite chair and sat beside her.

"There, there, Ma. S'all right. Mistakes happen. You're such a good cook, and everyone loves your bakin'. And Molly were only trying to help. How about I make ya a nice cuppa? That always makes ya feel better."

"That'd be nice, Sarah love," sighed Betsey, returning to her more normal self. "I don't know what I did." She sounded perplexed. "But I remembered summat from my mother's time and wanted to try out her old recipe."

"I'm sure 'twas a good 'un too, but looks like ya found the rancid dripping what were for the rubbish. I'll get rid of it all and set out a new lot of ingredients for you to make a fresh batch."

"I'm too tired now. Molly can do it. She's a good girl really, and cooks well."

Satisfied that the drama had passed, Sarah poured the boiling water over the tea in the pot and left it to stand while she swept the ruined pastry into the bowl, covered it with a cloth and took it out to the garbage in the back alley.

On her return, Ma looked at her intently between narrowed eyes as she handed her the cup of tea. "You look different? What you been up to?"

Sarah's stomach flipped and she felt her heart racing. "Do I? Dunno why? I ain't been sleeping well of late. Maybe I'm a wee bit tired."

Betsey took the cup and saucer and slurped some tea. "Maybe. But you're up to summat. I can tell."

"Where's Aunt Nettie today?" asked Sarah quickly, wanting to change the subject. These days Nettie used a horse and cart to get her into town. "Would she remember your mother's recipe?"

"What? Nettie? Not likely, she were never a decent cook."

"So where is she?" persisted Sarah wondering who had JJ.

"She's taken that lad of yours away. He were being such a pest wanting to know summat about summat. He's best out."

"He's an inquisitive boy. Likes to know things," his mother said proudly.

"Yeah, well he needs a play mate. Can't be 'round old women all the time. It's about time you had another."

This time, Sarah swore she felt the blood draining from her body.

"Will ya tell me about your ma?" gushed Sarah desperate to talk about anything else. "If she had such good recipes, she must have been a cook, like you. Did you get it from her?"

"Don't ya remember her? Well, maybe not. We didn't see her much once they moved back to the country. But let me see …"

Sarah had vague memories of her grandmother who'd died back in the '40s, but she couldn't say she knew her well, and certainly didn't remember spending time with her the way JJ did with his grandmother. She let Betsey prattle on about the past while her own mind drifted to more immediate issues.

Ma was clearly not well. The unexpected bouts of strange behaviour, like today, were increasing. How she hadn't noticed the stench of rotten offal in the bottom of the dripping bowl bewildered Sarah. But Ma still ruled the kitchen with an iron fist. She could still concoct the most wonderful pies, and her baking was excellent when she was in the mood, but then she'd give up and let Molly do all the cooking until the next time.

The irregularity of her actions was the difficult part to manage. Sarah checked the amount of laudanum Betsey used, and it didn't seem out of the ordinary or any more than what she'd taken for years. But one thing was certain, Betsey's intuition was as sharp as ever.

Whatever was happening with her mother, none of it was making Sarah's life any easier, and life would only get harder from here on.

16
When trouble comes knocking

May 1864

"You can't be seen in public! It ain't decent, I tell ya," growled an irate Betsey, who hadn't stopped complaining and scolding Sarah from the moment she began to show, demanding to know who the father was.

"I told you, Ma. Mr Clements came back, and …"

"I don't believe you. It's just not possible. How could he sneak away in the dead of night without being caught by his cap'n, find his way into the house w'out anyone else knowin', and leave you with child in just one night. Just not possible, tain't, not possible," she mumbled and went about her day.

With her earlier pregnancies, her da had been around and she hadn't been needed to serve in the taproom when she was so noticeably large. This time, as good as Amos was, she couldn't leave it all to him either. She decided to talk it over with Richard.

"What should I do?" she asked as the horse gently trotted along the narrow lane.

With the arrival of spring, the pair had taken to hiring a horse and brougham and going out into the country again.

On Rick's advice, since her da died, she'd made a point of hiring a gig or even a cart to carry goods every now and then, saying she had business to do, or meetings to attend, and it was too far or too time-consuming to walk. She'd become a regular sight around town, and no one batted an eyelid when they saw her.

"Why not hire another man, or a boy, to do all the heaving and cleaning?"

"Can I justify the cost?"

"Let's not get into that again, my love. You know whatever you need is yours to have."

To find herself financially secure, even in the background, was such a turnaround from her usual situation, she sometimes forgot. She was careful never to have obvious money to throw around, but if Betsey asked, she often explained away the little extra with a new boatload of sailors, or an unexpected discount on goods from the brewery.

Richard steered the horse off the lane and onto a track. They'd called a halt to their more intimate time together, but a picnic by the river or under the shade of a large tree had become her favourite times. They unloaded the basket of food and scrumpy, and Rick spread a blanket on the ground before helping her to sit and get comfortable, leaning against a tree for support.

They shared a few kisses and tucked into the picnic and talked about how much, apart from anything else, they enjoyed each other's company. After a while, Sarah's mind drifted back to her unavoidable situation.

"I'm sure most of the men coming into the pub don't care one way or the other, but Ma can't bear the thought of me breaking every rule in the book."

"Are you sure those rules are in a book, written down? Or is society pressured into certain roles and behaviours, women in particular, by those who think they know best? The churches and the wealthy have a lot to answer for, if you ask me."

Rick was certainly no conformist, but Sarah still felt guilty about so many things, some small, some not so, but she knew she'd broken one of the biggest conventions.

She listened to the insects chirping and watched the birds fly silently across the sky, unsure how to respond. *He* didn't have to carry the evidence of her transgression around with him. Nor would he have the responsibility of housing and raising the child.

"Don't fret so much, Sarah. Bristol is a big place. Last I heard, there are roughly a hundred and thirty thousand people living here. How many of those do you know personally, and how many are going to ostracise you because you are a woman having a baby?"

"I never realised the place was so big! I'd be lucky to know one hundred, if that, and like I said, most of them are the sailors who come into the pub. The women I know are my family and a few others. But I'm not just any woman having a baby, am I? I'm a widow and that takes a bit of explaining."

"Don't bother," he said, taking her chin between his fingers and kissing her gently and then more passionately.

By the time he'd finished kissing her, she'd lost the thread of their conversation and decided to enjoy the day regardless. She'd be back at home soon enough to face whatever the next dilemma turned out to be.

* * * * *

"There's a letter, Miss Sarah," said Molly two weeks later, passing her the hand-delivered note.

Sarah knew there'd be a pickle for her to sort out sooner or later and she held it in her trembling hand. But what she could do about it was another matter.

Iz know who the father be.
Cough up £100
Or 'twill be in paper

"Molly," Sarah called, "did you see who delivered it, or any message?"

"No message, miss, and 'twere a ragamuffin who brought it to back door."

A hundred pounds was a lot of money, but maybe Rick would be able to afford it. At least, she hoped he would. But he was just as likely to tell her to ignore it, and without a name or a way of contacting the person who'd made the demand, there was little else she could do. Her stomach roiled, and the little one kicked in complaint.

For the rest of the day, the words played over and over in her mind. She couldn't shake them, but what worried her most was the blackmailer coming back. He was bound to contact her again to collect the money. She was sure it was a he, somehow. She thought a woman would be more subtle. But if she didn't have the money ready, then what? She could probably skirt around street gossip, but if a notice appeared in the newspaper, then everyone would know. She couldn't take the risk.

She hesitated to send a message to Richard at the fire station in case the note writer was still watching, or she happened to use the same boy to deliver it and they'd put two and two together. One never knew. She dithered, and in her shilly-shallying made mistakes.

"Sorry," she said to Amos as she bumped into him, spilling beer everywhere.

"Sorry," she said to Molly as she spilt the jug of milk over the floor.

"Sorry," she said to JJ as she stepped on his toes. Picking him up, she snuggled into his neck. "Sorry, my sweet, I didn't mean to do that. Would you like us to go read a story together?"

Anything to take her mind off her worry. The child squealed in delight and wriggled out of her arms to run up the stairs ahead of her. The only person she hadn't said sorry to was Betsey. She sighed with relief that her mother had been out at one of her numerous church meetings and wouldn't know about the note.

The next day, after a restless night between the baby kicking and her mind seeking answers to her problem, she sought out Richard. She hired a brougham and, taking a circuitous route, travelled across town pretending to take in the sight of the suspension bridge she'd heard was finally nearing completion, and turned back towards the centre of town where she found a boy to take a message.

The wait seemed endless. She paced to and fro along the short pathway leading to the river edge where she'd suggested they meet, feeling conspicuous even though there was no one around.

"I came as soon as I could," said Rick, jumping out of his gig.

Sarah immediately began to worry that the two vehicles standing side by side made their meeting look even more sinful than it was.

"What's the urgency?" he demanded.

She thrust the note into his hand and continued her pacing and hand-clenching while he read it. He caught up with her and took hold of her arm.

"Slow down. Let's talk rationally about this."

"Oh, Rick, what am I going to do?" she wailed, fighting back the tears threatening to overpower her. "How do they know? How am I going to find the money? How ...?"

Rick pulled her closer into his arms. "Shh, it will be all right. I'm guessing this person doesn't know anything. It's a feeble attempt at extortion. Someone's jumped to the conclusion that since no one knows where your husband is, or even if he is alive, and hasn't been seen, then it must be another man. It's all speculation."

"But what if it's him? John. What if he ain't dead?"

"Sarah, my love. You are not making sense. Of course he's dead. A mariner lost at sea doesn't disappear for five years and then suddenly turn up."

Sarah knew he was right, but she'd never shaken the feeling of being abandoned. "But what if ..."

"What if nothing. The note's crudely written. There's no name. No way to contact them. All you can do is wait for them to contact you again and then deny it. You told your mother, and me for that matter, that your husband came back one night. That's the story you stick to."

"But …" She spun out of his arms, anxiety forcing her to keep moving. "What if they don't believe me?"

"Come on, Sarah. You can do this. Why wouldn't they believe you? How can they prove otherwise?"

Sarah wasn't convinced. "What if they do put summat in the newspaper? What then?"

"Don't worry about it. Even if they do, it's gossip at best. You just stick to your story about Mr Clements returning unexpectedly and there's nothing anyone can do. And I doubt the drinkers in your pub would be interested."

Sarah nodded. She really didn't have any option. She chewed her bottom lip, while studying the toes of her shoes. Rick's presence, a good foot or more above her head, steadied her. If he was calm about it, so should she be.

Taking her arm, he led her along the riverbank, the long grass catching the hem of her skirt releasing clouds of fresh seeds.

"Now, tell me," he said changing the subject. "How's that new lad going?"

They stopped under the shade of a tree by a simple bench and Sarah gratefully sat down. Her legs ached these days if she stood for too long. Rick took his seat beside her and stretched out his legs, using the tree behind him for support.

After their previous discussion, Rick had been insistent that Sarah couldn't – and shouldn't - manage with only Amos to help, the closer she got to her time, and for several months after, if he knew anything about babbers.

She'd tried not to laugh at his exceedingly limited knowledge of babies, but deep in her heart, she knew he was right. She was already far too large to be decent. Betsey had been complaining at her for some time, but the work needed doing and someone had to do it. Rick had sent a young man with huge brown eyes and spiky dark hair to her door to offer his services. He was one of the firemen's sons and keen to learn and be useful, or so he said.

"Amos likes him, but he's quite small. Are you sure he's eighteen?"

"That's what I'm told, and why should we not believe him?"

"No reason, I suppose. He arrives when he's needed, does what Amos asks and fits in around the place without any bother. I've seen Ada giving him the eye a couple of times, and I know she sneaks him an extra slice of whatever pie is going when she can."

"Do you mind? Technically, that's stealing."

"Maybe, but no. I always feed everyone anyway. Part of their wages, and if a growing lad needs more food, I'm not going to stop 'im."

Rick nodded. "More importantly to me, are you taking the time to rest?"

"When I can, but …"

He suddenly sat up and turned towards her. "Please agree with me that with both Amos and what's-his-name …"

"Eli," Sarah prompted.

"… Amos and Eli effectively doing all the physical work, that you are free to sit down, lie down and retire early when necessary."

"Well, yes, although the paperwork still needs doing."

"But you are sitting when you do that, correct?"

Sarah nodded. "Yes, but …"

"Then what is the 'but' all about."

"Ma." Sarah's shoulders sagged and she gave the muscles in her back a stretch. "Since I've got more time, she's decided she doesn't need to do so much around the place, so I'm having to spend more time caring for JJ and keeping a watchful eye on her so she doesn't upset Molly, and to a lesser degree Ada, although she doesn't have much to do with Ma. But I have to check Ada's done all the rooms properly. I'm up and down the stairs all the time."

Rick frowned and took her hand in his. "If I could I'd have a word with your mother …"

"You can't," gasped Sarah, interrupting.

"No, I can't, so you will have to, Sarah." He sounded exasperated. "You know better than me how important it is you rest at this stage." He waved his hand absently towards her stomach.

"I know you're concerned. Rick, and I understand, but I'm not fragile, like your wife, and our sort of people, working people, don't have the luxury to take time off. We have to carry on."

Sarah rarely mentioned his wife, but she knew his mind was comparing the two women and remembering the number of children they'd lost. Tragic as it was, infant mortality was commonplace and had no respect for class.

"My Mary Jane," she continued, "died of a disease, not through anything I did by working, and I worked a lot harder back then. I'll be al'right, Rick. I will. It's just all these other things are getting on top o' me. But I feel better for talking with you. I do, truly."

He raised her hand to his lips. "Very well. If you think you know best. But there's no need to worry about this note at all. In fact, I will take it and destroy it."

Having it gone from her sight would be a relief. She worried that Ma might find it and start up again about things.

"I'd better be going." Sarah waggled her ankles inside her boots and slowly stood.

They walked back to the horses, arm in arm, and Rick helped her into the vehicle.

"Take care, my dear. I don't want to lose you."

17
Life of joy

July 1864

This time around, her body knew what to do. Her pregnancy had gone even better than she could have hoped. No swollen ankles and none of the persistent back pain that had slowed her down the first time. She felt as fit and healthy as she ever had and put it down to the joy in her life.

She couldn't think of a more suitable word. Joy that the inn was turning a handsome profit this year; joy in the loyalty her staff showed, especially Molly and Amos, but even young Ada and Eli who were to wed soon, she'd discovered. They had all become like family to her.

Joy that JJ would soon have a playmate; joy that her mother had finally accepted the reality and said she was looking forward to a babber to hold, but most of all, joy in love.

She took the birth of her daughter a year almost to the day after Da's passing as a sign, and decided she would no longer wear mourning. At twenty-nine, she was too young to spend the rest of her life wearing black. She had worn it for five years already. First for her daughter Mary Jane, then for the loss of her husband, and after that her da. But she would put all that behind her now.

Rick became more ingrained in every pore as time passed. She couldn't imagine ever being without him. Whatever shallow emotion she once believed she held for John Clements was nothing in comparison. Rick had stirred feelings she didn't know existed or were possible. He was the other half of her: body, mind and soul, always in her heart and constantly in her thoughts. But more importantly, she trusted him.

Some would say her faith in him was blind, but she believed him when he'd vowed never to betray her.

"You have a daughter," said the midwife, disturbing her thoughts on life, and placed the baby in her mother's arms.

With the child snuggled against her breast, Sarah couldn't remember a thing about the birth, only the happiness having a daughter again brought her.

"Hello, darling girl," she murmured.

"What ya going to call her, then?" asked the midwife.

"Mary, after my first daughter, and Ann after her grandmother."

The midwife continued to put her things away and clean up after the birth. "I thought the grandmother's name was Betsey, or Elizabeth at least."

Engrossed in admiring her baby girl and memorising every detail Sarah wasn't listening.

"What was that?"

The midwife stopped and looked mockingly towards Sarah. "Where'd the Ann come from?"

"Her grandmother. Oh, I see. No, not my mother; from her father's side."

Now where did that lie come from?

"Well, I 'ope she was a nice person and led a long life, cos giving a babber a name that once belonged to someone else with trouble in their life is to pass it on to the child."

Sarah had never heard such rot in her life. Where on earth that had come from, she had no idea, but she wasn't going to allow such nonsense to influence her choice of name.

"I never knew her, but I like the name."

"Well, I never met an Ann that I liked yet. None o' them. And that includes me grandma and me sister," complained the midwife.

How that was relevant to Sarah's situation, she couldn't decide. "I'm sorry to hear that, but I can assure you my Mary Ann will be a lovely person with a lovely life. I shall make sure of it."

She was sure Rick would agree. All she had to do now was figure out how he could meet his latest daughter.

* * * * *

"Mary!" Sarah called as she entered the front door a couple of weeks later. "Are ya busy? I've brought your niece to show you. And show you one of the new outfits you made for me."

"I didn't expect you so soon," said Mary, greeting her sister in the hallway. "You look lovely, Sarah. The soft lemon suits you." Mary cooed over the baby. "Let me take her for a moment."

The two women made their way into the kitchen where the large table, pushed under the small window for better light, was, as usual, covered in Mary's sewing. Sarah noticed how bruised Mary's fingers appeared from where the needle often penetrated the skin.

Mary sat in the armchair by the fireplace with Mary Ann, leaving Sarah to put the kettle on the cooktop and make the tea.

"She's lovely," said Mary. "You forget how soft and smooth a baby's skin is, and her eyes are quite lively for her age. She's going to be dark, I think."

"I think so too," agreed Sarah. "Doesn't have much choice, really, with both parents being dark."

Mary ignored the reference to the girl's father. "How are things at home?"

"Not bad, I suppose. Ma dotes on her, which surprised me, considering all the moans and complaints about it while I was expecting. What is it about babbers that settles Ma? She loved all the babies, but she gets annoyed with JJ now he's coming up five."

"He'll be a bit too boisterous for Ma's taste, I suspect. She and Da were good with Ted when he was little, but they handed him straight back as soon as he got too much for them, until he were older and of use to them," said Mary, recalling the time she'd been separated from her son. She understood how it was necessary sometimes, like when she'd taken JJ for Sarah, and as it had been for two of hers at one time, but it still wasn't something a mother wanted.

The sisters continued to chat over a cup a tea, and cooed over Mary Ann while Sarah fed her, and Mary finished stitching a hem.

"It's been lovely having ya, Sarah. And I've loved seeing Mary Ann, but you're working up to something, I can tell. What is it?"

"Ah, Mary, my dear sister, who knows me so well. There is something I've been meaning to ask, and I know tis a huge imposition and putting you in an awkward situation, but I can't think of anything else if Mr Hunt is to see the child."

Mary raised her eyebrows. "You're not going to ask me to invite Mr Hunt into my home, are ya?"

Sarah had the grace to hang her head and blush, but backing away from what she believed in had never been her way, and she couldn't start now. "If you don't want to invite him here, I will understand, but Mary, ya have to help me. Can you take the perambulator and go for a walk and meet him somewhere or take Mary Ann to his work. If I go, anyone who sees me will know the truth. And I can't risk that with a spy in our midst."

"What's that?" asked Mary, picking up on Sarah's slip. "What spy? What ya talking about, girl?"

Sarah bit her bottom lip as was usual when she wondered what to say next. "I didn't want anyone to know – not even you. It's not fair, but I got this letter wanting money and threatening to tell everyone who the father is. But Richard, um, Mr Hunt that is, told me to ignore it as no one could know anything, especially after I put it about that John had come home for a night."

Mary changed the position of the bodice she was holding, opening it out so she could stitch another part. "You don't think anyone really believed that, do you?"

Sarah stiffened. "Maybe not, but there's no one who

can prove otherwise, is there? It's my word against theirs, and I should know my husband better than anyone."

"So when did you get this threat?" asked Mary uneasily. "Doesn't sound right to me."

"Several months back now. But I've not heard a thing since, honest. But then I've kept out of sight as much as possible. Amos is good with the customers, and young Eli is more than capable of doing the heavy work and cleaning up. I've only got to worry about the paperwork, and checking up Ada does all the rooms proper, and keep Ma from having a go at Molly all the time. Poor woman. Tis a wonder she stays. The things she has to put up with."

Mary shrugged, put down the bodice she was sewing and picked up a sleeve. "She's used to Ma's ways and doesn't let it get to her any more. Molly has it good, and she knows it. But about this letter? What's it got to do with you wanting me to meet Mr Hunt? I'm not so sure it's a good idea."

"Please, Mary, please? You could be out and about with a grandchild or minding her for someone else and say you're meeting him on business. No one would think twice about it. And you're more his age, so it wouldn't raise any suspicions."

"You've got it all worked out, haven't ya? But who d'ya think it is demanding money to keep secrets ya say they can't know?"

"If I knew that I wouldn't be so worrit, would I," snapped Sarah, her body tensing at the turn of conversation. "But I've no idea. It could be anyone, but who would watch me that closely? And since that one and only note, whoever they are ain't been back."

Sarah drew a deep breath trying to settle her nerves. Mary Ann fussed and grizzled at her mother's distress.

Suddenly overcome, Sarah stood. "Oh, don't worry about it. I'll think of something. It's not your burden. I'll get out of your hair."

"Oh, for heaven's sake, Sarah, sit down. I just want to know what's at stake, and I don't at all like the sound of you being watched. We'll have to nip that in the bud."

"I don't see how you can."

"As you said, there's a lot more I can get away with than you. It's just possible that Mr Hunt and I can solve this riddle and our newfound acquaintance might work in your favour."

* * * * *

A week later, Sarah paced Mary's hallway, counting the minutes as they passed, fretting about how the meeting was going and what she should do next. Even though it had been her idea, now the time had come she doubted the wisdom of Mary meeting Richard at all. So much could go wrong.

She trusted Mary, she had to, and she desperately wanted Rick to see his daughter, but how they would continue to meet and connect with each other in the future was beyond her for the moment. Most men left the child-rearing to a nanny, or at least its mother, if the household couldn't afford a helper, but she was stuck somewhere between. Certainly not middle class but a step above working class, since she had a living. But there was no room for a nanny.

Their household now bordered on overcrowding,

despite the fact she'd cut back on boarders, to cater for the extra staff she'd hired. After Da died, she'd disliked many of the long haul mariners, finding them far too boorish after being away for so many months or sometimes years at a time, so barred them from coming. A risk at the time, but she much preferred the local trow-men and travellers, who'd stay one or two nights, spend well and behave decently. Without the rougher elements, The White Hart had flourished. She was plentiful with the food, only sold good ales and looked after her regulars, giving them the odd discount, or a tip she'd heard about goods needing transport. The mistress's reputation as a great cook helped, even if Molly increasingly held the kitchen together, but the reward was a steady clientele.

At least she and JJ, and now Mary Ann, had a room of their own. Molly and Ada shared but Amos and Eli lived out, and Ma commandeered the upstairs front bedroom for herself.

Sarah turned at the sound of someone at the door, but it was only one of the family who lived upstairs. The only way Mary could make ends meet was to live in a shared housing situation in a big house with several other families. She was grateful to have the two larger downstairs rooms for herself, Ted, and her daughter Amey, even though both of them worked and brought funds home.

Finally, she heard Mary and rushed to open the door and help pull the perambulator inside. "How'd ya get on? What happened? What'd he say?"

"Steady on," said Mary, hanging up her coat and hat on the stand and pushing her gloves into a pocket. "Let me get inside before ya bombard me with questions. I'd kill for a cuppa."

"Oh yes, how silly of me, I should have got it ready before." Sarah rushed into the scullery and filled the kettle. After putting it on the range to heat, she went to peek at her daughter who was lying wide awake with her big dark eyes looking up. "How's my little girl, then?" she cooed, picking her up to feed.

Mary smiled. "She's been wonderful the whole time. Not a peep out of her at all. I think she likes the movement of the wheels."

Grinning with unwarranted pride, Sarah pulled out the carver chair beside the table. "Tell me everything," she begged as she sat.

"Whether you like it or not, I questioned him about his intentions."

"What!" squawked Sarah, making Mary Ann jump, but she soon snuggled back into Sarah's arms.

"Hush and listen," scolded Mary. "I think he's genuine, for a married man. He seems to truly care for you and was interested enough in the baby. He even touched her cheek," began Mary. "I don't think he'll desert you. But … he won't leave his wife either. He says he is honour-bound to look after her since she is so frail, and to provide a roof over her children's heads until such time as they make a life for themselves."

Sarah finished feeding Mary Ann and paced the room winding her. "I knew that. I wouldn't expect anything less from him. He's a decent man."

"Yeah. I think he is. I like him. I can see why you were drawn to him, but what now, Sarah? You can't go on seeing him. It's not right."

Sarah swaddled Mary Ann and put her down to sleep. Tears formed as she turned to Mary. "I know, but … Oh, Mary, I can't give him up. I love him, and I'd only be half alive if I did. I can't live like that again."

18

Excitement in town

September 1864

"I'm delighted to be given the opportunity," said Richard as he and Sarah discussed the forthcoming visit of the famous Dr Livingstone, accompanied by prominent members of the fancy-titled British Association for the Advancement of Science. "I am but a lowly fire engineer. But I have been associated with some of the various factories and numerous churches they will be visiting, and even the hospital, in a small capacity, advising them on fire protection. I will gladly take my place at the tail of the group inspecting the suspension bridge before it opens."

"It's what you deserve. You work hard and take care of people. But it looks like rain unfortunately," said Sarah, reading the details. "Be careful you don't slip, mind. They say the timber ain't down for foot traffic yet."

"I'm sure 'twill be perfectly safe, my dear."

In the three months since Mary Ann was born, Sarah had hardly seen Rick apart from the occasional meeting in the street or park, short and limiting by its very nature. On this occasion, she took advantage of the anniversary of the kitchen fire.

"I told Ma I was coming here," she giggled softly, "but not what I was really coming for."

"And what is that, Mrs Clements? What is it you have come for?" he asked with a happy grin.

Not to be drawn too quickly, she prevaricated. "Well, first of all, I need to renew my policy and ask you to put up a new fire mark on the building. The other one is very small and terribly old."

Rick stood from his desk and moved to sit beside Sarah on the sofa. "I can certainly do that for you, Mrs Clements, but is there anything else I can do for you while you are here?"

Taking her chin between his fingers he tilted her face towards his and kissed her gently. Every nerve in her body tingled at his touch and she restrained herself from throwing her arms around his neck and letting her rising passion take control.

"Are we alone?" she whispered, nodding towards the outer reception room where Richard's part-time assistant usually worked.

"I expect so; my clerk has usually gone by now, which is why I suggested you arrive at this time. But let me check."

Sarah heard Richard's footsteps as he walked across the wooden floor and caught the click of the lock. A few moments later he was back and had swept Sarah into his arms before she could say another word.

"My god, I've missed you," he murmured into her ear, and his hands explored her body. Sarah pulled away and, abandoning all pretence at decorum, quickly undid the buttons on her rose-pink jacket. Pulling it off, she dropped it on the floor with the sleeves inside out and undid her blouse, exposing her chemise and breasts for him to nestle into. "Ah, my love. I need you so much."

"I've yearned for this for months," she sighed as her love for him overtook her. She lay back on the sofa smiling, as she watched him remove his clothes.

"Is this what you came for, Mrs Clements?" he joked as he devoured as much of her as he could among the many layers of clothing.

"The service is excellent, Mr Hunt. I couldn't wish for better," she responded in kind, allowing her body, heart and mind to be transported.

"Oh Rick, my love. Whatever are we going to do?" she asked once she had restored her attire. "We can't keep doing this. It's so ..." She searched for a word. "Unworthy ... of our relationship."

"I agree. I wish we could do better, and we will. I promise. I will find rooms, somewhere private and discreet. Because I enjoy being with you whether or not we are ..." He hesitated. "Shall we say, intimate?" He smiled.

Sarah laughed. "Is that what you call it? I call it lovemaking, cos to me that's what this is. Love."

"Ah, yes but it also makes babies, and I don't think you are in a position to consider that again anytime soon."

"Maybe not, but I do want to spend more time with you and give Mary Ann a chance to get to know you."

"I think she's a little young for that, just yet. For now,

I'd prefer if it was just us. You know I'd be with you if I could, don't you?" he asked solemnly.

Sarah nodded. "Aye, I do, but can't be helped. We have to be practical. You've got your family, and I've got mine, and there's nothing can change that."

"I love how you are always so pragmatic."

"Prag what?" she asked. "What's that word mean?"

"Sensible."

"There no point being anything but," she replied. "We have to make the best of it."

"That we do," he agreed.

"Where you been?' demanded Betsey as soon as Sarah walked in.

"I told you. I was renewing the insurance. If something like that were to happen again, I need better cover."

Betsey huffed and grumped. "Well, you shouldn't be out and about. You should be here, working, and looking after those brats of yours."

Sarah held her temper. Just. "My children are not brats, and you have no right calling them that."

"I'll call anyone anything I want to. This is my 'ouse, and I'll do what I like."

"Not when it's my children. Now, who has Mary Ann and where is JJ?"

"Not my business, it seems. Find out for yourself. I'm off."

Sarah watched her mother plod her way upstairs, knowing that would be the last she'd see of her for many hours. She'd take some dinner up later if she didn't cause any more ruckus.

"Mary Ann's asleep, Miss Sarah, in the drawer over there," said Molly, pointing towards the open bottom drawer in the large chest where they kept the tablecloths. "I didn't know what else to do with her, and I couldn't just sit and hold her, and I couldn't leave the kitchen."

"Thank you, Molly. That's very good of you to keep an eye on her. And JJ, do you know where he is?"

"He's a one, that one. Such a ball of energy and always asking questions. 'What do I do with this and what is that for?' He's got a good brain, he has." Molly chuckled. "He took himself off to Aunt Mary's, he said. He were gone before I could stop him."

Sarah's heart sank a bit to think he was such a rascal, running around all the time, but he was so excited about turning five, he wanted to tell everyone he was having cake. But he knew the streets between here and Mary's and would never get lost, and kindly Mrs Croft on the corner always watched out for him and gave him biscuits. She would have to fulfil her promise to have a special cake just for him. Meanwhile, she wanted to check in on the taproom while Mary Ann slept.

December 1864

For the past month, the town had been a hive of excitement and activity with final plans for the grand opening of the Clifton Suspension Bridge. Tons of heavy rock were distributed along its length using a temporary tramway to test the strength of the span until engineers declared the result highly satisfactory. Teams of workers were busy painting all the ironwork in a rich chocolate brown, while the tollhouses at either end were rapidly being completed.

"The nobs are promising 'twill be a great day on the morrow," said Sarah, working in the taproom. If she was honest, she missed the camaraderie and the banter with the men, so she was looking forward to a few days serving drinks. "But if this 'ere rain don't let up, I can't see it somehow. It's not stopped raining for hours, and it's blimin' cold, 'n all."

Ada and Eli had chosen the first day of December to get married, and Sarah had given them two days off and a gift of linen. Molly was pleased to get her room back to herself, but for the celebrations the maid needed Ada in the kitchen, and Sarah needed Eli back behind the bar. Mary Ann still needed feeding.

Three men hurtled through the door, jackets pulled up over their caps and shook off the raindrops. "It's like a bleedin' river out there," said one, approaching the bar. "Can we have three pints, me maid?"

"Right chucking down, i'nit?" said Sarah, handing over the pints and collecting the coins. "Take your time, lovey. Tis cosy in here and you're welcome for as long as ya like."

"Thank ya, maid. Much obliged." The man tugged at his cap and went to find his mates.

Seeing no other customers for the minute, she turned to Amos. "I can't decide whether we'll be busier than usual, or quieter. They're saying we can expect thousands of people coming to watch."

"That's as maybe, but 'twill depend. But with Eli and me and yourself, we'll be gert, however it be."

Sarah twitched her head in agreement. "People are a funny lot. They'll moan about the weather when it suits and then go out in the worst of it."

"Aye. Tis true that. But we'll do a proper job, Missus Sarah. That we will. You'll see."

The day of the official opening Sarah stood at the door listening to the peal of church bells and watching the rain. It had eased, but anyone out in it for long would still get wet through. The flags and banners hanging from many of the buildings added brightness to a dull day, and she could hear the voices of sightseers starting to arrive. A festival atmosphere filled the air, even this early in the day.

"What time's the parade supposed to start?" asked Amos, rearranging furniture and stacking up more mugs, pots, tankards and any other drinking vessel he could lay his hands on.

Sarah glanced around at the clock. "Ten-thirty, I think, but there's some military display afore that behind us in Queen's Square. We might get a bit o' trade out of that, but otherwise we're gonna have to wait till it's over."

"You might be able to nip out and have a quick gawp. They reckon more'n a hundred thousand people will come along to watch."

"So might you, if we're lucky. We can take it turn abouts, although once it leaves Queen's Park and heads off the other way, there'll be no chance to follow. I suspect neither of us might get near seeing anything if that many people are in town."

Sarah knew from what Richard had said that every one of the trades and friendly societies, including the police and fire brigades, would be represented and marching along the designated routes. He would be amongst them, and she wished she could watch him, but she doubted she would even see him, let alone view the parade. They were gathering early, he said, in the Old Market, to arrange themselves in the right order. Once he got caught up there, he might not get away until much later.

She could hear the faint sound of bands tuning up in the distance, and she imagined the likes of The Oddfellows and other such societies standing ready and waiting with their insignia flags, scarves and silver regalia. Richard told her that many of the tradespeople had working models fitted to carts to demonstrate their goods. Thousands were expected to take part, including the Chair and Directors of the Bridge Company, numerous dignitaries, guests and the military, and the procession would extend fully two to three miles. She'd never seen anything so big in her life.

All day long, people came in through the front doors chattering about what they'd seen, keen to have a drink and some hearty food.

"Did you see it, Missus Sarah?" asked one of her regulars. "At the end of the procession was what was called Mr Ginnet's Triumphal Car, whoever he might be. It were right clever, though, I can tell ya. 'Twere a float pulled by eight horses with Britannia seated on a globe and figures from the continents all round."

Sarah made appropriate noises saying it sounded wonderful but was too busy to chat. Next up she heard,

"Would ya believe it? Nearly half a mile 'n more after the advanced guard of artillerymen were going into Park Street, the company of riflemen bringing up the rear only just come out from Thunderbolt Street."

"That would've been a gert sight, I'm sure." She handed over the drinks and took the coins. "I'll get your food over to you dreckly."

"I'm glad I didn't follow 'em all the way," said another man. "Too many people for my likin'. Took over forty minutes to pass as it were. They'll be lucky to get there in time for the presentations and medal ceremony for those boys from the 'ospital school."

By midday, the sun had come out and, shortly after, they could hear the boom of the four eighteen-pound artillery guns, and several people rushed out to listen.

"I'm right gratified to have so many customers through the door," said Sarah to Amos in a quieter moment, "but they won't see anything from out on the Back. They'd need to go along to the Downs, but I'm told it's packed tight, and has been since early morning."

"Bin a gert day, though, Missus Sarah. I've sent Eli to grab some food and take a mo'. He's a good lad, does a proper job."

"Good to hear it. Why don't you do the same and I'll hold the fort here?"

A short time later, new arrivals entered.

"Al'right, me luvver?" said Sarah in welcome.

"Aye. Tis much quieter around 'ere. Glad I am to find a spot to rest me weary legs, and the missus. Could we have two scrumpies, please."

"Exciting, i'nit?" grinned his wife. "We just come from the Downs as it's heaving over there with all the entertainment. You should've seen it. Shooting galleries, and peepshows, and acrobats up to their tricks, and loads of street vendors selling souvenir gewgaws."

The man smiled indulgently. "We got some, didn't we? But the pickpockets were up to their tricks too, and from Cumberland Basin to the bridge, the river was full of steamships decked in bunting. I won't forget in a hurry."

As they wandered off, Sarah overheard the woman say she'd liked the flags of all the different nations and the flowers and greenery decorating the approach.

Sarah wondered if there'd be any let-up. Her feet were killing her already, and the day was only half over. The evening drinkers hadn't yet arrived. With Amos and Eli at full stretch, between serving drinks, she'd been racing back and forth to the kitchen for food, and Mary Ann had demanded more of her today. Fortunately, it was one of Ma's good days, and she and Molly were working as a team producing pies and roast meats, and bread, and any number of pickles and cheeses. But Sarah'd not had time to eat. She swallowed a mug of scrumpy and hoped that would hold her.

Eventually, Sarah locked the door behind the last drinker and flopped down onto one of the settles. Eli had stretched himself along the length of another one, and Amos sat in a solid captain's chair nursing a tankard.

"I'm glad we don't have days like that all the time," said Sarah, taking a gulp of scrumpy. "I'm all in."

"Me and Eli too. We's might be knackered but there's good coin in the tin, mind," said Amos. "That 'as to be good for all of us."

"How's that?" asked Sarah wearily.

"Well, the brewery gotta be happy with the increased sales, which means any threat to the licence has been thoroughly dispelled."

"Hadn't thought of it that way. But true. They can't cancel my licence while I'm making 'em money, can they?"

Amos grinned. "No they can't, Missus Sarah." He raised his mug to her. She tapped hers against his in reply. "You get to stay, and me and Eli get to keep our jobs."

Sarah's spirits perked up at the thought.

"Wish I could've seen the electric lights, mind," mumbled Eli under his arm thrown across his eyes.

"Customers told me they weren't much good," said Amos. "Too dim to reach far, and the wind blew out the magnesium lights."

"What about the fireworks? They'd 'ave been gert."

"Ne'er ya mind lad, there'll be another time."

"There's a room upstairs not used tonight if you'd like to stay," offered Sarah. "We'll need to be up and going again for another day."

"Aye, that I will," answered Amos, "if you're sure you don't mind, missus."

Sarah pushed herself to her feet and slouched over to the bar to find Amos had already wiped it down and restacked the drinkware. Grateful for his help, she reached for the money box thinking she'd pay them both an extra h'penny or so and saw a note poking out from under the bar mat. "Who delivered this, Amos?"

He looked up as she was unfolding the piece of paper. "Dunno. Found it when I was clearing up. What's it be?" he asked as her face turned white.

"Nothing," she answered, thrusting the note into her pocket. "Tis nothing."

Except it was something. She'd received another threat.

I ain't forgot.

19

Another turn of events

December 1864

"I'm quite frightened, Rick. After all these months, I thought the threat had gone, like you said it would, but now he's back. And I'm scared summat bad's gonna 'appen. I can feel it."

She and Rick stood on a high point on the Downs overlooking the bridge where people now freely walked and horse-drawn vehicles clip-clopped their way across. Gone were the trappings of the opening ceremony, leaving just the awe-inspiring beauty of the bridge. The gilded nuts on the chain links gleamed in the sunshine. But Sarah felt change was in the offing, and she worried that more road traffic would mean fewer boats, and less trade at The White Hart.

"I still say there's little this … this … person, whoever they are, can do," said Richard. "No one can prove anything. You've maintained all along that your husband came home, and that's that."

"Except she's coming up six months old and no one's

seen hide nor hair of 'im since. And you and I both know he's not ever coming back!" she wailed. "Oh, I've made such a mess of things. He'd been missing for nigh on five years, then I say he's back and I'm expecting, and then he don't come back after, so is he dead for a second time? Has there been another shipwreck that took 'im? And how can I say he's dead and get the magistrate to make it official if word gets out he's supposed to be the father of my baby? How do I know that letter writer won't spill the beans? And now I'll 'ave to wait another seven years before I can make the declaration."

Sarah drew a long breath after blurting out all the worries that had been building up in her mind since the day she knew she was pregnant. "I know tis foolish, but I feel so alone at times. I've people everywhere but tis me who has the burden."

The spot where they were standing was too public for Rick to take her in his arms; to tell her she was not alone; that he would always be with her; that he would look after her; as he'd so often said in the past. She understood that, but it didn't help her mood that he hadn't offered her physical comfort. The growing feeling of desolation stirred sourness in her stomach and choked the words in her throat. She seemed always on the verge of tears and utterly exhausted.

"Mrs Clements," he said sternly. She turned towards him in surprise. "You must control your hysteria. You are upsetting the balance of all you hold dear. Now pull yourself together, and let's carry on as we always have done."

Sarah stared at him, aghast. The man who had been her guiding light, her strength, and her love; the father of her illegitimate child – for that's what she was in the eyes of the law – was accusing her of being hysterical. She struggled to get her head around the thought he would berate her at a time like this, her heart beating so loudly she could hear it in her ears. But he hadn't finished.

"I can't have you behaving like my wife does and falling apart at the slightest suggestion of anything out of the ordinary. It doesn't become you."

Sarah gasped with pain and shock, but anger built within. She didn't need him turning on her.

"How can you say such things to me? You've never compared me with your wife before, and I don't appreciate it now."

"Then behave. Show the gumption I first saw in you and admired, and loved. And stop worrying and complaining all the time."

Sarah took a deep breath, ignoring the terse, impatient tone in his voice, and pulled her shoulders back, gathering all the dignity she could. "I'd like you to take me home, now, if you would be so kind."

They rode home in silence. He dropped her in Queen's Square, and she walked the remaining distance seething with rage.

No sooner had she stepped through the door, before she'd even had a chance to remove her gloves, let alone her hat and coat, Molly rushed to take both her hands in hers.

"Oh, Missus Sarah, the mistress 'as taken a real bad turn, she 'as. I dunno know what to do. She won't listen to nuffin' I say, and she's been screamin' her 'ead off summat awful."

"Don't fret, Molly. You always do so well with her, it's not your fault. I'll see what I can do. Where is she?"

"In her bedchamber."

Sarah found Betsey clutching her head and pacing. Low moans emanated from her throat, more like a growl than any words. She was clearly agitated.

"Ma, what's wrong? What can I do to help?"

Stripping off her gloves, Sarah tried to stop the pacing and held her mother by her upper arms.

A red-eyed, flushed face stared back at her. "Medicine," she breathed. "Hurts."

"What hurts, Ma?"

Betsey shook her arms free and, letting out a high-pitched scream, clutched her head once more. Still groaning, she began pacing again. Sarah looked for Ma's laudanum bottle and found it lying empty on the bedside table.

"Come lie down, Ma, while I run 'n get more medicine." Easing her mother onto the bed, she shut the curtains to block the light that seemed a bother. "I'll get some help. Try to sleep now."

Sarah watched her mother relax as whatever pained her released its grip. She tiptoed from the room, scurried down the stairs and out the front doors, calling out to Amos. "The mistress is ill."

Luckily the apothecary was in as she raced through the door, sending the bell clanging wildly. "Please come!" she cried. "My mother is very ill. I need medicine but someone needs to see her and tell me what to do."

"I don't usually do house calls," said the man behind the counter.

"Please, sir. Please come. I'm at me wits' end, I am."

Her breathing was rapid and she had trouble getting all the words out. She glanced between the man and his wife, who she knew, pleading, "I don't know what's right or what's best. Please, sir."

After sharing a word with his wife, he agreed.

"Take this, dear," said his wife, handing him his bag, having refilled it with various bottles. "I know Mrs Daniels. You'll need it."

With the medicine bag in hand, the pair left the pharmacy. Sarah tugged at his sleeve to hurry him along and within minutes they were back at the inn. She led him up the stairs, carefully opening the door first and peeped inside. Ma lay tossing and turning on the bed, seemingly in delirium. Her eyes were shut tightly, and small moans escaped as she moved.

"Come," she said to the man, opening the door wide. "See for yourself."

The apothecary moved to the other side of the bed, testing Ma's temperature with the back of his hand on her forehead, then lifted Ma's eyelids one at a time, after which he checked her pulse with his fingers on her wrist. Next, he took out the stethoscope and proceeded to listen to her chest.

"Can you sit her up?" he asked, standing back.

"Come on, Ma, sit up?" she whispered putting her arm under her mother's shoulders.

Betsey moaned and opened her eyes, glaring at Sarah vaguely, but their combined effort finally sat her upright.

Placing the stethoscope on Betsey's back, he listened in several places before he folded it up and placed it back in the bag. He then checked both of Ma's ankles as she fell back into the pillows.

In the silence, Sarah stood in a muddle of anxiety. She grasped her hands together, fingers flexing over the backs while her heart continued to thud. For all her faults, Ma was Ma, and she couldn't lose her, not yet. Not while she had so much on her plate to worry about.

"How long has she been like this?"

Sarah jumped at the sound of the man's voice. "She's not um … hasn't been as bad as this before," she stammered. "Only a matter of hours maybe."

"And before this?"

"She's always been sad and had her bad days, when she stayed in bed, since I were young after she lost her little ones. But since my da died last year, she's been getting worse. Sometimes she forgets where she is and thinks Da – and my young daughter who died backalong – are still with us."

"I see. How often does she get confused?"

Sarah hesitated, not wanting to condemn her mother. "Not that often. She's still a great cook and makes the best pies, but our housekeeper keeps an eye on her in case she doesn't finish what she's doing."

He picked up the empty laudanum bottle and sniffed it. "How much of this does she take?"

The apothecary's questions were starting to alarm Sarah. She didn't quite know what she was supposed to say or if anything she was saying would make things better or worse. "Measured amounts. She's been really good about not taking too much since she had a fright a while ago. There was a fire, and …"

"I see."

"What's wrong with her, sir?"

He reached into his bag and pulled out a bottle. "I'd say she is suffering from brain fever. Give her a few drops of this whenever she gets agitated. It's a stronger form of laudanum. There's not much else I can do. Be prepared. She will deteriorate over time, but this will help her relax."

He closed his bag, and put his hat on. "Good day to you."

Sarah stared out the window after he'd gone, praying he was wrong and Ma would get well again, but knowing she would not.

With only a matter of days until Christmas, she questioned what she'd done wrong. Why was Christmas always so hard? Not since the days when Mary Jane had laughed and giggled over the brightly coloured ribbons had Sarah found the peace and happiness the season promised. This Christmas would be no different. Except this time, she would have Ma to look after as well as the cooking, the children and all the other duties the bar demanded.

March 1865

She could hold out no longer.

For weeks she'd be so angry with Richard, she'd refused to see him. While Ma hadn't deteriorated in that time, neither had she improved. The head pains plagued her less often while she took the opium, but if she wasn't in her bedchamber, she sat in her favourite chair in the kitchen and watched. Molly pushed more work onto Ada and stepped smoothly into Ma's shoes as far as the cooking was concerned, but Sarah found the extra workload exhausting.

Mary did what she could to help with the children, usually having them under her feet while she worked, but was of little help at the inn. She would sit with Ma and talk with her often during the day, but the nights were the most difficult for Sarah when Betsey took to wandering.

Richard left her endless messages and wrote long letters after that fateful meeting last December. He had apologised for his outburst and his false accusations, explaining that the pressure of business and increasing difficulties at home had allowed him to lose his temper when he shouldn't have. He constantly begged her to forgive him and allow him to visit her and apologise in person.

She had not replied. Not spoken to him. Not seen him. She tried to put him out of her mind. She knew continuing with their relationship was wrong and would cause further grief. But oh, how often she missed him, longed for him. She dreamt about him at night, and her determination was finally broken as spring approached.

The morning was still young and the overnight temperature had barely risen when she sent a message.

"I came as quick as I could," panted Rick, his breath misting in the air.

"I need as many people as you can find to help look for Ma. She's gone. No one saw her leave, but the perambulator and Mary Ann are missing." The fear of losing her daughter was greater than her worry about her mother.

"Please, Rick. I promise I won't get hysterical, and I won't ask anything else of you, but please," she whispered looking over her shoulder to make sure she wasn't overheard, "find our daughter."

Sarah sucked in her breath as a sob threatened to escape. She would not break down in front of Rick. She would not show weakness, but she nearly melted at the sight of him. If the situation hadn't been so dire, she would have thrown herself into his arms and told him she loved him and had forgiven him.

"Leave it with me. I'll get the fire brigade out."

With that, he was gone, and Sarah was left trying to pretend she had the situation under control. Deciding her only option was to keep busy, or her resolve would fail, she began cleaning everything in sight.

An hour later, as Sarah's nerves threatened to explode, Rick returned with Ma at his side, pushing the perambulator, while he carried nine-month-old Mary Ann in his arms. The girl had obviously been crying but she was now quite content cuddled up against him, her head resting on his shoulder.

"Thank you," she whispered with a wide smile as she took the child into her arms. She made a series of cooing noises to soothe her own jitters as much as to put the girl at ease. "Where did you find them?" she asked when she was satisfied that Mary Ann was no worse for her escapade.

"Not far. Down by the old market. They were quite safe, sitting on a stile. Your mother said she'd come to get fresh vegetables."

A tentative smile crossed Sarah's face. "I remember, we used to do that when I was a child. Once a week, we'd go to the markets with this old thing, so we didn't have to lug 'em back." She nudged the perambulator with her foot. "She must have thought she still did that."

She turned to her mother, whom Molly had settled into her usual chair. "Ma, I hear you've been to the markets."

She looked at Sarah curiously. "Well, some'un has to. Your da can't. He has work to do. But summat wasn't right cos no one was there, and young Sarah was in the carriage when she should've been at home. This fine gentleman escorted me back, y'know."

"That was nice of him, 'n all. But my Lord … what an outing you've had, but next time if ya tell me when ya want to go to the markets, we can go together, like we used to. It'll be better with the two of us."

"Ere, ah'd kill for a cuppa. All that walking 'as fair taken it out o' me, I can tell ya. Where's that kitchen girl?"

"I'm 'ere, mistress," said Molly. "I'll make us a cuppa in a jiffy."

Ma seemed satisfied that all was as it should be, laid her head back and fell asleep where she sat.

Sarah motioned to Rick to follow her, and they slipped into the snug that wasn't likely to be occupied at this time of day. She sat Mary Ann on her knee.

"I'm ever so grateful," she began. "You don't know how worried I was. But we've no time to talk. I'll need to feed this little one so we can't linger."

He took her hand in his and kissed it. "As long as you promise me we will talk. I've regretted every day we've been apart. You have no idea how unhappy I've been, especially knowing it was all my fault." He pulled her closer. "Truly, Sarah, I can't live without you. Promise me we'll meet soon."

She fixed her eyes on his, trying to determine how genuine he was, and saw the same longing she carried in her heart. "I promise."

20
The end of an era

July 1865

When she finally visited Richard's offices, taking Mary Ann with her saying she needed to say a proper thank you to him for coming to her rescue and finding Ma and the child so quickly, Sarah's resolve had lasted no more than a few minutes. The stilted conversation scarcely concealing the nervous tension emanating between them, they willingly fell into each other's arms.

'I'm sorry,' Richard had muttered. 'Truly, I should not have spoken to you like that. None of it is your fault, and I've failed you when I promised I wouldn't. It won't happen again.'

Now, three months on, celebrating Mary Ann's first birthday with a picnic in the countryside far from prying eyes, she knew her body had changed and suspected she was pregnant again. She wouldn't tell him yet. Although she knew her love for him was real, and believed utterly in his love for her, they couldn't openly show it or share such moments of happiness, except in private.

"I must get going," he said as they packed up the picnic. "My wife has not been at all well, rather like your mother, I fear, but more melancholic rather than confused. It's a lot for my daughter to cope with as well as being mother to the younger two."

"It must be hard on your namesake. He's still a boy."

"He's had very little to do with his mother, if I'm honest. Sarah Ann has always looked after him, and Isabella is so engrossed in her studies, little else matters to her."

Sarah often worried that her presence would affect the lives of those hapless children, by taking their father's attention away from them. Although they weren't poor financially and had more than enough social opportunities, she understood the lack of a mother's love. She'd always known she was the last of many and not the preferred child, but Da's love had more than made up for it. She hoped Richard showed his children that he loved them, but melancholia had a habit of depriving not only the sufferer, but the entire household, of any warmth.

"I've been meaning to tell you," she said as the horse trotted home. "I've had a letter from the brewery. They want to visit for some reason. They didn't say why exactly."

"When are they coming?"

"Next week."

"Let me know how it goes." He pulled the carriage to a halt and helped Sarah down. "You've not heard anything more from our erstwhile blackmailer, have you?"

"No. Thank goodness. Maybe he's given up. It's been months."

"I told you not to worry, didn't I?"

A week later, her world came crashing down.

Two men from the brewery wandered around the pub, inspecting every corner, wanting to see the guest rooms upstairs, and queried Amos on the hours he worked and what his tasks were. They finally returned to the bar and stood in front of her. Shoulder to shoulder, like a barrier, with stern faces.

"We hear you are frequently absent and that you entertain men," said the older of the two.

"Whadya have to say for yourself?" asked the shorter, meaner-looking one.

Sarah stared at them vacantly for a moment, before spluttering, "I'm hardly absent." Her mind worked overtime to think of what to say that would appease these uncompromising men. "I work in other parts of the inn, keeping the patrons fed and the bedchambers clean and refreshed. And this place is always full of men. They drink here, they eat here, and they stay here. I don't understand what you're suggesting. Are you not satisfied with the returns?"

"The returns are worthy. I can't dispute that," said the older man. "But it's not the returns we're concerned about, it is the reputation of the licence holder."

"I beg your pardon?" Sarah's stomach clenched as a shiver of alarm ran through her.

"Like I said, we've heard you're often not here and entertain men, and not in the taproom, like you tried to suggest."

"Yeah, and your worker confirmed he works on his own most days." The accusatory tone of the second man gave her the creeps.

"I told you, I have other work to do," she defended

with a shudder. "Amos manages the bar when we are quieter, which gives me a chance to do everything else. I can't expect Amos to make beds or clean, now can I?"

A hard gleam entered the man's eyes at her tone. "How you run your household is your problem. But when customers complain, then it's our problem."

"Who's complained? Are you gonna tell me that? And how many? Because maybe then I'd understand what this all this about." Ire at her treatment rose with every word.

The man stood straighter. "You are being insolent, madam. Control yourself. It is not your place to question. You are to simply answer our queries and behave in a far more becoming manner. No wonder customers are dissatisfied."

Sarah bit back the immediate response that formed on the tip of her tongue. She couldn't risk aggravating them further.

"My apologies then, sirs. I did not intend any disrespect, but you have taken me by surprise."

"Exactly our purpose," snarled the vile one.

Sarah gathered herself and tried another tack. "May I offer you any refreshment? You must be thirsty at least, and maybe you'd like a slice of pie. We have a reputation for serving the best pie in the area."

"No," said the older man, adding, "er … thank you," as an after-thought. "But it is that reputation you're talking about that concerns us."

"We've bin makin' enquiries," added the more menacing of the two, "and we don't like what we hear."

Sarah's legs wobbled and she screwed her hands tightly into her skirt.

"I'm sorry to hear that. And I don't wish to be rude, but how can I defend myself against what I don't know?"

The men looked at each other; the older one, who appeared to be the senior of the two, nodded.

"The brewery gave you a chance after your father died, for his sake. But to our mind, you've not lived up to our expectations, and ..."

"We 'ereby give notice," the other man interrupted, "for ya to vacate these premises by end of nex' month." Withdrawing a piece of paper from his satchel, he placed it on the bar with a sneer.

Sarah gasped and grabbed the bar counter for support as the blood pumping around her body seemed to drain away.

"My licence," she began. "I hold a legitimate licence. How can you do this? I have children ... and responsibilities ... and my mother isn't well."

"None of that is of concern to us," replied the senior agent. "You can transfer your licence at the renewal date, but as this is our premises, we are fully in our rights to ask you to leave. We have been very generous as it is, allowing you to stay longer. We could have asked you to leave immediately but were aware of your, shall we say ... situation."

"But why?" she breathed. "If the returns are good."

An iniquitous grin spread across the younger man's face. Did she detect a lecherous look in his eyes? "You had a child last year. Correct?"

Sarah swallowed hard and instinctively put her hands on her stomach. "I did. Yes."

"But it says here," he looked at another paper in his hand, "you're a widow." He took a step forward, his finger pointing. "So who's is it? Eh? That's what I'd like to know? Who's is it? Who ...?"

The older man restrained the other's arm.

While softer, his tone was no less inflexible. "We cannot condone illicit behaviour, Mrs Clements, under any circumstances. Good day to you."

She watched them go before she bent almost double from the pain of knowing she had failed everyone. It nearly brought her to her knees, but no amount of weeping and wailing, self-reproach or remorse, would make any difference.

She had to fight.

August 1865

Sarah had begged the brewery to reconsider, to no avail. Richard had written to them in her defence, which had alarmed her considerably. "What if they guess it's you?" but he'd shrugged off her concerns.

Amos had also written in support, saying how much he'd valued working with her and would like her to continue as landlord, but nothing swayed them from their decision. Amos was told his job was safe even when the temporary manager came in.

"I'm that sorry, Missus Sarah. I'd much prefer to be working with you than some other bloke."

"It's not your fault, Amos," she reassured him. "Just look after yourself, mind. I don't want you on my conscience too."

To make matters worse, she had admitted she was once again pregnant, and it would be visible to everyone within a matter of weeks. This time, there was no pretending John had come home. It was far too late for a ruse like that to work again.

Mary was less understanding. "Didn't I warn you no good would come of a relationship with that man?"

"Wouldn't have mattered," said Sarah. "Someone was out to get me, and they did."

"What ya talking about?"

Sarah then explained she'd received another threatening note. "They were so far apart and so long ago, I'd put them out of my mind. Mr Hunt believed they were empty threats, and I should ignore them. Which I did, and look where it got me."

"Oh, Sarah, love, I'm real sorry. Do ya have any idea who was threatening ya?"

"None. I've never upset anyone that I know of."

Sarah sighed with the weight of the world on her shoulders. Molly and Ada would still have their jobs, Eli too, from what Amos said. It was just her they wanted out. Her and her children, and Ma.

"I haven't found a way to tell Ma yet," mumbled Sarah, hoping Mary would offer. "She's reasonably stable at the moment. The headaches leave her alone most of the time if she takes the morphine, but she is still confused by the children's names. She keeps thinking they are hers, but who I am supposed to be, I haven't worked out."

"Aunt Nettie has been good with her, hasn't she?"

"Very much so. She's kept me sane at times and knowing I can call on her whenever Ma gets upset is the gift from God I prayed for. She talks to Ma about the times when they were little and growing up together.

And she's the only one who can mention Da without upsetting her."

"Then let her tell Ma. Have you made any plans? Do you know where you're going to live? Time's running out, mind."

Sarah stared at her boots peeping out from under her skirt, thinking they needed a good polish, but she'd not had the time, or the inclination. Wrapped in despondency, Sarah's spirit was at its lowest ebb. "I know, but I can't make a decision about anything. I don't trust myself any more."

"I've been making enquiries," said Richard who had brazenly come to the pub to talk to her.

"You shouldn't be here," said Sarah, looking around nervously in case anyone was watching. "You might be seen."

"Even if I am, the damage is done. Whoever was threatening you has won. But you need a home to go to." She filled a mug with beer and passed it across the bar as if he was simply another customer. "Ta, but listen. There's a place over by St Agnes Park that's for sale."

"But, Ri–" Sarah stopped herself and began again. "Mr Hunt, I appreciate your advice, but I can't afford to buy a place."

"I'm not suggesting you do. I wish to invest in a business."

She eyed him suspiciously. She wouldn't be bought, not now. "What business?"

"It's a relatively humble place with a few rooms to let, and is available for a modest price, but it requires a licence holder to manage it." He paused long enough for her to take in what he'd said. "If I purchased it, would you agree to manage it on my behalf?"

Possibility ruffled her thoughts. Her gaze met the warm, soft eyes that had captured her heart in the first place, and the generous smile creasing his face offered her the certainty she craved. "Tell me more."

While Richard's proposal had merit, the clincher came the following day. Swaggering and smug, the man strode into the place with nary a word until he came face to face with Amos.

"From now on, ya do fings my way. Got it?" A mean scowl marred his face, as he pointed a crooked finger towards Amos.

"And who might you be, to be tellin' me what to do?" countered Amos calmly.

"I'm your new boss, that's who. I'm taking over from that hussy who thinks she's better than anyone else roundabout. So don't give me no lip."

"Are ya now?" queried Amos. "So, other than twat, what's ya name?"

Sarah emerged from the shadows behind Amos distracting the man from whatever he was going to say in reply to the insult.

"Owen Davidson," she said slowly, comprehension dawning. He was her nemesis. The one who sought her downfall. Now she understood. "You've a nerve coming in here."

Spluttering with rage, his head twisted in her direction. "I told ya I'd get ya, bitch, an' I did. Now, tis time you was gone."

Her knees were shaking as she lifted her head. "I'm still landlord til end of the month and you're not welcome. Now git and don't come back."

Owen took a step towards her, shoulders hunched, finger pointing.

Amos stepped between them. "You 'eard the lady. Git, afore some'un gets hurt. And it won't be me."

Small, beady eyes switched between the two as the man contemplated his next move. "Just you wait. You'll see, ya will. I'm not one to be nobbled."

As he stormed out the doors, leaving them swinging, Sarah knew she hadn't heard the last of him.

21

A beginning and an end

September 1865

Within days, Sarah had packed up their personal belongings, taking only what was theirs, including Betsey's favourite china, said farewell to a tearful Molly, awarding her with a few extra coins for her loyalty, and moved to The George.

Richard had been correct when he'd described it as modest, but the two-storey, white-washed corner property in a row of terrace houses would suit her new lifestyle nicely. Although less than two miles from the Welsh Back, she didn't know the area well, and hoped no one would recognise her or know her story.

"Come along now, Betsey," said Nettie who had taken it upon herself to make sure the move went as smoothly as possible for her sister. "Your room's at the top in the front, just like you've always 'ad. And there be a lovely park across the ways for ya to look at."

Betsey struggled up the stairs, muttering all the way, and disappeared into the bedchamber. The men had delivered all their furniture the day before, and Sarah hoped Ma would like her room.

Nettie called down, "She found her chair and is as 'appy as a pig in muck."

Sarah laughed at Aunt Nettie's new phrase that she'd overheard a farmer say at the markets, and sighed in relief. "Good to know."

She suspected she'd be up and down those stairs a great deal, even with her burgeoning figure, but as long as Betsey was settled, life would be easier.

Of the remaining five rooms, she'd chosen the smallest and darkest one at the back for herself and the children. Looking around, she had ideas on how to brighten it up in time. She plonked the two suitcases on the floor before poking her nose into the other rooms available for let. She had plans to put her own touches on those rooms too. One was already occupied by a woman she'd yet to meet, who'd been resident there for some time and wanted to stay on.

'Twill be nice to have some female company, thought Sarah as she ran down the stairs wanting to get a few things sorted before the children arrived.

On the ground floor, the front two rooms had been converted to a lounge with a small bar and space for no more than a dozen people. A fireplace, an assortment of round tables surrounded by ladder-back and carver chairs, and two comfortable armchairs gave it a cosy feel. The clientele here would be nothing like the mariners she'd grown up with, but she was ready for a change of pace. And being a free house, she wasn't beholden to any brewery. As long as the Licensing Board was happy, so was she.

At the back, Sarah inspected the surprisingly well-equipped kitchen, with running water, a scullery and pantry, and a door leading to the outhouse in a small backyard with its own side entrance for deliveries. Beside the scullery was a narrow room with a tin bath and a washstand with a jug and ewer, which all the tenants could use. Sarah was grateful, as it would save her lugging pails of hot water up the stairs all the time. Next to it was a small private sitting room, where she would thankfully retreat at the end of her day, and the crib for the new baby would fit in the nook under the stairs.

Satisfied she'd made the right decision, despite her concerns that Rick was the owner and technically her employer, she delighted in the knowledge he would be able to visit her without impediment and they would be closer than ever.

She hugged that thought to her jaded heart.

"Al'right, Sarah. Are ya there?" called Mary, coming through the front door, straight through the lounge and along the corridor into the kitchen. "I've brought ya a pot of stew and bread to tide you over."

Following behind came six-year-old JJ who valiantly carried a basket full of Mary's gifts.

"Ta ever so much, Mary. And you too, my son," she added, taking the basket from him. He beamed with pride.

"My word, this is a fancy kitchen," Mary added, placing the stew on the cooking range.

"Tis 'n all. Never expected anything like it, if I'm honest."

"Gimme an 'and to lift the carriage in afore Mary Ann wakes. She fell asleep on the way over. But JJ did very well. Didn't ya lad?" said Mary, ruffling the boy's hair.

Mary stayed for a couple of hours helping Sarah unpack and put things where they belonged. JJ raced up and down the stairs, chattering to Aunt Nettie before she left and patiently sitting with his grandma happily reading a book.

"He loves his readin', don't he?" said Mary.

"Always has done," agreed Sarah. "Took to it like a duck to water right from the start. I reckon he could be a teacher in years to come. Tis in his nature."

Tasks completed, Mary said goodbye, promising to return when she had the opportunity. "But I'm a bit on the hop with sewing at the mo'."

"Don't worry about me. I'm doin' fine. Thanks for your help today."

"Good luck to ya, then."

Sarah had barely turned around and began preparing the bar for customers when Rick appeared.

"Mrs Clements." He raised his hat and smiled. "I thought to see how the move in was going."

Sarah's whole body quivered at the sight of him. "Almost settled and ready for customers. Can I offer you refreshments?"

"No, I won't stay today. You will have lots more to do, I'm sure. I've put a notice in the newspaper on your behalf that The George is now back in business, and you have rooms available."

"Tis kind of you, for sure. Havin' a full house will be good. There's two rooms available – unless …"

"Al'right, me luvver?" said a woman's voice. "You be the new landlady then?" she asked, coming straight up to the counter. Sarah guessed the woman was in her late fifties or early sixties, short with a rounded body; she looked up at Richard. "I'm Mrs Binns, Ethel Binns. I'm in the big room upstairs. And who's this fella? Ain't seen ya before. You taking a room or what?"

The rapid chatter alerted Sarah to the woman's nature. She'd have to watch what she told her or it'd be all over the street before tomorrow.

"Hello, Mrs Binns. I'm Mrs Sarah Clements, and that's right, I'm the new landlady. This gentleman …" she saw Rick give his head a short shake and changed what she was going to say, "… is my husband, Mr Clements. He's a commercial traveller and is often away, but you'll see him around from time to time."

Sarah inwardly shook at her audacity and avoided looking at Rick who she knew was eyeing her quizzically, but what else could she say? He clearly hadn't wanted to give the woman his name or reveal his connection to the tavern, so what choice did she have? In fact, she was quite proud of her quick thinking.

"Well, good to meet ya both. Lots of travellers stayed 'ere in the past, comin' and goin' like the wind through the windows. I quite like travellers, they got lots of interesting tales to tell."

"And what do you do, Mrs Binns?" asked Sarah.

"I do charring, lovey, but me old bones are getting weary of it, I can tell ya."

Sarah wondered if the woman might come in useful to her, if she was clever. Greying curls peeked out from under the mob cap she'd wrapped around her hair. A full-size pinny was tied around her waist, over which she wore a coat and carried a bulky bag.

"I hope you'll be happy living here. My elderly mother is upstairs in the front room, but she suffers from the ah … the vapours, so you might not see her so much. And I have a boy John Jacob, we call him JJ, and a daughter Mary Ann who's fifteen months old."

"And I see you're expecting again, too," sniffed Mrs Binns. "That'll be a shock to some. A woman with young children running a place like this, but it's all the same to me. It don't matter one jot, it don't. I like children. Not that I had any of me own, ya understand, but they make the world go round."

Sarah stifled a laugh. "They do that, Mrs Binns."

"Call me Ethel, lovey. If we's to live together we might as well be on first names."

"Thank you, and you may call me Sarah."

"I'll be away upstairs then. Shall I pop in and say g'day to your good mother? I'll be back down later for me usual sherry. I do so enjoy a drop in the evenings and a good natter. Makes for a good life."

"Ma might be sleeping," said Sarah, "so maybe leave it for another time, but I'll look forward to seeing you again later."

Richard and Sarah watched the woman go through the door into the rest of the house, and once they were convinced she was out of earshot, let go their repressed laughs.

"I think you'd better watch that one," said Rick, "but what on earth possessed you to introduce me as your husband, for God's sake?"

Sarah turned serious at his implied displeasure. "Because in everything but name, you are. You lie in my bed, you are the father of me daughter … and this one coming," she added, placing her hands over her stomach. "And how else are we to explain your comings and goings? Or aren't you going to visit me no more?" All her insecurities, and the mostly buried disquiet over what would happen to her and the children if ever Richard should cast her off, surfaced in a flash. Her eyes glistened with barely concealed anger. "Coming here was your idea. I thought it would make it easier for you, but if you're done with me, then be on your way."

Richard had the grace to look penitent. "Sarah, my love, I could never be done with you. How many times must I reassure you of that? I want to be with you every moment. But I can't, so maybe you have hit on a solution. I'd never have thought of it, but a commercial traveller could be a good ploy."

Mollified by his response, she softened. "It didn't take her long to see I was with child even so soon, so it wouldn't take her long to notice how often you're here. At least now she has no reason to question me."

"You astound me with your logic and practical sense. I do so love you. Don't ever think you can get rid of me."

October 1865

A full month had passed in a whirl as Sarah settled into a routine. The George was more boarding house than pub, where she served breakfast to whoever was staying, but not an evening meal. She had a small midday crowd, who ate the bread and pickles she offered, or a pie on certain days, but the evenings were when the bar came into its own. Anytime from four o'clock on, regulars would drift in to have their drop, go home for their tea and return bringing their family with them.

Rick, too, was a regular caller, coming in each week as if he'd finished his rounds. He'd stay two nights and then be gone again. Sarah cherished those nights, although they had to be far more discreet and infinitely quieter since walls, and children, had ears.

The tavern was clearly the social hub of the community, and she quickly learnt who everyone was and where they worked, and whatever other piece of gossip Ethel could impart.

"Honestly, Ethel," asked Sarah one time early on in their friendship, "is there anyone you don't know?"

"Prob'ly thousands, lovey. I only knows them I meet in the street, or at the shops, or wherever I 'appen to be, but I'm a friendly type, mind. I like to talk to people and then they talk back and before you know, we're best of friends."

"I'm sure they are. Ma has certainly taken to you and enjoys your chats," said Sarah, thankful for the moments Ethel distracted Ma from her fits.

"Anythin' to help, lovey. She's ever so poorly, i'nit? Must be a right worry for you 'n all. Some days I can't make sense of what she's saying. It don't make no difference, mind. I just chatter on and when she catches up, she's as right as rain again."

Sarah had let the other rooms out to commercial travellers whom she discovered came and went and could disappear for weeks before they returned. She'd give consideration to doubling up on their bookings once she figured out their routine, but Ethel was a daily fixture.

Without fail, she was down for breakfast at seven o'clock, full of chatter about what she'd heard the night before, except when the men who were the source of her information were at breakfast at the same time. Then she'd head off to char for part of the day, and in the evenings, she'd help Sarah tidy up in the bar and wash the glasses before she went up to bed.

In many ways, Sarah felt happier than she had in a while. She had more time to spend with JJ and Mary Ann, and while Ma kept to her room more often than not, which meant regular trips up and down the stairs, Sarah had less work to do chasing after her or cleaning up a disaster in the kitchen. JJ spent time reading to her every day, and even Mary Ann could be left safely in the room with her if the door was shut. The girl crawled around the place, pulling herself up when she could and instinctively Ma knew when the child needed saving. She would scoop the girl up, and they'd lie together on the bed and sleep.

Ethel made herself invaluable. When Sarah needed to clean or cook or go shopping, the woman was there keeping an eye on Ma and the children, but sometimes she tuned out of the constant chatter, and would miss something Ethel had said until reminded.

"Did you hear what I said, missy? It pays to listen, or you might not learn what you ought to know."

Sarah shook her head at some of Ethel's turns of phrase, but she was endearing in her own special way.

Engrossed in her pie making, Sarah was once again not listening when Ethel came in.

"Are ya with me, lovey?"

"Sorry, Ethel, I were miles away. What did you say?"

"I popped in to say g'day to our Betsey, and she's not good. Not good at all. I'd say she's starting to go, lovey. Prepare yerself, cos I'd say she's not long."

Sarah's heart sank. She'd known it was coming and tried to ignore the signs, hoping Ma would rally again like she'd done in the past. She'd noticed Ma had started taking more laudanum, and she was constantly running to the apothecary for a new supply. The headaches were the worst part. Ma would hold her head and groan, sometimes for hours after she'd gone to bed. Well into the night, Sarah lay in her own room listening, knowing there was nothing she could do.

But was she ready to lose her mother? Was anyone ever ready to say goodbye to the one person who'd been a constant throughout their entire life?

"I'd better call for Mary," said Sarah, wiping the flour off her hands on her apron. "And Aunt Nettie."

"You do that, lovey. You need family round ya at a time like this."

Sarah trod the stairs slowly, not wanting to face what was ahead, but the moment she looked at her mother lying on the bed she knew Ethel was right. She'd not long to go. She'd not told Ma she was pregnant again, and since Sarah was still only barely showing, she hadn't noticed. At least, now she wouldn't have to bear the shame of knowing her daughter had borne two children with a man who wasn't her husband.

Sarah pulled up a chair from against the wall and sat next to her mother's bed, taking Ma's hand in her own. It was almost weightless, and white, cool to the touch. When had Ma lost so much weight? They'd only been in this house a matter of weeks. How hadn't she noticed? While she sat there talking aloud about her memories of growing up, she felt Ma slipping.

Mary and Nettie arrived, and they took it in turns to sit with Betsey, catch a quick nap or grab something to eat. Sarah checked on the children, but Ethel had them in hand until they were tucked up in bed. She didn't remember how the evening trade had gone, but somehow, she must have done it. The hours ticked by slowly as they waited for the inevitable, praying it wouldn't happen, knowing there was a force greater than them making the call.

On Tuesday 10th October, Betsey left this world aged seventy-four, to join her husband and lost children.

The sisters clung to each other in silent acceptance. Nettie knelt beside the bed in prayer. They would grieve in time, but Ma had not been herself since the day Da had died two years earlier. Her mind had gone with him then, only her body had kept going, and now that had gone too.

In many ways, it was a blessing, and Sarah suddenly felt a huge sense of liberation, promptly followed by guilt that such selfish thoughts should enter her head. She was sad her mother had gone, but also relieved she suffered no longer. She would mourn her as she should, but for once, Sarah's life was her own and she was free to live and love as she chose. And she loved deeply.

Part Three

Turmoil and Peace

22

When love is all that matters

April 1868

"Can you believe it?" Sarah busied herself tidying the bar, hoping to release some of her distress, while Aunt Nettie sat in the armchair by the fire. "That poor boy is drowned and the father gets off scot-free."

"That I can't," agreed Nettie. "Not after all the evidence. Not guilty, huh! I don't believe it, mind. He were a right nasty man, that Blackmore."

"I wish I'd never let him have a room here. I feel I was part responsible for the boy's death."

"Now don't take it on yourself like that, Sarah dear. You couldn't have known. And you did give him notice beforehand, mind."

The murder of that boy, and she did consider it murder never mind what any court said, had haunted Sarah for months. Called, as they both had been, to give evidence against the man and testify to his ill-treatment of the boy in general, Sarah was sure he'd be convicted.

"And to think of all that time we've given up – you and me both – to do our civic duty, and for nought. Tain't right. Tain't fair. Tain't …" continued Nettie.

"Life ain't fair, though, is it, aunt? If it were, I'd still be at The White Hart."

Nettie looked at Sarah softly. "Maybe, maybe not. But I'd say you're better off here. You've an easier life, the people are nicer, and ya wouldn't have wanted more babbers back there."

"You're right, I know, but I can't help wondering if Ma would have lived longer if we'd stayed."

"I doubt it, in all's truth. She suffered with that brain fever for a long time, mind. The doctor told ya 'twould take her sooner or later. She were lucky to've lived with it as long as she 'ad. Don't blame yerself for that either, me girl."

"At least that Owen Davidson got his comeuppance," said Sarah with a small smile. "Amos did well to get the regulars to sign that statement telling the brewery what Davidson was like and how they didn't want him there."

Nettie nodded in agreement. "Your da and you had a good loyal crowd, you did. I'm glad Amos got to take over the manager's role."

"Me too. He deserved it."

Sarah's thoughts drifted back to the good years she'd had growing up. Now, reflecting on her sixteen-year-old self, half a lifetime ago, who'd promised her da to never let him down, and the young woman who'd rejected a life of children, drudgery and loss, she now counted her blessings, despite the pain of losing two.

"How people like Blackmore could harm their children is beyond me," she said, bringing herself to the present.

She couldn't imagine being without her beautiful JJ who at eight was the kindest of souls. A bit of a scallywag, always off somewhere to investigate something new, but bright and inquisitive. Nor four-year-old Mary Ann who had such a calm and quiet nature, but she worried most about her namesake, nicknamed Sadie. Coming up two, she was a grizzly child who never seemed to settle easily.

As if sensing her thoughts, Ethel came into the taproom carrying the little one. "She's been that fretful I thought maybe the lil' mite was missing her ma. Have you a mo' to take her while I finish in the kitchen?"

Over the years, Ethel had become a close friend as well as ally and servant. After Ma died, Ethel had been a godsend of sense and practicality. As Sarah's pregnancy had advanced and she found herself more cumbersome, she'd offered Ethel a role in the household, and they'd never looked back.

'I'd be honoured, that I would,' Ethel had said that day. 'It'd be like looking after me own place after all this time, and you and the kiddies are special to me now, they is. And with room and found. 'Tis generous of ya, 'twill do me well enough. I'll be happy for the rest of me days. And I won't let ya down, mind. You can rely on me.'

Sarah took the child from Ethel and sat beside Nettie near the fireplace with the girl on her knee. As she had after the birth of Mary Jane, Sarah had once again come out of mourning when Sadie was born, even though only six months had passed since her mother had gone. To her mind, a birth was something to celebrate, and colour, however subtle, like the dove grey she wore, made her feel lighter.

"Let me know when you're done, Ethel. She might be less of a handful by then, cos I'm expecting a crowd soon."

"I'll do me best and be quick as I can, I will, but methinks you should be putting your feet up. You've had such a stressful time, and you, Nettie. I haven't forgotten you in all this, but our Sarah is too kind-hearted for her own good sometimes."

"She is that," agreed Nettie, always happy to chat with Ethel. The two could blather for hours if she let them, thought Sarah intervening.

"Maybe later, but there's work to do for now, so I think we'd better get on."

"Right ya are, Sarah. Right ya are. I'll be back to the kitchen then. Mr Richard'll be home later wanting his supper."

"I'd better be leaving, then," said Nettie, pulling herself to her feet. At seventy-two, she found her joints stiff at times, but with a husband and two boarders at home in Bitton, she had more than enough to keep her occupied.

"I appreciate you coming with me all these times," said Sarah. "You've been very good to me over the years and especially since Ma left us."

"You've always been special to me, Sarah, me dear. Always."

"And you to me, aunt. I'll send for a cab to take you home."

"Ta ever so." She paused as she reached for her coat off the stand by the door. "Forgive me, my dear. It's not my place and not my business, but are you sure you should still be keepin' up this charade with Mr ..."

"Clements," Sarah put in quickly. Ethel still considered him her husband, or if she didn't, then she'd been wise enough not to say anything. "And yes, aunt. After all we've been through, the answer is yes."

"Very well. I shan't mention it again, but I know your mother wasn't happy about it, and it goes against all Christian morals."

"So I've been told, aunt. Many times, but I think it's a tad too late for such concerns."

With the passage of time, even without a body, she'd accepted John was dead. She longed to make it official – but ... there was always a 'but'. She'd registered Mary Ann under John's name so she'd need to wait another few years before she could complete the legal paperwork.

After Nettie had left, little Sadie was persuaded to have some milk and mush, and finally went to sleep. Mary Ann and JJ were given their tea and sent upstairs to play while Sarah managed the bar. Ethel would put them to bed in time, and JJ would keep them occupied until then.

With nothing of great importance or interest being discussed tonight, the evening seemed to drag on. By nine o'clock, Sarah was watching the door, wondering when Rick would be coming. He struggled to get away some nights. Although he never told her the full reason, she suspected that either his daughter or her mother had learnt of his liaison with her and made it difficult for him. An attack of the vapours could prevent him coming at all. But tonight, she wanted him by her side. He knew how to calm her frazzled nerves.

The bell over the door alerted her to his arrival. Overcome at the sight of him, a sigh of utter contentment lifted her heart, setting it thumping in her ears. She watched him make his way across the room, stopping to say hello to a couple of the regulars who'd got to know him over the years, but she knew his attention was all hers.

"Good evening, Mrs Clements," he finally said with that look he reserved for her and that same generous smile he'd given her the first day they'd met five years ago. If someone had told her at the time that she would fall deeper in love with this man day by day, carry two children by him, and would leave The White Hart because of him, she wouldn't have believed it possible. And in all that time, he had stood by her as he'd promised. She stood behind the bar at The George because of him, she felt whole because of him, and had never regretted one moment because of him.

"It's good to see you home again. Supper is ready for you if you wish to eat now. Or maybe you'd like to freshen up first?"

"Supper first would be grand. I'll just sit here by you and eat, and I'll have a pint of your best ale, Mrs Clements. Thirsty work it's been this week."

"Let me take your hat and coat, and I'll fetch ya a plate."

Richard stayed seated at the bar until the last of the customers left. One of the good things about The George was a closing time of 10 pm. Often on the Back she'd be lucky to be closed before midnight.

Sarah slid the bolt home seconds before Rick wrapped his arms around her and pulled her to him. "I've waited for this all week."

Between kisses, she put out the lamps, and step by

step led him out of the bar and up the stairs, noticing a light still shone under the kitchen door.

"Shh," she said as she closed the bedroom door quietly. "Ethel's still up, and we mustn't wake the children. I'll just go check on them."

After Ma passed and with the imminent arrival of Sadie, Sarah moved into the front room, leaving the room she'd once shared for the three children. Moving towards JJ's bed, she smoothed back the hair from his forehead and kissed him and turned to the cot. Only Mary Ann lay in it.

"Ethel must have Sadie," she said as she entered her bedchamber. "She's been niggly all day. I hope she's not ailing."

Rick wasn't interested in Sadie or the other children at that point. He had already hung up his clothes and was lying in the bed. He immediately held the coverlet open for Sarah to join him. Undressing fully, she slipped into his arms, whispering words of longing.

Their first joining was hurried and quickly over, but soon after they began to explore each other's bodies. None of the so-called modesty she'd been told was necessary in women for her. Rick brought her alive with his touch, and she revelled in every caress and learnt what he liked in return.

The wilful creak on the only stair to groan, and a deliberate cough alerted Sarah of Ethel's presence. She giggled against Rick's mouth. "Stop for a minute, until Ethel's settled. She must be putting Sadie down first."

The men renting the rooms on the other side of the hallway towards the back wouldn't have noticed or heard anything untoward, but Ethel knew exactly what was going on. But since she was someone who took delight in the happiness of others, she ignored it all. Sarah suspected she used it as a foil for her own lack of personal happiness, but she'd had never once complained or hinted that her life was anything other than enjoyable.

"That woman … even with all her chatter … is a surprising soul of discretion. No one else I know of … would approve of what you and I do," muttered Richard, still kissing her in parts that heated her skin from head to toe.

"She thinks you're me husband, remember," said Sarah.

Even though she sometimes had moments of guilt that she was taking Rick from his other family, she doubted any other couple celebrated their love as much as the two of them, or in such a manner.

"Now, where were we?" he murmured, his touch removing all thoughts from her mind and setting her body alight until the fire exploded and they fell asleep entangled in each other's limbs.

March 1869

The birth of her second son increased Sarah's feeling of completeness.

In the six years she'd known Richard, her happiness had only grown. When they'd first met she'd had no idea, or intention, that she would give birth to three children by him, even if they all carried her Clements name. The thought still astonished her, knowing he had three other much older children who carried his name in another part of Bristol.

His eldest daughter, the one who had been companion to her mother, had married last year. Richard had said he was glad to escape the madness filling the house with plans that would surely bankrupt him. But he'd survived, both financially and socially, and even admitted he'd enjoyed the occasion, while she'd simply valued the extra time he spent with her.

"What would you like to call him?" she asked.

"Alfred."

Sarah blinked at the instantaneous answer. "That was quick. There's no one by that name in the family. Have you been thinking about possibilities?"

"A bit. And that's what I want to avoid, repeating the same family names over and over through the generations."

"I've been thinking of that too. I know it's common to name a son after his father, but you've already done that. And I'd like our son to be different. Alfred it is."

Solemn JJ had taken it on himself to be the protector of the younger children. "Hi, Alfred. Nice to meet you," he said as he stared into his brother's eyes. "'Twill be fun havin' a brother. I hope we will be friends growing up."

Sarah choked up at her son's maturity. When did he get to be so grown-up?

Instinctively, as the eldest, he'd known when Sarah was busy or flustered or upset, that he could make a difference to the running of the household by entertaining the younger ones or by overseeing whatever they needed. When *he* needed help, he turned to Ethel, who adored him. But then she adored the girls too.

"I enjoy reading to the others, Mama," he explained when she thanked him for keeping his siblings occupied while she and Ethel were busy. "It helps my reading and understanding as well. When they ask what something means, I have to make sure I know. The dictionary Papa bought me is very useful."

Sarah was in awe of JJ's command of language and that he spoke so beautifully. Only sometimes did she give herself credit for reading to him when he was young, which had inspired his love of books.

"And I shall read to Alfred when he is bigger."

Mary Ann was less impressed and distinctly uncooperative. "It's a boy. What are we supposed to do with a boy? Sadie and I wanted a sister we could play with."

"JJ's a boy," Sarah pointed out. "And you've always liked him, haven't you? Why don't you want Alfred?"

"Yes, but he's older. And he looks after us. Babbers just mean noise and smelly bottoms."

Sarah suppressed a laugh. "He'll grow I promise. Just like Sadie did."

Before long, the extended family settled into their routine again. She and Richard continued their life ostensibly as husband and wife, the children called him Papa, including JJ, who'd known no other father. They all accepted that he went away to work and was only home once a week at best, and Ethel chattered on as much as ever.

"Ere, but it's a happy house we live in. Never known one like it, I haven't. I hear all about the arguments in some households, and the bashings that some women get, usually for next to nuffin', mind. But I never known no one as easy going as your Mr Clements, and you, me lovey, are a precious gem."

Sarah blushed at the compliment. Other than Richard, and possibly her da, nobody had thought that highly of her. She thanked the Lord for her blessings, never once doubting the Lord's approval, even if some of the earthly beings who worshipped Him condemned her.

23

A mother's heartbreak

October 1870

Five years to the day, since her mother passed away, Sarah's thoughts centred entirely on her daughter Sadie. The child had first complained of a sore throat and headache, and Sarah noticed a nasty red rash, which quickly spread across chest and abdomen. Her little face was bloated and painfully bright red as the child tossed from side to side moaning in discomfort.

"Shh … my sweet angel, sleep easy, my darling child," murmured Sarah, hoping her voice would calm the child.

Sarah had read about the latest outbreak of scarlatina in the newspapers and had followed the instructions as best she could, isolating herself and Sadie from the others. She used rags, which were burned straight away after a single use, to wipe the child's nose and mouth, and made sure she washed her own hands thoroughly with carbolic soap. She cleaned every surface with disinfectant, soaked the used sheets and the child's nightshirt in Condy's Fluid and diligently rubbed Sadie's body with camphorated oil twice a day. But in her heart, she knew she was losing the battle. Sadie just wasn't strong enough to fight the infection.

For three days, Sarah sat quietly with her daughter, leaving Ethel to manage the other children. She'd reluctantly put a closed sign on the door, since she couldn't risk infecting her guests and patrons with the disease. She'd even banned Richard from visiting. His memories of Sadie would remain beautiful, as the last time he'd seen her she was well, and the next time he would see her …

Sarah stopped her train of thought, sucking in her breath at the pain that physically tore at her body. The next time, Sadie would be in a coffin. She wept softly, trying to let the sorrow go before she had to face the world.

On a cold autumn day, with leaves scattering in the wind, another of her children was prayed over, blessed and laid to rest. Sarah refused to stay away, as custom decreed, and walked behind the hearse to the church, but the minister wouldn't allow her at the interment. She wasn't the only black-clad and veiled mother there that day, standing outside the cemetery, watching.

And Richard was there somewhere too, she sensed. She wouldn't look for him or acknowledge him, but she felt his love. She needed his strength, because even knowing how many other children had died in no way lessened her pain; if anything, a greater sadness overcame her.But such was life, and Sarah needed to get on with her life for the sake of her other children – JJ, Mary Ann and Alfred.

She thought then of her own mother, and how loss had changed her into another person. Back at home, surrounded by her sister Mary, Ted and his wife, Aunt Nettie, various other old friends and relations, and her loyal friend Ethel, she hoped she was stronger, but only time would tell.

A week later, as she began closing up for the night, dousing all the lamps except for one candle, she took a moment to stand at the open door and look up at the night sky. Covered in cloud, as it was, she couldn't see the stars she knew were there but wished upon them that Sadie's soul was safe in their keeping.

With a whoosh, a dark figure pushed her backwards. She lost her balance and fell heavily onto the floor, sending a chair flying. The gust of air as the door shut extinguished the last remaining light. In the gloom, she couldn't see her attacker clearly, but she could smell the rancid, unwashed body and the stink of stale beer.

Before she had a chance to get to her feet, the man placed one hand on her chest, pinning her down. He roughly pushed her skirts and petticoats up with the other and sat astride her knees.

"Bitch. I knew I'd find ya one day if I were patient. And now I have, ya gonna wish you'd never crossed me," he cursed, and spat in her face.

Hardly able to breathe with the weight of him, but aware her hands were free, Sarah began to pound any part of his body she could reach. "Ger-off, me … you lout … ger-off!" she roared, recognising her nemesis.

But he just laughed, sat heavier on her knees and punched her in the diaphragm. Gasping for air, her arms dropped like a stone to clutch her stomach.

"Thawt yerself clever, didn't ya? Hiding away over 'ere. Thawt I woudna find ya. That I'd gone away … but I 'adn't, see." His words slurred the more he talked. "But I saw ya, at the boneyard. And 'im, standin' by the wall. I guessed it were 'im all along, I did. Didn't see me, though, did ya? Too full of yerself to notice."

He gave a foul chuckle, his breath nauseating. Sarah raised her arm to cover her nose seconds before he slapped her hard, jerking her head to one side. Without his hand on her chest, she filled her lungs and screamed, only to receive a second slap that twisted her head back the other way. Giddy with shock, her brain scrambled to think of a way out of her situation.

"Keep quiet, or 'twill be all the worse for ya," he snarled. "There's no one to help. I know, see. And he ain't 'ere neiver. Followed him didn't I, and you. Those nippers of yours'll be easy meat after you. Think ya smart, but you'll see."

At the threat to her children, Sarah struggled even harder, looking for her opportunity as the man shifted his weight. A rough hand ran up her inner thigh. Self-protection kicked in and she sat bolt upright and began screaming and shouting and pummelling. "No! Stop! Stop, I say!" Her arms flailed in all directions before he got hold of them and forced her down on her back, his face inches from hers. He pinned her wrists between them and pressed a hand around her throat.

"I'll knock ya senseless if ya try that again. But I want ya to suffer every minute of what's gonna 'appen to ya."

She lay helpless, praying it would be over soon, sensing the worse was to come. He removed his hand from her throat and twisted his head away. He seemed to be fishing in his pocket, but the relentless pressure on her chest kept her from drawing anything other than a shallow breath. Without air, she'd soon faint. Her brain started fogging up and she closed her eyes, thinking she heard a muted sound.

Before she had time to identify what it might be, a screaming banshee crashed through the internal door. The diffused light from the hallway lifting the darkness enough to see by. Sarah suddenly able to breathe, filled her lungs and tried to pinpoint what was happening.

"Get away!" screamed Ethel. "Get away, you monster! Out! I tell ya. Out!"

With each utterance, Ethel brought the rolling pin down on the unsuspecting man's back and shoulders. He raised his arms to protect himself. Feeling his weight shift, Sarah pushed herself up on one elbow.

"Stop, Ethel," she croaked, her lungs gasping. "Stop," she tried again louder.

Ethel turned slightly at the sound of Sarah's voice. The rolling pin continued its trajectory, struck the back of the man's head and laid him out flat. "What?"

"Stop. If you kill him, you'll hang."

"Oh, Lordy me." Ethel threw the rolling pin onto the floor with a clatter and knelt beside Sarah taking her upper body in her arms. "Oh Sarah, I'm sorry I didn't hear nuffin' sooner. I were upstairs with the kiddies. I only came down to get an 'ot chocolate. That's when I heard you shouting. Did he harm ya, lovey? Are you al'right? 'Ere, let me help you. Oh my, what an awful thing."

Checking that Sarah could support her upper body before she let go, Ethel scrambled to her feet and ran around to the other side of Sarah and pushed until the man's body slid off Sarah's legs. "Can you move, lovey? Can you get up now?"

Ethel pulled a chair out from a nearby table and helped Sarah to her feet and made her sit down. She relit a couple of lamps so they could see more clearly and stood beside Sarah, a concerned hand on her shoulder.

The two stared in silence at the still body splayed in front of them, blood oozing from the head wound.

"Do'ya think I killed him?"

"Dunno. Check if he's breathing." Sarah rested one arm on the table and leant forward, still trying to ease the pain in her diaphragm and lungs.

Ethel bent down and put her hand tentatively on his chest. "I think he is."

Sarah let out a relieved giggle. "You certainly gave him what for."

Ethel pulled herself up to her full five feet and grimaced. "No one comes into me home and treats ma family like that without answering to me. He were lucky, 'e were. But how'd 'e get in?"

"I was standing at the door looking at the sky when he attacked."

Ethel tutted, but refrained from reprimanding her. "Do ya know him?"

Sarah nodded. "His name's Owen Davidson. He used to work for me until I fired him. He's had it in for me ever since, but 'twas years ago. Used to send me threatening letters and got me kicked out of my previous place. Before Ma passed. I thought he'd gone long time since."

Ethel shook her head. "What hatred some people build up inside 'em. Right betwaddles me, it do. But what we gonna do now? We can't leave him lying there, and I'm gonna have to clean up that rug." She picked up the chair that Sarah had knocked over at the start and inspected it. "And this'll need mending 'n all. But by the by, where are ya hurting, lovey? Did he do any … er, damage."

Sarah shuddered at what Ethel was hinting at. He had been close … but she needed to put it out of her mind. "Only my pride, and a few bruises. My ribs are hurting, and I'll have a right ol' shiner by tomorrow."

Ethel touched her eye, looking at the injury. "I'll get a cold compress for that, but bruises'll heal. Are you sure you're not hurt elsewhere?"

Sarah shook her head and tried to stand but immediately felt dizzy.

Putting her arm around Sarah to steady her, Ethel said, "Easy, girl. Not so fast. Sit there for a mo' longer." She went to the bar and poured a glass of brandy. "Drink this. 'Twill make you feel better and put some strength into ya. Always a good drop to lift the spirits, I say. And a good night's sleep, and it'll all look better tomorrow."

Sarah smiled as much as her aching face would let her. "I'm sure it will, but we have to move *that* first." She kicked out at the body with the toe of her boot. "I don't know how hard you hit him or when he'll wake up, but he's not staying there. I don't want the children coming down and seeing him."

"And I'd better scrub the floor tonight too. If that blood dries 'twill be murder to get off." Ethel clamped her hand over her mouth aware of what she'd just said. "I nearly did murder him, didn't I?"

"Maybe. But you didn't." As if to prove her point, Sarah pushed him with her foot, and they heard a low groan. "Let's drag him out into the street. We can't do anything tonight, and I'll talk to the police in the morning."

They each tucked their skirts up between their legs, grabbed one arm each and tugged and pulled until they had momentum. They hauled him head first out the door. Once on the stoop, Ethel checked the street for anyone out and about, but it appeared empty in the blackness of a cloudy night. She sniffed the air. "Nobody about. Not surprising really, it'll rain later."

They pulled harder, nearly lost control as he slithered down the two front steps and dragged him out across the footpath. They pushed him over, where he fell face down into the gutter.

"Good riddance to ya," said Ethel, spitting on her hands and rubbing them together. "Now let's get you to bed, lovey."

Sarah slept solidly and was woken by Ethel bringing her a cup of tea.

"Ah, you're awake at last. How are ya this morning?"

Sarah eased her body into a different position and found every muscle protesting at the movement. "Sore. Everywhere. But I'll get up soon and help you. I'll just drink my tea first. Thanks ever so much." Sarah took the cup and saucer from Ethel and sipped the hot drink.

"You'll do no such thing. You're to stay abed till I say so. The place is all scrubbed bright as a new pin. You'd never know anything had happened. The children are sorted. They've had their breakfast, and JJ'll be on his way to school soon. It's been right chucking it down all night, it has. I'm surprised it didn't wake ya, but better that it didn't. Better you slept."

Ethel opened the curtains on a thoroughly wet and grey day and gasped.

"What is it?" asked Sarah, alert to something in Ethel's reaction.

"That man," she whispered, "he's still there."

Sarah carefully manoeuvered herself out of bed and tentatively walked to the window.

Ethel continued chattering as Sarah looked down at the street. The gutter was running high, and rainwater gushed over the still body of Owen Davidson.

"I thought he'd have picked himself by now and scarpered before the police were called. You gonna tell them, lovey, are ya? He broke into your home and attacked you. He were in the wrong and he needs 'is just rewards."

"If I wasn't, I'd better now. I think this time he really is dead." Sarah began, before remembering what Ethel had said. "Quick, stop JJ from going out the front door. Send him through the side gate. I don't want him seeing that."

"Oh, Lordy," muttered Ethel, doing as she was asked. "Oh, Lordy, me, what a predicament. JJ!" she called as she hurried down the stairs. "JJ. Wait!"

The police were called. Sarah couldn't stand the thought of the body lying in the street outside her home any longer. She couldn't imagine what people would say when they found out.

"Sit down, Mrs Clements, you look very pale. Are you sure you are up to answering some questions?"

asked the sergeant after writing down that he'd seen the bruises on her face.

Grateful that he appeared sympathetic to her plight, she attempted a shaky smile. "Thank you, sergeant, but the sooner we get this over with, the better."

"Right, then. Can ya tell me in your own words what happened here."

As succinctly as possible, Sarah related the events of the evening before. "I have no idea why the odious man attacked me, sergeant." She put her hand to her chest, which still hurt, but the gesture was intended to reinforce her words. "And I don't know what would have happened if my servant hadn't been able to help me."

He busily wrote what she'd told him in his notebook, licking his pencil from time to time. "But you said you knew him."

Sarah agreed. "More than five years backalong. I've not seen him since."

"And you say he was alive when he left the premises."

"Yes, most definitely." She didn't add that she and Ethel had dragged him unconscious outside, but she had shown the sergeant the broken chair. If he wanted to know more, he could ask. She wouldn't lie to the police, but she wasn't going to get Ethel into trouble if she could avoid it either.

"I've called the undertaker to take the body away, and we'll see what the doctor has to say about the cause of death, but it looks to me like he fell and cracked his 'ead."

"He was certainly drunk," added Sarah, suddenly wanting the policeman gone as soon as possible. "Is there anything else, because I have to get ready to open for the midday regulars, if it's all the same to you?"

"Yes, ma'am. Go ahead. I'm sure it'll be fine. I believe we have everything we need. I suspect the blow to 'is head didn't kill him. It didn't look that bad to me. He more likely drowned. Pity for 'im it rained so 'ard last night."

Hidden by her full skirts, Sarah crossed her fingers, hoping the sergeant was right. Neither she nor Ethel could be blamed for the rain. "Indeed."

The sergeant put his notebook away, repositioned his helmet, took a last look around and wished her good day.

"Good day to you, sergeant. I appreciate the consideration." She smiled again hesitantly. "I am quite shaken. You see, I am also mourning my young daughter who passed only days ago," finished Sarah, hoping to further engage his sympathy.

"My condolences, ma'am. We'll try not to bother you further, but if I have more questions, I will advise you."

"Thank you, sergeant, that is most kind of you."

Shortly after the police officer had left, Richard arrived at her door in answer to the note she'd sent saying she needed to see him, but not explaining why.

"Sarah. Are you all right? Why did you need to see me?" He pulled up short when he saw the bruises on her face and the black eye developing. "You're hurt. Oh, my God, Sarah. How did you get those?"

"It could have been much worse," she whispered. "But don't fuss over me and don't give me any sympathy or I'll break down and be useless to anyone. It's over, Rick. It's finally over."

"What's over? Are you going to tell me what this is all about?"

"Not now. I can't go through it again. The police have only just left."

"Police? What were they doing here?"

Sarah conceded she'd have to tell him something. "I'll tell you the whole story later, but a drunk came in here at closing time. He got a bit belligerent, so I tossed him out, and this morning he was found dead in the gutter."

Richard gasped, "Oh, you poor girl," and reached out to hold her, but she flinched away.

"Ooh, no. Sorry. I'm a bit sore right now." She placed a hand on his chest. "I will tell you everything, I promise. And I am not really harmed, just a bit battered and weary. But I have to carry on." She glanced towards the door. "Have they removed the um ... er him ... yet? I haven't dared look."

"There was nothing in the street I could see as I came in."

Her shoulders sagged with relief. "Good. Hopefully, no one else saw anything either."

"The children? Ethel? Are they okay?"

"Yes." Her eyes glistened as her thoughts turned to sweet Sadie. "I miss her already. I'm glad you were there to say goodbye. I sensed it."

He squinched his face, a similar grief etching his face. "I couldn't stay away."

"Can you come back tonight?" She held her hands clenched in front of her pleadingly.

"Wild horses couldn't keep me away."

24
A decade passes

April 1871

One Sunday evening at the start of April, the enumerator knocked at her door asking for details of who was in the household.

She remembered the first time she'd been asked, or rather her da had in those days, back in 1851. She'd been sixteen, and life felt full of promise. Officially her nephew, Mary's boy Ted, was living with them then, but with less than two years between them, they were more like friends or siblings back then. They'd mostly gone their separate ways these days, but she saw him occasionally. Molly, her loyal kitchen maid, had been fourteen, and several of the mariners who frequented the inn lodged upstairs. Waiting ahead was marriage, and children and a life of her own. She would never have imagined her life to turn out the way it had.

A decade later, she was the one who had provided the information for the census. The pain and uncertainty and disappointment rushed back. After much indecision she'd announced herself a widow, even without having evidence of her husband's death. She'd lied about her parents' ages, for their sakes, but she knew they were into their seventies and their health was failing. The workload had fallen on her, and the death of her first daughter, Mary Jane, had nearly been her undoing. Mary had eased the burden by having JJ live with her, but oh, how she'd missed her son.

Now another decade had passed, and the man was back with his official sheets of paper.

"Only three of us here this evening," Sarah had answered. "Myself, Sarah Clements. I'm a widow," she said confidently, knowing that John had finally been officially declared dead. "I'm … um, thirty-six, I think. My son John Jacob is eleven, and my daughter Mary Ann is six."

She hadn't imagined she would lose both parents in the interim, or that she would bury two children, but the joy of having three children with the man she truly loved had made it all worthwhile. Except now, her youngest, two-year-old Alfred, was not with her. She still mulled over the wisdom of sending him to stay with a widowed cousin she barely knew, but Richard, backed up by Ethel, had insisted.

"Won't be for long, lovey. Just till you get your strength back. You can't do it all, you just can't, and you need to take care of yourself or everything you've worked for, and everything you ever wanted in life will go to waste." Ethel had never been one to hold back and she'd always been honest with Sarah. Reluctantly, she'd agreed. The last few months had been some of the most difficult she'd ever known.

The man went away satisfied, but as she shut the door, Sarah once again wondered how such few facts could ever reflect the reality of her life. Not with two people missing, if only temporarily.

The police had continued their investigations and after several delays, both she and Ethel were eventually brought before the magistrates at the Petty Sessions in February last, to explain the events of the night, yet again. The room seemed constantly in an uproar with people shouting and cussing. She heard male voices shout 'lock 'em up!' and 'give 'em a good beatin!' and women who shouted 'serves the bleeder right'. Who the comments were directed at, she wasn't certain, but the noise, the aggression and the proceedings upset her greatly.

Sarah gave her statement almost word for word to the one she'd given before. She'd replayed the scene so often in her head, she could never forget. Sarah had let the sergeant assume the broken chair had sent her assailant packing but Ethel, as usual, couldn't stop talking and let it slip that she'd attacked him with a rolling pin.

"Only in defence, your honour," said Sarah promptly, scared her friend would be charged with assault. "She's a good woman. He'd have turned on her too, quick as lightning he would, if he'd not been stopped. My life depended on it."

The judge, or whatever he was called, sitting in the middle looked at her over the rim of his glasses. Sarah trembled under his gaze. "You have said under oath that the victim was alive when he left your premises. Is that correct?"

Sarah didn't understand the workings of the legal system so, apart from that one man, she didn't know who anyone was or what they did. Hoping to win him over, she never took her eyes off his.

"Yes, your honour. I swear he was alive when he went through my door." She crossed her fingers and said a quick prayer. She wasn't lying, just not quite telling the whole truth as she'd sworn to.

After consulting with his colleagues, the one wearing the white curly wig nodded. "Very well. I bring down a verdict of accidental death by drowning after falling in a drunken stupor." He wrote something on the papers in front of him. Then looked back at Sarah and Ethel. "You are discharged."

He banged his gavel and shouted, "Next!"

Sarah stood still for several moments, in shock, trying to unlock her knees and quell her churning stomach. Ethel nudged her.

"He said we can go. Come on, lovey, let's get out of here." Ethel waited but Sarah still didn't answer. "Come on, we gotta go," she said again, tugging at her arm.

A court orderly or some such waved them on, and another woman was led to the stand.

"I can't believe it's over. That it's really over," whispered Sarah as they walked outside into a surprisingly sunny day.

"Me neither, lovey. I thought I was a goner there for a mo'."

"Hope I'm not dreaming."

The whole experience lingered with Sarah, both the night of the attack and the terror of standing in the dock, and she suffered greatly. Unexpected noises made her jump, sometimes she'd squeal with fright, and she slept badly, reimagining the scene in her nightmares.

Her tender stomach and broken rib, where he'd punched her, according to the doctor prevented her from eating much and she began to lose weight, until even the children noticed.

"You have to eat, Mama," said JJ with Mary Ann nodding in agreement. "You are very thin and pale. I'm worried about you."

Ethel too was always on at her, offering a tonic for this and that, but for all his love and kindness, and understanding, the day she collapsed in the barroom was the final straw for Richard.

"Enough, Sarah. This has to stop." He towered over the bed as she lay helplessly where she'd been placed. Despite his apparent gruffness, she knew he cared. "I will not let you be so casual with your health any longer. Do you hear me?"

"I'm not doing it deliberately, Rick. But I can't stop thinking about what might have happened."

"But it didn't, Sarah, my love. It didn't. And it's not going to. Ever. But you are no good to the children, or to me, in this state. And we don't want to lose you."

"I know, dear heart. And I don't want to lose you either. I promise I'll try harder."

"If you don't, then know this: I will admit you to the asylum."

Fear settled in Sarah's abdomen, and her eyes dilated. She'd heard terrible things about that place. "No! Please, Rick, no. Please don't do that. I promise I will get better, but not the asylum, please. I beg you. It has a fearful reputation for locking people up and treating them bad."

"Fear not," he soothed, realising his error. "I do not mean the local asylum, my dear. I know of a private one at Brislington, run by Dr Fox. It's a place of rest and recuperation, where you can walk in the gardens, and talk with others like yourself, and has nothing to do with punishment. It will cost a significant amount, but I would part with it all to have you well."

Sarah relaxed a little, but she still didn't want to be parted from Rick or the children, or Ethel, or her livelihood, or ... the more she thought about it, the more anxious she became.

"That does sound nicer, but I'd really rather stay here." She grabbed his sleeve in her fist, her eyes bulging in alarm. "Please, Rick. Let me stay here."

"I'll consider it. But only if you will allow Alfred to be sent away to stay with someone while you get better."

Sarah gasped. "What! No. I couldn't do that. He's still little."

"He's two, Sarah, and at his most demanding stage. I've seen you running around after him. He wears you out. JJ does amazing things with him, but he's still a child and has his studies to think of, and Mary Ann is too young to be pushed aside while you manage Alfred."

"But I don't ..." she began, knowing Richard was right. Alfred knew how to run rings around her and test her patience.

He frowned. "If you want to stay at home, then Alfred goes away while you recuperate. The faster you get better, the quicker he comes home. It won't be for long, Sarah, I promise. Now, I'll take my leave. You need to rest. Ethel will bring you some broth. I want you to eat it all – and I'll find out if you don't – and then you are to sleep. Hear me?" He kissed her gently on the forehead. "Consider your choices carefully, my love."

Sarah pulled her thoughts back to why she was alone, her heart close to breaking. Ethel had left four days ago, taking Alfred with her to the village where both his grandparents had grown up and where family still remained. A cousin, recently widowed, gladly agreed to take her child and add to her own brood, once the offer of payment had been included.

Would she accept payment to look after someone else's child? she wondered. More than likely, since how else would they pay for his needs?

A few days later Ethel returned. "'Tis right good to be back," she said, giving Sarah a big hug. "And what a journey! I tell ya. But it all went well, considering, and they were such lovely people and so willing to help. Alfred was happy to have all the fields to run in, and animals around him, he was. He'll be off like a shot, I can tell ya. The cottage they live in is clean and well cared for and that cousin of yours is a chipper thing, and her cooking is fine. Alfred'll eat well, that's for certain. The wee nipper will share a room with the older boy. I have no worries at all, I don't and neither should you."

Ethel continued to sing the praises of the village she'd visited, the fresh air, the country living, the fresh food. "Apart from farms, the iron works and the mill, there's loads of cordwainers and carpenters in that town. Odd really, that so many should do the same sort o' work. But there ya have it."

"I'm sure you are right, Ethel. My Alfred will do well, and that's what breaks my heart. I'm sure he won't even miss me while I'm aching with loss all the time. I want us all together."

"And you will be, lovey, just as soon as we get you well again."

Sarah wanted to get well, she wanted to work, to raise her children. She was still young, wasn't she? But she was worn down. Recently, Richard had been promoted to superintendent, a prestigious position with an increased wage, but the extra responsibility kept him busier than ever. Some weeks she didn't see him because he'd been attending so many fires, a lot of which seemed to happen at night.

She worried sometimes that, being in his mid-fifties, the late nights and hard work might affect his health, but he remained as healthy, handsome and charming as ever. In all their eight years together, she'd never once doubted their relationship, as shocking as society regarded it; she considered love an essential part of living.

As the year progressed through summer, she ate better, her strength returned, and Richard's loving hands eventually gave her fresh hope. The first time Richard had attempted to tickle her inner leg after the attack, she'd withdrawn, memories of the rough hand that had touched her making her shudder. He caressed her with such gentleness, such skill. His soothing hand persevered, calmly, encouragingly, until she'd responded, and they reaped the reward together.

"You are so beautiful, and enticing." His hands followed the curve of her hips, the bones still too sharp for his liking, on down her leg and up her inner thigh, leading to a frenzy of passion that left her exhausted but so, so contented.

"If you keep improving as much as you have, I think Alfred should be able to come home for Christmas. Would you like that?"

Sarah threw her arms around his neck and kissed him rapidly on his neck, face, lips, anywhere she could in her excitement. "That would be wonderful. Oh, yes, Rick, please. At Christmas, we should all be together."

With that hope in her heart, Sarah was determined to get well.

25

A changing world

1872

Bristol was growing and changing, and most of it for the better. The *Bristol Times and Mirror* reported daily on any event that added to the culture of the city, in addition to the usual business, crime and gossip.

A regular column about who was seen attending concerts at the beautiful Colston Hall, now approaching five years old and proving very popular, claimed her attention. Sarah knew the building from the outside. She'd been told it had been designed in the Bristol Byzantine style, but she'd never ventured inside.

The sports section highlighted the latest successes of the Gloucestershire County Cricket Club, not that she was knew anything about cricket, but it seemed JJ had taken an interest. He would talk to Richard about it endlessly, and they would sometimes go and watch a match together. If it wasn't the sport, then the next thing she knew, JJ was talking about the recently opened Bristol Museum and Library, a merger of older establishments involving the sciences and art, but in new premises.

"It's not far, Mama, I can walk, honestly. Please can I go and see? There's so much interesting stuff there and I want to learn all I can."

"Very well. But be back here before dark."

After that, whenever he wasn't at school, he'd be off somewhere investigating. Sarah could hardly keep up with the boy's enthusiasm for learning, and her belief that he would be a teacher one day became stronger with every passing year. And if JJ's jabber at everything new that excited him wasn't enough, she had Rick expounding on the wonderful benefits of the new harbour railway connecting the docks and wharves throughout Bristol, meaning that shifting freight would be so much easier. As if she cared. But what was good for Bristol was good for her family.

Despite all her efforts and vastly improved physical and mental state of health, her life had changed too. Far more drastically than she'd ever intended or hoped for.

Christmas had been a wonderful event, especially with Alfred home as Rick had promised. She and the children had decorated The George with garlands of greenery and tied bright red ribbons around to hang from the mantelpiece and doorways and along the front of the bar. The house was filled with squeals of laughter.

They'd sung carols, and played parlour games and Ethel had cooked a fine roast dinner of goose with chestnutty confections, and a Christmas plum pudding. She missed Rick, but that was her burden to bear. Only she knew she was sharing him with another family, but he came to see the children the following day.

By the end of winter, the signs confirmed she was pregnant again. The knowledge boosted her spirits, and she began to plan, but plans had a habit of going awry. The annual licence renewal came up and she reapplied at the magistrates as usual, only this time she attended in person.

"You are Mrs Clements of The George in Thomas Street, I believe," began the adjudicator.

"I am, yes," she smiled confidently. "And have been for the past many years."

He looked at her standing at the table before him and muttered something she didn't quite hear.

"And you are the same Mrs Clements who was up before the courts only last year after a man died outside your premises?"

Sarah's heart thudded in her ears. She swallowed to ease her throat, sensing things were not going the way they usually did, and licked her lips. "Yes. That's correct, but the verdict was accidental death. It had nothing to do with me. I was discharged."

"I'm not sure that is quite correct," he said, emphasising the 'quite'. "As I seem to recall, the man was inside your premises prior to his … um … accident."

Sarah refrained from answering. She wasn't going to get caught up defending herself in public to the licensing board. She'd been discharged and that was that!

"And tell me, Mrs Clements, if I'm not being indelicate, but are you, er … with child?"

Sarah blushed to her roots to be asked such a thing in public. She didn't think she was large enough yet for someone to notice, and she'd worn a cloak deliberately.

"How is that any of your business, sir?"

"It's very much my business. The behaviour of our licence holders is paramount to the reputation of the association."

Pompous pillock, thought Sarah, wondering how to answer, but she needn't have bothered. He'd made up his mind.

"You are listed here as a widow, so I am to assume therefore that your dead husband is not the father." The sneer crossing his face warned her seconds before he announced, "Application denied." He rubber-stamped his notebook and wrote something before calling, "Next!"

With her heart in her stomach, she had no option but to move on.

Sarah wandered home in a daze. What would she do now? She'd never known anything other than running a pub and boarding house. She had three children to consider, and another one on the way, and while Ethel wasn't her direct responsibility she felt obligated to include her in any future decisions. But without a licence, she could no longer manage The George. She would have to move. But to where?

She had savings. She'd been diligent about that over the years, and while Richard's support helped cover the costs for the children, the business had paid its own way and gave him a profitable return.

Was she now to become a tenant in someone else's house with no means of supporting herself?

"Oh, Lordy me," began Ethel. "Lordy me, what a terrible shame it is, 'n all. Terrible shame. The locals won't be 'appy about it, I can tell ya."

"But what about you, Ethel? I don't know if …"

"Now don't you worry your 'ead about me, lovey, not at all." Ethel buzzed around the kitchen, throwing things into pots getting ready for dinner and put the kettle on the cooktop. "A nice cuppa will do us well, now, won't it? While we think about things."

"But Ethel ..."

"There's no buts 'bout me, lovey, I tell ya. I'm getting on now and maybe it's time I went to me sister's place. She's still living in the old place our folks used to live in. Tiny village tis, but everybody knows everyone and there's lots to chatter about. She's older than me and needs help, she does, but while I was needed 'ere, I stayed. Cos you and the kiddies mean the world to me, but all things come to an end. Don't they?"

Ethel never stopped moving the whole time she was talking. She placed a cup of tea on the table in front of Sarah and pushed a plate of biscuits towards her.

"Now don't you cry none, you hear me, cos you'll set me off 'n all if'n you do, and that won't do for any one of us. Not at all. And we can't upset the kiddies, and JJ'll spot summat's up the minute he gets in the door."

For once Sarah was grateful for Ethel's ebullience. She sipped on her tea and pondered her future, but she would do nothing without Richard's approval, and he'd not be back for days.

When Richard did hear about the outcome, he was livid. "How can some jumped-up clerk decide someone's future like that?"

"Happens all the time, Rick. Landlords lose their licence here and move on to there, depending on how many pubs there are in one area, or whether summat happened the licensing board didn't like. Obviously, finding a dead body in the street outside this place didn't go in my favour, and neither did this." She patted her stomach. "I'm going to have to look around and find somewhere else. Or maybe I'll just run a boarding house and don't bother with a licence ..."

Her thoughts drifted. Life would be easier in many ways, without having to conform to set hours, or manage unruly customers, not that she'd had many of those since she'd been at The George, but she'd miss the camaraderie of the barroom.

"Is that what you truly want to do?" he asked. "Wouldn't you rather just run a house full of busy children? There'll be four soon. If I sell The George, would Ethel stay on to help you?"

"No, she's decided to go to her sister's. She says her sister's health is poorly and she's needed. I don't know whether to believe her or not. I didn't know she had a sister, even after all these years."

Later that evening, as they lay in bed, Sarah was still upset by the whole turn of events. They had both written to the board challenging the decision, but the latest letter confirmed a final decision. Sarah was out.

Unable to comfort her in their usual way due to her cumbersome size, Richard settled for the intimacy of conversation in the dark, and simply held her hand. Softly, he tried to soothe her worries. "I promise I'll look after you, my love. You don't have to worry. Will you let me?"

This time Sarah squeezed his hand and murmured yes, so softly she wasn't sure Rick had heard her until he shifted his weight onto his elbow and kissed her gently.

* * * * *

Richard again came to her rescue. "I've found a tidy little two-up, two-down terrace cottage over in Redcliffe. It's near the church, and there's an infants' and girls' school nearby if you want to send the younger children there. Will you look at it?"

Sarah simply nodded. Without even seeing it, she knew the rooms would be small, the space cramped and beds would need to be shared. It would be less than what she'd known, at least inns and boarding houses tended to have more rooms, and most likely the outhouse would need to be shared, but she'd manage. She had to. She needed somewhere to birth the next child who was close to full term.

Needing less than she had at The George, the move went as smoothly as it could, given the difficulty of getting some of the furniture into the right rooms. But JJ was a blessing and kept the kiddies out of the way while she sorted the house. At least it was clean – more or less. She'd do better after the baby was born but she didn't have the strength or energy to do much before that.

"So, here we are my little chickies," said Sarah, dishing up a plate of stew. She cut some fresh bread and handed them each a chunk to dip in the gravy. "Eat up. This is our new home. Tis a bit smaller, I know, but there's just us now. No more me working and you having to fend for yourselves. No more boarders and customers and people coming and going; no more chatter. Just us. Won't that be grand?"

By the time she finished what started off as a positive view on the situation, she was close to tears. She would miss all those things, and the people who had brought her enjoyment for much of the last twenty years. And she would miss Ethel's chatter and adult conversation and … Stop it, she thought to herself. Stop. It can't be helped.

"I don't like it, Mama," said Mary Ann, screwing up her nose at the congealing food before her as she swirled the bread around. "It's not nice like our other place. Why do we have to live here? Why couldn't we stay?"

Clenching her fists to keep control of her voice and her temper, she snapped, "Because we couldn't, that's all. Now eat your dinner and be done."

"It'll be good you don't have to work any more, Mama, what with the new baby 'n all," said JJ. "And I'll help with the chores when you need me too."

She smiled at her boy and ruffled his hair. "You're a good lad, and kindly to offer, but let's see how we go, shall we, because you need to keep up those studies of yours."

She took a wet cloth from the bucket and wiped Alfred's hands and face and lifted him off the chair so he could play.

Mary Ann pushed her plate away. "Don't want it. It's horrid. Like this place. Like you. I hate it." The girl burst into tears and ran up the stairs to the bed she would share with her mother.

Sarah listened helplessly. Nothing was going to be the same. Nothing.

Beatrice made her way into the world in the autumn barely a month after they'd moved. Sarah, delighted she had a new daughter, had chosen a name unlike any of the others. Somehow it made her more special.

"And you are special, my dear Beatrice. You will grow up in a whole new world to the one I knew. I hope you will be happy."

Mary Ann had turned into a stubborn and silent thorn in Sarah's side. She refused to see anything good about anything and always wanted to go back to The George.

Richard took her aside and tried to cajole her. "Mary Ann, I do understand why you are upset and I'm sorry it has to be, but this behaviour of yours is not good enough. Your mother is not to blame. For reasons you would not understand, you have to accept this is where you now live. You have a new sister, and I want you to be a big girl and help your mama look after her. Will you do that?"

Mary Ann glared at her father, arms folded and pouty lipped. "Why should I?"

Richard's patience was wearing thin. "Because, Mary Ann, that's what I have told you to do. And I suggest you do not cross me. I have been very lenient, knowing how upset you are, but I will not tolerate rudeness or disobedience. You will behave nicely. Is that clear? Now go outside and let your mother rest."

While Beatrice thrived, and JJ turned into a surprisingly considerate and helpful young man, Mary Ann remained truculent and objectionable. Sarah had no idea what to do to turn her around. She wouldn't even play with Alfred any longer, and Sarah found herself shouting at the girl more often than not. Which didn't help. She knew that, but she couldn't admit to anyone that she felt as angry and disillusioned and friendless in this strange part of town as her daughter did.

The only bright light in the drudgery was Richard. With him in her arms, her world seemed beyond compare.

26
When time catches ip

January 1874

After Beatrice was born, and without the encumbrance of a constant stream of customers, incessant demands and strange hours, it turned out that Sarah found a community where she lived. Not only at the local church, but also along the street where other kiddies played and went to school. Mothers standing outside chatting about where to find the best bargains, complaining about the behaviour of children these days, and gossiping about the latest scandal in the newspapers, welcomed her.

The local shop was a hive of information, and she made sure to visit most days. It filled her need to be with people and was where she picked up topics of conversation she might otherwise not have known about. Like her mother, Mary Ann was now flourishing having found new friends of her own, and thankfully had returned to her normal sunny self.

How Richard managed to meet the expense of the grammar school JJ attended, the small school her daughter went to, pay the rent, and whatever his other household cost him, she never asked. She just enjoyed his visits, and talked about whatever he happened upon and discovered she knew about. If anything, their love grew stronger, more settled, more content. But within months, despite their precautions, which had failed in the past, Sarah knew she was pregnant again.

This time things didn't go as smoothly.

In the depth of a cold December, days before her fortieth birthday, Sarah remembered going into labour. She sent the younger children to various houses along the street, and JJ to tell his papa at work. After that, the hours became a blur of pain, voices in the distance that didn't make sense, and a feeling of floating.

She had no recollection of the events over the next hours and days until she woke in a strange room, lying on a strange bed, with the smell of carbolic in her nostrils.

"Mrs Clements. You were lucky. I thought we would lose you," said the stern-faced doctor standing beside her. "However, there is considerable damage, and I recommend this be your last child."

Sarah squeezed her eyes shut as tears leaked from the corners and ran down the side of her face.

"You must abstain, or the next one will kill you," continued the doctor, not unkindly, but adamantly. "Do you understand me?"

What choice did she have? Sarah nodded and clenched her hands amongst the blankets, already thinking about how completely fulfilling the intimate part of their relationship had been, and how she was supposed to feel without it.

"May I see my child?" she asked, suddenly dreading the answer. Had it lived? She pressed her body into the mattress, trying to escape the answer, fearing the worst.

"Certainly. He is a robust boy and that was a greater part of the problem. Nurse, please bring Mrs Clements her son."

A son! Sarah's heart leapt and her breasts tingled with the anticipation of feeding the newest arrival, if she had the strength to sit up.

"I wish you good day, Mrs Clements, but please do heed my words," said the doctor before departing.

Shortly after, the nurse appeared with her baby in a basket, which she put on the floor. "Now then, I'll help sit you up." She grabbed Sarah's arm and slipped her own hand under her charge's armpit and lifted, while the other hand plumped up pillows behind her. "There, that's better, now, i'nit?"

Carefully lifting the baby from the basket, she placed the boy in Sarah's arms. As with her other children, love filled her soul. Never mind how many she'd had, and this little one was number eight if she included her first who had never taken a breath, she'd not lost her awe and joy. Each one was a miracle to be celebrated, even if this one's arrival had nearly been the death of her.

"I shall call you Sidney," she whispered to the boy in her arms. Like her other two sons, she firmly believed they would all become successful in life, given the chance and she was determined to give them every chance she – and Richard – could.

January 1875

The year progressed with little to give it note. No great moments but no bad ones either, except for Richard.

While she had once enjoyed the Sunday classes and reading to the children, Sarah had long ago given up on the teachings of the church. From a young age she'd learnt it frowned on the way she lived her life. The more pious the congregation, the more reprobation she received.

Recently, she had returned on occasions, for moments of solitude, not to the big church nearby, but a smaller and more welcoming one. One that had become the centre of the community, where people met, where children were taught, and where she could live her life more truthfully. She maintained the story she'd begun when she'd entered The George: her husband Mr Clements was a travelling salesman and was away sometimes for weeks at a time. No one doubted her, and she was accepted into a community for probably the first time in her life.

But she worried about Richard.

After Sidney's birth, to her surprise, he had been the most understanding of men.

"My love, whatever is necessary to protect your life is what we must do."

"Are you telling me, you agree with the doctor and think we should abstain? Not do what we have always done for over a decade? I don't think I can do that." She flushed at her brazenness, but she simply couldn't imagine never having Richard's hand caress her body again.

He chuckled. "I didn't quite say that. But I do think the boy should be your last child." His fingers traced her jawline and followed down her breastbone. "There are other ways."

Lost in the intensity of his ardour, she learnt new techniques to fulfil desire.

He became serious later on and broke one of his cardinal rules. He spoke of his other family. "I am a fortunate man, Sarah. I have had two women who love me and willingly gave me many children. But I have also seen the destruction of one woman who produced nine children, of which only three are with us today. She became detached. She no longer took pleasure in what life had to offer. Living became a chore. She is only half the person I married, the person who aided my need to better myself and become the person I am today. Which is why I can never desert her. She deserves my support."

"You don't need to explain, Rick ..." Her words were cut off by a gentle finger pressed to her mouth.

"I know what it's like to lose children. A mother is expected to grieve, a father less so. Society assumes we have less attachment, and we do in some ways, as we don't nurture them in the same way. But they are no less a product of us. I grieved for every one of my lost children, their lost potential, and felt a failure because I couldn't protect them the way I expected to."

He paused, deep in thought. Sarah let the silence between them linger, not wanting to disturb such deep revelations.

"I suffered too, watching two mothers grieve. You and I have been more fortunate, losing only Sadie, and before her, your Mary Jane. But even one child lost is one too many." He sighed and shifted his position, the weight of all he was saying heavy in his heart.

"What I'm trying to say is, I love you. I don't want to lose you. I would never forgive myself if you were to die having another child. So you will not. That is my promise to you. And my other promise to you is that one day you will become my lawful wife if the Good Lord allows me to outlive my first one."

Tears ran down Sarah's face. She had given her life to this man and never regretted a single moment. She'd always understood how much she had risked in becoming his lover, and the life of penury she would endure if he ever stopped loving her. But none of that mattered any longer. In her wildest dreams, she'd never thought she could love and be loved so deeply, so fully, so completely, that her life would become more important to him than anything else.

How or why she was so special to him, she didn't know, but at fifty-eight years of age, she prayed he would live long enough to keep his promise. She loved him with all her heart, body and mind.

She had no words to convey what was in her heart. Not now, at least. She was too choked up. She turned to him, kissed him softly and together they once more found fulfilment in each other.

Summer 1875

Life continued its normal routine, the seasons changed, the children grew, and Richard remained an integral part of their lives.

Since that night, when he had spoken of his family with such meaning, he began to talk about them more often. Careful not to use their names, especially in front of her children, she began to realise how well informed he was about them and committed to their success. His eldest was happily married to a bookbinder.

"She has a girl the same age as Alfred," he said proudly, "and a son a few months older than Beatrice."

Sarah muttered the right words, but wondered how this man had such capacity to be father to young children and a grandfather to children of the same age, and genuinely be part of all their lives.

His son, barely five years older than JJ, was learning to be an engraver and would have a secure, well-paid future.

Some weeks later, he was less cautious.

"The girl is a Queen's Scholar, no less. Such a clever girl. She intends to be a teacher, which I wholeheartedly endorse."

"Who wants to be a teacher?" asked JJ, perking his ears up as he entered the living room.

"No one you know," answered his mother, seeing Richard looking a little blank while he thought of an appropriate reply.

"I think I'd like to become a teacher. I enjoy learning, and I think everyone should have a chance to learn, boy or girl and from any class."

Astounded that her fifteen-year-old son should have such progressive ideas, she smiled broadly at him. She had believed he could be a teacher since he'd been small. "I think that would be an excellent idea."

"So do I, young man," said Richard, clapping the boy

on his shoulder enthusiastically. "So do I. I'm glad your education has brought you to this conclusion."

"All thanks to you, Papa. I'm ever so grateful you sent me to grammar school, but Mary Ann is coming along nicely at the girls' school too. I help her sometimes when she's stuck."

"That's very generous, JJ. I know how hard you study."

"That's why I know I'd like to be a teacher. I like helping."

Sarah shivered. Richard's two parallel lives seemed inextricably entwined.

Gradually, as Christmas came and went, and they celebrated Sidney's second birthday, she began to think about whether Richard's children could be baptised. She'd taken Mary Ann along to the church for a blessing, listing John as the child's father. It had been the story at the time, so she believed that naming her husband would quieten all gossip and ensure the girl was accepted. And she'd been right.

But wee Sadie had died without the church's blessing. Sarah didn't think it would matter. An innocent child would surely be granted God's love, but now she began to worry. Had Sadie been taken as punishment for her sins?

So far, Alfred, Beatrice and Sidney were healthy, active, noisy children, but what if one of them fell sick? What if another one was taken? She didn't want to be maudlin, but neither did she want to risk God's wrath.

"Rick, dearest, would you be willing for the youngest three to be baptised?"

"Where?" he asked with a frown, looking a little startled.

Seated beside him at the table, she took his hand in hers. "My local church. It's small and welcoming, and we could have it all done when they have a blessing day. We'd blend into the crowd without notice."

"If that's what you want," he said, once again granting her whatever she thought best for the children. "But no fuss. I don't want it to become spread around the neighbourhood. And ..." He paused, clearly reflecting on something. "... I'm sorry to ask this of you, but it's for your protection as much as mine, and for the protection of the older children."

"Yes, what is it?"

"That they keep the name Clements."

Sarah smiled as his diffidence. "Of course. I'd never once thought otherwise."

Shortly after, she approached the priest and asked him to bless her children. Plans were put in place and a date agreed on some months hence.

And so it was in October 1876, Alfred, Beatrice and Sidney were baptised together at St Raphael's Church, with their parents listed as Richard and Sarah Clements.

Both parents beamed with pride, but unbeknown to Sarah, a shadow loomed over their future.

27

More changes

As Sarah shut the door on the enumerator, she wondered where all the years had gone. So much had changed for her since the last census. Some for the better, like this house she was living in, others not so favourable.

It'd be five years ago now, reflected Sarah, since a law was passed that all terrace houses should have individual water closets. She'd rejoiced in the thought, having decided the two-up, two-down cottage was too small after the birth of the two youngest. She set out to find a home large enough for herself and five children with its own facility.

At that time, the then two-year-old horse-drawn tramways system had been a great boon for getting around the place and seeing other areas of Bristol. It had taken her a while, but Sarah had finally chosen this place, on the other side of the river near Bath Bridge, within an easy walk of a tram stop – and this one was hers.

Still a terrace house, but longer, with more rooms, its own small courtyard with entrances front and back, and the all-important water closet and indoor running water. But not long after she'd moved their belongings, adding touches here and there to make it her own, Richard presented her with a conundrum.

"It's ended up being a bit of a paradox. The better we were at our job, the more it made sense that we should hand over the provision of an efficient water supply for firefighting to the local authorities. We knew this back in 1875, it's just taken another couple of years to negotiate ourselves out of a job."

"Is that why the council charges a fire rate now?"

Richard nodded, while Sarah continued with her next question. "What does this mean for you?"

"I'll be out of a job, I suppose," he shrugged. "All five of the insurance companies, the Imperial, the Liverpool & London, the Royal, the West and us at the Sun, sent a joint letter to the city council giving them notice. The fire brigades'll all be disbanded within a few months."

Sarah cherished the still lean body of the man who was already well past sixty, observing the lines around his eyes and mouth; soft grey eyes that still regarded her with warmth and lips she loved to kiss.

"What will you do?" she asked with genuine concern.

"I'll probably go back to the docks where I started. It's what I know best, and they're always looking for labour." He seemed nonchalant about it, but the thought upset her.

"You can't do that. You're too …" She was about to say 'old' and then changed her mind. He wasn't old, not really, not compared with some other men of his age.

His hair had greyed, but to her he looked even more distinguished. "Too good," she finished, "too clever, for that."

If anything, it was she who felt old and dowdy at times. Her eyes, once sparkling like molasses in the sunlight, were surrounded by shadows and lines, and her hair had faded from the rich mahogany it once was. She was no longer the young widow Richard met eighteen years ago, but never mind how bad she felt, Richard always told her she was still beautiful to him.

"You think too highly of me, my dear. There's no shame in labouring."

"Maybe not, but labouring is physical work and you're not the young man you once were."

He chuckled. "You've noticed, I see." As usual her heart melted at his self-effacing nature. "But no, I don't want to do the physical work, I'll get a senior stevedoring role managing the teams and making sure they do a proper job. There's a knack to getting it right. Overload a ship or tie down an unbalanced load and you could lose both ship and crew."

Sarah knew all too well the heartache of crew lost at sea.

Since then, Richard seemed even stronger than he had been, certainly more weathered, tanned and with deeper creases in his skin, but he enjoyed the work, or so he said, and was content.

But for herself, she wasn't so sure.

In the three years since they'd been in this house, Sarah had accepted her place in life as a mother whose role was to provide warmth and nurturing to her family. Not that she saw Richard any more frequently, or that he stayed any longer, and she never had asked for anything more than he had to give. But today she'd wished for something more momentous to say.

The census man had checked her status; widow, number of people in the house; one adult, four children, and asked what her occupation was; she'd said none. Then she wished she'd said she did something, anything other than wait; wait for Richard, wait for her children to leave, wait for something to happen. Thirty years on, she recalled her younger self, fantasising about a different life. One that would take her somewhere exotic, that would bring her love and not involve hard work and heartache. These days, she had a great deal of love, and warmth and companionship, of that she was certain, but along with that came hard work and the sorrow of lost children. But now her children were grown, one gone out on his own and the others away from the house all day, she missed them dreadfully.

JJ had raised the idea with her before talking with Richard. 'I wish to go to London to study, to learn to become a teacher.'

Sarah swallowed the instant response that had come to her lips. She couldn't say no, outright. She'd need a reason. 'Why London?'

'It has the best programme, I've been told, and I've checked it all out to be certain and believe it's the right decision. But it does mean I'd have to live in, and it will take several years of training .'

Sarah felt as if she was losing part of herself. 'Well, you'd better talk to Papa about it," she'd said, knowing Richard would be thrilled and totally supportive.

And so it had been.

JJ had left for London to study at St John's at the start of the year, and even with the other four children at home, she missed him greatly. She was lonely, and her days seemed long with everyone out of the house. Mary Ann was working to become a stay maker, thanks to Mary, but she'd insisted Alfred, and the younger two, complete their schooling.

The largest shadow that hung over her was the day a woman of about thirty approached her while she was standing at the school gate waiting for Beatrice. Sarah didn't always meet her daughter to walk her home, and she never met the boys who would walk together. Alfred had been adamant he didn't need his mother watching over him. It would be too embarrassing, and he would look after Sidney, and Beatrice.

"Are you Mrs Clements? Mrs Sarah Clements?"

The woman's mid-brown hair was tied back in a neat bun, her plain dress was of good quality without any suggestion of wealth, but it was her eyes that drew Sarah. A hauntingly soft blue-grey, and features that seemed familiar, but she knew she'd never met this woman before.

"I am. Forgive me, but who might you be? And how do you know my name?"

The woman smiled knowingly. "I've known about you for some time," she said, not unkindly, "but it's only recently become clear."

Sarah still looked confused.

"I am a teacher," she stated, as if that piece of information alone might help.

"How interesting. My son has recently gone to college in London to learn to become a teacher," said Sarah, still struggling to find a connection.

"I know."

Now Sarah was utterly perplexed. "How do you know that?"

"I just do."

Beginning to get irritated with the woman's abstruse words and intense scrutiny, she snapped. "What do you want from me? Who are you?"

"Like I said, I am a teacher. I believe my half-sister, Beatrice, is in my class."

Sarah's heart sank like a stone into her stomach, putting pressure on her bladder and turning her knees to jelly. "Half … sister …?" she stuttered.

"I do believe that's what the progeny of a father who has a child with another woman is called."

Suddenly Sarah recognised the eyes. They were Richard's eyes.

"Ah, I see you you've twigged. Beatrice reminded me so much of me when I was younger, I had to wonder if I was seeing things, but no. It's true. And there are others, are there not?"

Throughout, the woman had remained calm, with a slightly disinterested tone in her voice, but her eyes gave her away. Sarah knew those eyes and their moods. Sadness, regret and curiosity warred with each other, but curiosity was possibly the stronger emotion.

Sarah held her nerve and her ground. "I repeat, what do you want from me?"

"Nothing. There's nothing you could do or say that will change the situation, for better or worse, so let's not pretend, shall we."

Richard's daughter continued scrutinising Sarah from head to toe, searching her face, looking for …

Sarah didn't know what. "I will not betray your secret to my mother. She is too frail for that. Nor will I tell my brother, who is likely to want to challenge our father, which would not be ideal. My sister and I know of your existence, and of our half-siblings, and have done for some time. Grudgingly, we have accepted our father's need of your companionship and affection. He doesn't get that at home, but that doesn't mean we would accept any disruption to our lifestyle. But understand this. Should pressure be put upon our father to change his situation while my mother still lives, we will not be so generous." She smiled as disarmingly as her father.

Sarah met her gaze, her emotions confused, but she felt threatened. "I am too self-respecting and proud of my family to consider such a disgraceful suggestion. Good day to you." Sarah turned on her heel. Beatrice would have to walk home by herself. Sarah was too angry, too embarrassed, and far too distraught to behave normally for a while. She would have to walk until she was once again calm.

"You should have told me," berated Sarah, feeling all of her forty-six years.

"I admit I was wrong. Yes, I should have told you," he shrugged his shoulders, looking somewhat chastened, but the hands held out in supplication belied any true remorse. "But I didn't think it would matter. I never thought the girls would ever get to meet you."

"Well obviously one did."

"Not until recently. I don't think the girls ever put you and me together. It was the children."

"The children?" repeated Sarah in a daze, trying to figure out how his daughter knew her children, but clearly, she did.

"At the library."

"The library?" Sarah was beginning to think her brain has turned to mush. She couldn't follow his line of thinking.

"Yes. JJ had gone there seeking information about teacher training. Quite why he had Alfred with him, I have no idea, but my daughter was also at the library."

"When was this?"

"You remember that conversation we were having about my first family and JJ walked in asking who wanted to be a teacher?"

Sarah gawped. "That had to be years ago. Before we moved here."

"Probably. Something like that." His dismissal of the whole situation had begun to annoy and alarm her.

"Are you saying your daughter knew about us then?"

"Not quite. She came home and said she'd seen a boy who was the spitting image of her brother. They laughed over it and she teased him about who else would want anyone who looked like him. He's five years older than JJ, but Alf would have been roughly the same age as when the siblings were growing up together. There are similarities. But nothing more was said so I assumed she'd forgotten about it."

"But then what happened?" Sarah insisted. "How does she know who I am?"

"She doesn't, exactly."

Sarah thumped her hand on the table, her eyes like balls of fire. "Don't lie to me. You never have, so don't start now, because she certainly does know." His sigh of exasperation stirred a flame. "You're not getting out of this, so tell me how she knows."

"I told her."

"What!" Sarah couldn't believe her ears. After all the years they'd taken care not to be seen together as a family, to know as little as possible about the other to protect her and the children, all the times Papa was missing from their lives, and ... he had betrayed her.

Richard tried to take her in his arms, to comfort her the way he always had done, but she backed away, flailing her arms wildly hitting him on arms, head, chest, wherever her blows randomly landed.

"How could you! How could you?" Tears fell down her face and she sat on the chair, hands covering her face, defeated.

He knelt before her and wrapped his arms around her, murmuring soft words of love and reassurance.

She rested her head on his shoulder, until the tears slowed. She took his habitually immaculate white handkerchief from him and dabbed her eyes. "What happens now?" she asked far more calmly than she felt, but she needed to know. "Does she want you to leave me?"

"No. Nothing like that. We carry on as we have always done. I told her, and her sister, because they had already guessed." He rose and paced and rubbed his hands through his hair. "How often does Alfie walk with Bea and Sid?"

"Quite a bit. The boys walk home from school together, and Bea too if I don't get her. Why?"

"My daughter, the one you met, changed schools a while ago and, as you've found out, Bea ended up in her class. Something about the child drew them together and Bea innocently talked about her mama, and her papa who was away at work. Then she saw Alf and Sid waiting outside the gates and watched Bea join them, and recognised Alf again. From there, it didn't take much."

"Why now? You've always denied it in the past."

He shook his head, pulled up a chair next to her and sat. He took her hands in his. "That's not quite true. I've never had to say anything. I was never questioned, but the two girls got together and demanded to know the truth. Intelligent girls who finally worked out why I was away from them so much when they were little. Bea said much the same things, and once my eldest had seen Bea and realised how much like her baby sister she was … I don't know, it just all came out."

"Are you sure their mother doesn't know?" Sarah's head thumped, she thought she would pass out with the strain.

"No!" He sounded shocked. "And she never will. They promised never to tell their mother. And I promised to never leave while their mother was alive."

"Are you certain?"

"Absolutely."

"Well, we'll have to leave it there then, won't we? But Bea is changing schools. I won't have her open to taunts."

28
As life moves on

March 1886

As February came to an end, a great snowstorm hit the country, delivering freezing temperatures and inches deep snow. Getting anywhere was difficult as the snow turned to slush and ice, but with JJ back living at home and Alfred working, funds were more plentiful than they'd ever been.

"Mama," said Mary Ann hesitantly late one afternoon as she returned home from work as the weather began to clear. "I'd like you to meet someone. He's … um … waiting at the door."

"What's he doing out there in this weather? For goodness' sake girl, bring whoever it is in, and let's be getting on with things. Tis bitter, it is."

Mary Ann opened the door and let in a lanky young man. "This is Joseph, Mr Williams."

"How d'ya do?" Sarah extended her hand, which Joseph shook with some surprise.

"We don't stand on airs and graces here, Mr Williams,

and I'm right glad to meet you. What work d'ya do?"

Hesitant and fiddling with his cap, he finally found the words. "I work as a solicitor's clerk in a law firm."

"'Tis a fine job you have there. And are you wanting to walk out with my girl? Is that why you're here?"

"It is, Mrs Clements, it is. If'n it be all the same to you."

"As long as you take care of her and treat her well, I'll be happy with her choice, but if I hear you've been unkind towards her, you'll be out on your ear, law or no law. Do I make myself clear?"

"Mama," gasped Mary Ann, shocked at her mother's pronouncement.

"Don't Mama me in that tone. I'm only looking out for you. I know the difference between being treated well and not, and I will only accept the best for you." She turned to Mr Williams. "Do you understand what I'm saying?"

"Yes, ma'am, Mrs Clements, and I would never treat Mary Ann, er, that is Miss Clements badly. Not ever."

Sarah had watched him keenly, the way he glanced nervously at Mary Ann and the look in his eye. She listened to the intensity of his voice, rather than the words, and liked the way he met her gaze. Sarah expected a wedding before the year was out.

"Put the kettle on love, and let's have a cuppa and a chat."

She and Richard continued their relationship, still mostly independently, but always devoted as if nothing had ever been said. The children looked forward to his return and welcomed him the same way they always had done, and she gladly received him in her bed.

"I've missed you," she said as they cuddled under the warm blankets after an evening of catching up, eating and talking as a family.

"I often wish I could be with you more, but we do well, don't we?"

"We do. We do very well."

A moan escaped as his caresses began their knowing journey and ecstasy was theirs once more, even if in a different and lesser way than when they were younger and more fervent.

"Even after all these years, you are still so beautiful, and I love you," murmured Richard.

How they had maintained such a long-standing connection was never discussed. It just was. From the beginning, through all the ups and downs, the heartbreak and the tragedies, they had never faltered, taking strength from each other. Sarah had decided long ago, she would rather be happy with the man she loved who she rarely saw, than be with a man who didn't love her and likely would beat her and treat the children badly.

As spring progressed and the weather warmed up, Sarah decided to visit her ageing sister Mary. Once her rod to lean on, someone who knew her well and never judged, and the only one who knew her secret, Mary now shared a house with her daughter and son-in-law and three young grandchildren on the outskirts of Bristol.

Over the years, Mary's strength had deteriorated but her mind was as sharp as ever. It wasn't easy to get between their two homes without time and cost, and finding a quiet opportunity to talk the way they used to about personal matters was not simple either.

"Al'right, Mary, my dear. How you be today?"

"Sister dearest, what a pleasure. My old bones suffer greatly in the cold, but I do like sitting out in the sun when it shines."

Sarah had settled Mary into a chair with cushions and a rug and carried out a tray of tea things into the rear courtyard. It was hardly a garden, more a paved area away from the outhouse and a few vegetables growing, but at least they could talk more freely outside.

"How's that young man of yours?" asked Mary.

Sarah blinked and then laughed. "He's hardly young? He's nearly as old as you, and you keep telling me how old you've got now you've turned seventy."

Sarah looked lovingly at her sister, her grey hair tied back in a bun and wearing a lace cap. Her face was criss-crossed with lines, many of them smile lines, and she still had a glimmer in her eyes, although they too looked rheumy and sunken with the pale rings of old age. She was four years older than Richard, but she might have been a decade or more, going on appearances.

"He's doing well. Working on the docks still, says he's managing the teams who do all the hard work. I hope he's right. He's not getting any younger either."

They fell into casual chatter about the children, and her grandchildren and how many more opportunities there were for them these days compared with when they were young.

"Beatrice is doing well with her schooling, but she's always sewing something. She says to say hello and to give you her love. And Mary Ann has a fella."

Mary had retired from dressmaking roughly a decade ago, about the time Mary Ann showed interest in learning how to sew, before she found work as a stay maker. When Beatrice showed aptitude saying she wanted to become a dressmaker herself, Mary had encouraged them, gifting her machine, along with many of her tools and patterns and teaching them her tricks of the trade. Sarah reaped the rewards. She was their dummy. On her they tried out new ideas, learnt how to fit and design, and she received a new dress in the latest colour and style.

"That's nice for you dear. And JJ? Has he anyone?"

"Not that I know of, he hasn't said anyway. He seems focused on his teaching, and Alfie's working as a clerk for an ordnance survey company, and into his maps and such."

Sarah didn't mention Miss Hunt, but she'd never forgotten their meeting. Beatrice and Sidney had changed schools, and Sarah never saw the woman again, but her presence always sat on Sarah's shoulders even after all these years. Everywhere she went, she was fearful the woman would unexpectedly reappear and this time demand she finish her relationship with Richard. She had no logical reason to think that she would. Miss Hunt had not been unkind or unduly threatening. The worry was entirely in Sarah's mind, but she couldn't shake it, although she had mellowed considerably towards Richard's first family.

"I'd better be going," she said after an hour, "or I'll never get back in time."

"'Tis been wonderful to see ya," said Mary, reaching for her hand and squeezing it. "And good to know you're content in your own unconventional way. You've done well for yerself, Sarah."

Tears filled Sarah's eyes as she bent to help her sister up from her chair and guide her inside. Mary's approval filled Sarah's heart.

As Sarah had predicted, Mary Ann's young man had proposed, and the house was filled with a flurry of activity.

"Reminds me of when my eldest got married," muttered Richard with irritation. "At least I could come here to get away from it, but these days when I come here, it's enough to send me away again."

"Oh, stop it. You are not the ogre you're pretending to be. And it's what all young girls dream of. Don't destroy her happiness. There's time yet for her to learn about the realities of life for herself. Not everyone is like us."

The place was covered in fabrics and frills and paper patterns. Scissors and sewing materials cluttered the table as Mary Ann began making her own dress, with Beatrice helping.

"I know the trend is to have a white dress since Queen Victoria wore her beautiful one," said Mary Ann, "but I've decided on a soft blue taffeta with darker blue and gold trims."

"That'll look lovely, and bring out the blue in your eyes nicely," said Sarah. "Especially if you wear a royal blue cape. It'll be chilly so you'll need one."

"If I make it well, I should be able to wear it again with a few adjustments."

"You know Papa is willing for you to have a special wedding dress," Sarah reminded her. "But the cape could be reused."

"Aye, but that's too much to expect. I'm happy with a more useful but lavish gown that I can alter."

"You are such a wise girl. I'm proud of ya."

"Where do we start," asked Beatrice keen to show off her skills.

"I need to finish the corset first," Mary Ann explained to her sister knowledgeably, showing her one already half done. "It's got to fit tight into the waist, and then we need the underskirt for the bustle to support the draping at the back. Without that, we can't know the size to cut the panels for the bodice."

Much to the frustration of the three males in the household, who were frequently banished from the parlour and sometimes the kitchen, the sewing lessons went on day and night whenever time allowed. Beatrice was put to sewing seams, the clacking of the sewing machine in the background, while Mary Ann tackled the tricky tasks of cutting, shaping and turning corners and points.

Sarah and Richard talked about his role in Mary Ann's nuptials but decided it would be better if he didn't attend.

"We've told everyone that Mary Ann is your husband John's child, remember?" he said kindly. "I may have been responsible for her upbringing and many of the costs, but legally, she is not mine."

"I know, and I agree, and your um …" Sarah paused. She didn't like to think of Richard's wife and daughters at a time like this, but they couldn't be ignored. "The others wouldn't be too understanding, I suspect, but I will miss you greatly."

The weeks passed and Mary Ann's outfit, from the stockings, through to the petticoats, to the dress itself, began taking shape, but the girls still weren't satisfied.

"But Mama, I have to have a new dress," said Beatrice pleadingly. "It would be shameful to wear one of my day dresses that everyone has seen," she wailed.

Sarah admitted her daughter's dresses were all now outdated and worn, and rather young in style. She agreed the girl could have a new dress made from a primrose brocade, with a blue wool cape.

Beatrice bounced up and down, already babbling about the trims she would use. She loved sewing and creating but where her skill had come from, Sarah didn't know and put it all down to Mary's teachings.

"And you must have a new dress too, Mama," said Mary Ann, holding up a beautiful silk and wool fabric in a rich purple shade. "And I'll highlight it with lavender and golds."

"I'm sure such a gown would be beautiful," sighed Sarah, "but I don't need a new one."

"Yes, you do, Mama," insisted Mary Ann. "And I'm going to make it for you, whether you like it or not."

Finally, after months of hard work, frustration and arguments, it all came together and the finished garments were ready.

Amid a flurry of chatter and excitement, two days after Christmas on a cold but clear winter's day, they donned their bonnets, buttoned up boots, attached capes and pulled on their muffs. Sarah checked her sons' clothing, retying neckties, smoothing down the freshly made cotton shirts, and brushing their jackets until she was happy.

With Sarah's fifty-second birthday only two days away, her eyes now sparkling with glee, the womenfolk

315

walked arm in arm with the men of the family the short distance to the church to witness the happy couple joined in matrimony.

While Sarah missed Richard's reassuring presence, she proudly watched JJ sign his name to the register in support of his sister.

Sarah's happiness knew no bounds.

July 1887

Six months later, during a glorious summer with dry, sunny weather, Sarah was preparing to go to Mary Ann's home. Two-thirds of the way through her pregnancy with her first child, Mary Ann was struggling with the heat, her ankles had swollen badly, and she found it difficult to get around. After the doctor told her to keep her feet up as much as possible, Sarah had gladly taken on many of the everyday chores.

She'd missed the girl and her bright chatter since the wedding, even if Beatrice was as lively in a different way. But with free time on her hands during the day, she liked to feel useful, and it helped chase away the loneliness.

Vague, disconnected thoughts tripped through her mind as she worked. Sidney was coming up fourteen, and Beatrice had already left school and was earning her keep as a dressmaker. They no longer needed her to nurture them the way she once had, but what would she do without them? She had so many unanswered questions that nagged at her during her long empty days.

"Don't dwell on the might-bes, Sarah my love," Richard would tell her constantly. "Deal with each event as it happens."

She knew he was right, but that didn't stop her hoping that Bea would continue to live at home, or worrying that she would marry young and leave. Sidney was already hankering after a carpenter's apprentice job, which could take him somewhere far away.

The evenings were special times, thanks to John Jacob, and a time when wide-ranging discussions on topics he introduced from school would be debated. But he was now twenty-eight, and Sarah was convinced he would find a bride soon and would leave her hearth.

Children leaving home was the natural progression, but she still feared the day, even if she was about to become a grandmother. In itself, that brought its share of worries, but overriding those was the delightful anticipation of a new baby, a new generation to nurture and love.

In the middle of loading her basket with tonics and salves, and some home-made jams and pickles to take to Mary Ann's, a knock on the door interrupted her. Startled, she wondered who it could be at this time of day. The children, although she could hardly call any of them that any more, wouldn't be home for hours, and it couldn't be Richard.

Bare moments later, a second more urgent knock on the door made her jump, and she put down the jar in her hand and went to the door.

"Message for Mrs Clements," said the young boy. "Are you 'er? I'm to 'and it to Mrs Clements only. Mrs Sarah Clements."

"Yes, that's me."

He thrust the sealed note into her hand and ran off down the road, his messenger bag draped over his head thumping up and down on his leg as he went.

Sarah stared at the plain note with only her name on the front. It gave no clue as to the sender. Her hand shook as she held it, and intuition told her she needed to sit down before she opened it.

Moving back along the corridor to the kitchen, she picked up the letter opener from the hall table as she passed. Her stomach fluttered as she lifted the seal, the stark words filling her with sadness and disquietude, overlaid with optimism. Torn between opposing emotions, she struggled to decide how she felt.

She cast her eyes back to the note in her hand and shuddered.

My wife has died.

Those four words would change her life. What she didn't know was, would it for the better or worse? She burst into tears, knowing the next twelve months would bring some very dark days.

29

Love reaps its own rewards

October 1887

The summer faded fast, followed by an unusually cold and wet autumn. Sarah felt as if the tears of the world were falling at her feet and the ice in her veins barely allowed her to breathe.

For weeks after receiving the news, she hadn't seen Richard. The odd note arrived promising he hadn't forgotten her, but his family were grieving and he needed to be there for them. She had no grounds to complain. She wasn't grieving; she'd not known the woman, but she grieved for Richard – her loyal, steadfast, dependable man – except he wasn't *her* man. He belonged to someone else and always had done.

She'd forced herself to continue life as normal. She baked and shopped; she visited Mary Ann regularly and her sister Mary once to tell her the news; she scrubbed and cleaned, she kept busy.

She explained Richard's absence by saying he been called away on business. She suspected JJ knew more than he was letting on, but he didn't say anything and supported her.

Autumn deepened and the bitter cold set in, even when the days were sunny. Mary Ann went into labour, and every inch of Sarah's body contracted and ached alongside her daughter as she helped her granddaughter into the world that October.

"Isn't she beautiful, Mama?" whispered a besotted Mary Ann as Sarah laid the infant in her arms.

"She is, like all newborns are to their mothers."

Sarah wasn't convinced that everyone agreed with the sentiment, but to a mother, her first child is her joy and happiness in those moments.

"Have you chosen a name yet?"

"We have. We are calling her Ellen."

Sarah approved. The bringer of light. She made a wish that Ellen would bring light into their lives.

Every night she returned home, and every morning she would retrace her footsteps, back to Mary Ann's, willing to do anything to help her manage the new baby. Only it soon became obvious she really wasn't needed, and Sarah's usefulness diminished.

When Richard came, he would quickly remove his black armband, so he didn't need to explain to Bea and Sid why he was wearing one for so long, but as the months passed, he began to relax.

By the time Christmas came around, and they celebrated both Sidney's and her own birthday, Richard seemed almost back to his old self.

"I've given this a great deal of thought," he said one night as they lay melded into each other. For the first time in months, she felt warm inside and out, but something about his tone sent a shiver down her spine.

"What about exactly?" she murmured, her hands trying to distract him.

"Us. The children. Our lives."

Her body tensed, and he ran his fingers up and down her arm to reassure her.

"There's nothing to worry about." He kissed her softly, pulling her closer. "But my life has changed so much, I've had to think about what that means."

"For whom?"

"All of us, of course. With two of mine married and the third telling me she's accepted a teaching post with its own accommodation, I have no need to house them any longer. But I, that is, we as a family, will need to uphold a year's mourning period."

"Naturally," agreed Sarah, thinking of her one and only meeting with the Miss Hunt, wondering where the conversation was going.

"That leaves us with only Alfie, Bea and Sid to consider."

"And JJ," added Sarah, giving thought to her eldest boy.

Richard chuckled. "I hardly think John needs you to look after him. He's well set up. Remind me, how old is Alfie now?"

"He'll be nineteen in March, Bea is coming up sixteen and Sid a year younger. Why?"

"I think we should tell them."

"Tell them?" she echoed, a chill settling in her bones once again.

"Yes. It's time the children knew about us. All of them."

321

Sarah sat bolt upright, blood pumping. "What?" she gulped. "How will we do that? What will they think of me? It's al'right for you, men can get away with anything, but they'll be shocked with me. They will."

Richard chuckled again. She could almost see his smile in the dark. "Possibly. But probably not. I'm sure they've worked it out by now. Boys talk, and if my two girls know, so do yours."

Sarah blanched. "How do you know that?" Not that she was sure she wanted to know.

"Because they told me so."

"Our girls said that?"

He nodded. "And my girls, after their mother died, told me I was free."

Sarah's mouth fell open as her mind raced to find a rational explanation for such bizarre behaviour.

"I can't do anything until August, when mourning ends," continued Richard, unaware of the turmoil he'd created, "but after that we can make plans."

"Plans?" Sarah hoped, prayed, wished for Richard to tell her what his plans were, but she had no control over his decisions at all.

"To be together, of course. What did you think I meant?" he said laughingly as he took her in his arms. "To be together like this."

His kiss ended the conversation as his fingers explored.

In the following months, her world spun into another spin. Sarah had resisted meeting his eldest daughter for as long as she could, and had refused to allow the younger children to meet their half-siblings. It sounded so wrong.

But after a surprising turn of events, Richard finally won her over.

* * * * *

"She has a plan for us," said Richard making himself at home in her kitchen.

She placed a cup of tea in front of him. "Who?"

"My daughter."

Richard was being obtuse again and her fragile patience was near breaking.

"Which one? Mrs Sutton or Miss Hunt?" persisted Sarah.

"Does it matter?" He knew she didn't want to meet Miss Hunt again in a hurry, still irrationally fretting she would not be accepted by her. "She's quite nice, you know, and no threat to you."

Sarah folded her arms and glared at him.

"Mrs Sutton. All right?"

Sarah relaxed a little. The older daughter was a far more approachable woman with two children similar in age to Alfie and Bea.

"She wants me to retire from the docks, and …"

"Well, I fully agree with her on that. You are past seventy now. Surely, such a job is no longer necessary."

"I have been thinking about it," said Richard, taking a piece of cake from the plate and pushing his cup forward for her to pour another cuppa for him. "But I don't wanna sit idly at home either."

Sarah waited for him to finish pondering.

"Anyway, she says I should get out of the house where I am, and move near them."

Sarah carefully picked up the dirty crockery and took it to the Butler sink and pumped some water in to rinse them. Adding hot water from the kettle on the cooking range, she washed them thoroughly not wanting to look at him while she asked her questions. "Is that what you want to do? Be near your daughter and family. Is she intending to take care of you, and do the cooking and cleaning, and washing and such? I would have thought she had enough on her plate."

"I don't think she has any of that in mind at all," he replied, sounding surprised, "and neither do I."

Sarah wiped the dishes and put them away on the Welsh dresser before sitting down again.

"No, no," Richard continued. "What she has in mind is that I should apply for the verger's job at Christ Church with St Ewen, where we go to pray. The cottage next door to them on Clifton Hill is available, and I thought …"

"Go on." Sarah had butterflies in her stomach, her ears rang with the beat of her heart, and she broke into a sticky dampness. For a moment, she thought she might die on the spot, but logically she knew it was simply her nerves running wild.

Richard turned his bewitching grey eyes towards her. "If I do all that … Sarah, my love. Do you think … um, would you consider … if I did that, would you marry me?"

Feeling like a youngster again, pining for her first love, she wanted to jump up and down and run around and scream, but while her insides were doing just that, her brain was responding much more calmly. She had loved him for so long, the idea of being Mrs Hunt to the end of her days would be the fulfilment of her dreams. Even if it meant living next to his daughter. She would – had – sacrificed everything to be with him; another sacrifice would be barely noticeable.

"I would, yes." Her reply was quietly given. For most of her life, she'd questioned if the day would ever come. And now it was here, she wondered how much difference it would make after all.

Richard rose, walked around to her chair, bent down and kissed her gently on the lips. "Thank you. You have made me a very happy man and will for the rest of my days."

16 October 1888

Twenty-five years after they had first met, Richard and Sarah were wed.

They chose a church unknown to them, with a congregation equally unknown, where the rector they prayed with was officiating that day. Refusing a new gown, she wore the purple outfit her daughter had made two years earlier. Alongside her, John Jacob stood witness to the proceedings.

Standing on either side of the chancel were strangers, and others being married that day. They hadn't wanted anyone there from the past who might mar their day with some unkind comment. This day was theirs, and theirs alone. A day to mark their constancy and steadfastness. A day for looking forward together.

She had lived her life defying the traditional customs and practices in the name of love. Her life had been one of make-believe and dissemblance, because of one man; the man who stood beside her.

She needn't have been concerned about the children finding out about each other. The older ones, finally admitting they had known, or rather guessed, many years ago as they began to understand relationships better.

JJ summed it up for them all. "Mama, if the two of you have kept your love for each other alive for two and a half decades, with all the difficulties that entailed, then you deserve happiness at this time in your lives."

Sarah turned to Richard and reached for his hand. Their eyes met and no words were needed. Love had conquered.

Epilogue

"Time to go, my darling," whispered Sarah sitting at Richard's bedside, holding his hand, allowing the memories to fill her mind.

Since their marriage, seventeen years earlier, life had been kind to them.

As she'd expected, their routine hadn't changed all that much, except Richard was now by her side every day and shared her bed every night. JJ, Alfred, Beatrice and Sidney had continued to live with them after the wedding until John Jacob married on Boxing Day the following year.

"I'm so proud of my boy," she said to Richard. "He came from such humble beginnings backalong, when I was a young victualler's daughter on the Welsh Back. I'm ever so grateful my da made sure I could read and write, and I could spur JJ on. But for him to be a fully trained teacher now is beyond my wildest dreams."

"I remember," replied her beloved, his eyes gazing at her with the constancy she'd come to cherish. "You were always curious, always wanting to know more, always encouraging JJ in his studies. It's all because of you."

Around them, Bristol and the rest of Britain was moving on. Schooling for children under ten had been made compulsory, ensuring JJ had a job for life. Electric light was touted as the next big change affecting the lives of hundreds of thousands of people. Not that she understood how it worked, even if JJ had explained it to her, but she recognised its potential and hoped it would be something she could enjoy one day.

More importantly for her, changes to the Married Women's Property Act meant she could keep all her own money and assets in her own name, even after marriage and in the event of being widowed again. She dreaded the thought but knew she would be.

Alfie married his Ada eighteen months later and presented Sarah with another grandchild before the end of the year. What a great day their wedding had been, Sarah remembered, thinking about the beauty of St Mary Redcliffe Church and how she'd been drawn to it in the earlier years after she'd left The George. She could still hear the organ music echoing after many celebrations at the same church.

In quick succession, she'd become a grandmother to seven, with three from Mary Ann, three from JJ and one from Alfie. She idolised every one of them and spent as much time as she could with them.

Richard had two grandchildren of his own, from before they'd wed, one more after the Miss Hunt Sarah had once feared, but had become an ally, had married five years after them, but his boy never had any children, much to his regret. But to him, grandchildren were someone else's problem.

"I'm too old now to be a playmate or a teacher. What I know they don't want to know, and what they talk about, I don't understand."

Sarah could sympathise with that feeling, but while hers were young, she'd enjoy them. "I worry about Bea, though. She shows no sign of wanting to marry. She's never even had a bloke that I know of."

"She's doing all right for herself. She's a great dressmaker and is totally independent, and could live anywhere. But she stays with us and helps you take care of me, and keeps you company when I'm out."

Richard was always out. For the first few years, he'd walked down the hill every day to the church and performed his duties as sexton and verger. They seemed to vary, cross over and interchange. Sometimes, he would oversee the grounds and the gravediggers – she'd insisted he not once consider doing the digging himself – but someone had to manage the paperwork, the gardens and the workers – and ring the bells. She loved the sound of the bells calling people to prayer, but when it tolled for someone departed, she counted every one, determining whether female or male and how old they were.

Other times, he would be busy organising the week's numerous duties for the clerics, caring for the church's sacred vessels, planning the logistical details for the service, and leading the Sunday procession. He'd been in his element, but as the years passed, the walk back up the hill took its toll. He transferred his service to St Andrew, across the road from where they lived. At least then, he could come home in between duties and rest when needed.

"That's what has kept me alive for so long," he professed. "That, and you, my love. Especially you."

In amongst the happiness that life had bestowed upon her, were tragedies Sarah struggled to come to terms with. First, she mourned the death of her faithful sister Mary, who had finally given in to old age. A year later, in 1896, a smallpox epidemic raged through the city. Mary Ann had succumbed and passed away at the age of thirty-two, leaving her husband with three daughters, one only two years old.

Sarah had first wept, then withdrawn into herself as she came to terms with her loss.

"Take your time, love," urged Richard. "You can't hurry grief."

For the sake of Mary Ann, she had stepped in to help, but within a short time, her widower took a new wife who didn't appreciate Sarah's interference, as she called it.

"Don't cry, Sarah," comforted Richard. "I understand your loss. Mary Ann was a special girl to me too; she was our first, despite what the documents say. But the others need you. You can't let them down."

Sarah had dried her tears and pulled herself together. She still insisted on seeing her grandchildren, whatever her former son-in-law said, but she had never been one to wallow in self-pity either, and forged on, supporting those who wanted her.

She'd taken an avid interest in the suffragette movement and wholeheartedly supported their campaign, but the powers that be hadn't accepted that women could be as informed and active in government as their male counterparts. They would need to fight on.

She'd breathed many sighs of relief that none of her sons had been called to fight the Boers in South Africa. The daily casualty reports upset her greatly.

"The waste of young lives is appalling," she'd bemoaned to Richard. "I remember all the talk at The White Hart when the Crimean War was at its height back in the '50s. Dreadful times with terrible tales, and it seems they haven't learnt anything."

"War is a natural construct of man's greed," said Richard. "Power is the paramount gift, and glory the reward for sacrifice."

"Well, I'm glad I'm not a man then, as I don't want either," argued Sarah, simply happy to have her sons beside her.

Then the death of Queen Victoria in May 1901 brought the country to a standstill. She hadn't given much thought to the fact the Queen was ageing and might one day die. She'd been on the throne for so long, Victoria had become an institution, someone who had given her name and blessing to so much in life: its style, its beliefs, its behaviours, until she was no more, and everyone grieved her passing.

Sarah too, until her own heart was broken once more. Not so much a personal loss this time, but the helpless agony of watching her youngest boy, Sid, weep over the loss of his new bride a mere six months after their wedding. A little over two years earlier, he had left their home full of joy and hope and optimism. He was doing well as a carpenter and had great plans for the future, only to return, a few months later, to the home he'd always shared with his parents and sister, and where he stayed, woebegone and defeated.

As always, Richard had comforted Sarah, talked when she wanted to, reminisced about the good times and allowed her to put loss into perspective. He and Sid would take walks together. She never knew what Richard said to him, neither let on, but while Sid took little enjoyment from life, he valued his work, and his handicraft benefited from the hours of patient and meticulous woodworking.

But nothing in her life had prepared her to say goodbye to Richard. Despite the loss of both parents, a young husband, three children, and her sister, as well as aunts and cousins, neighbours and friends, she had never given a thought as to how life would continue without Richard.

For forty-two years, since he'd first set eyes on her as a young widow of twenty-seven, Richard had loved, cherished and protected her, and given her a reason for being. In return, she had shared him, borne five children, and idolised him.

But life as she knew it, ended that day.

In the spring of 1905, Sarah's lifelong love affair came to an end. At the age of eighty-nine, Richard breathed his last. But she wouldn't complain. They'd had a good life together. She would lay him down across the road at St Andrew's cemetery, next to his first wife, as his family wished. Where he lay didn't matter to her; he would always live in her heart.

"Goodbye, my darling. Rest in peace. I love you still."

* * * * *

On 24 December 1907, five days before her birthday, Sarah Daniels, Clements, Hunt, aged seventy-one, joined her beloved Richard.

* * * * * * * * *

Thank You

If you enjoyed Sarah's story, then you will love reading about the girls in The New Zealand Immigrant Collection:

- ✦ *Brigid The Girl from County Clare*
- ✦ *Gwenna the Welsh Confectioner,* and its sequel
- ✦ *The Costumier's Gift,* where the secrets of the past are laid bare.

Sarah's Destiny is the first in
THE ANCESTORS Series.

Look out for **Martha** – Book Two – coming soon.

* * * * * * * *

Available at
www.amazon.com/vickyadin   www.vickyadin.co.nz

Please consider leaving a customer review.
I'd be delighted if you would sign up for
my newsletter on my website
www.vickyadin.co.nz

Other Books by Vicky Adin

THE ART OF SECRETS SERIES

Emma's willingness to help others discover the mysteries of their past sometimes puts her in harm's way. Yet curiosity spurs her to solve the riddles of her clients' family trees – even the ones where she is threatened and everything she cares about is put in jeopardy.

Emma, the journalist in **The Art of Secrets** (**Book 1**) is a broken-hearted young woman who finally comes to terms with the painful truth about herself, thanks to her adversary, Charlotte Day.

Some years later, in her role as family historian and biographer of other people's family histories, a friend asks Emma to find an ancestor, **Elinor** (**Book 2**).

In **Lucy** (**Book 3**) Emma pursues her passion for revealing secrets, which tests her loyalty to her family and friends while she unravels Paige's intriguing past.

THE NEW ZEALAND IMMIGRANT COLLECTION

If you enjoy multi-generational family sagas, inspired by immigrant journeys to foreign lands, then you will love these stand-alone stories set in New Zealand.

Become engrossed in this collection of suspenseful family saga fiction about overcoming the odds.

Journey alongside one of the immigrants as they cross the oceans for a better life, or follow their heirs as they uncover the secrets of bygone days in stories that bring the past alive. You won't be disappointed.

All available at
www.amazon.com/vickyadin   www.vickyadin.co.nz

About the Author

Vicky Adin is a family historian in love with the past. Like the characters in her stories, she too is an immigrant to New Zealand, arriving a century after her first protagonists, and ready to start a new life.

Born in Wales, she grew up in Cornwall until aged 12. Her family emigrated to New Zealand, a country she would call home. Vicky draws on her affinity for these places, in her writing. Fast forward a few years, and she marries a fourth-generation Kiwi bloke with Irish, Scottish and English ancestors and her passion for genealogy flourishes.

The further she digs into the past, the more she wants to record the lives of the people who were the foundations of her new country. Not just her own ancestors, but all those who braved the oceans and became pioneers in a raw new land. Her research into life as it was for those immigrants in the mid-to-late 1800s and early 1900s gave her enough material to write for many years about the land left behind and the birth of a new nation.

Her first book, *The Disenchanted Soldier,* is the most biographical of all her books, inspired by her husband's great-grandfather. For the rest, while the history of the time is accurate, the characters are fictionalised to fit with the events and happenings as they occurred.

Vicky holds an MA(Hons) in English, is a lover of art, antiques, gardens, good food and red wine. She and her husband travel throughout New Zealand in their caravan and travel the world when they can. She hopes younger generations get as much enjoyment learning about the past through her stories, as she did when writing about it.

Author's Note

Sarah's story is a biographical-fiction account of the life of one of the author's ancestors. Surnames and some other names have been changed to protect any descendants who might be unaware of her story: one of true love, constancy and devotion.

The personal facts, and timeline, as written, have been gleaned from numerous birth, marriage and death certificates, ten-yearly census records, business directories, lists of victuallers, licence holders and newspaper reports, and many other sources. Between these facts are unaccounted-for years where dramatic licence has been taken.

Thorough research helped paint a picture of Victorian life and Bristol at the time Sarah lived there, and fill in some of those gaps. The history of Bristol is similarly factual and taken from historical records, but whether Sarah or any of her family were involved in any of the events cannot be proven and that aspect has been fictionalised to suit the story.

Sarah's love interest was named Richard, and his life story is also as close to the facts as is possible to glean two centuries later. Sarah did employ various staff throughout, but those mentioned in this story – from Molly, through Owen Davidson and Amos Baker, to Ethel Binns – and her interactions and encounters with them are fictional. Whereas the story of Sarah giving evidence against a man named Blackmore, who was found innocent of the murder of his son, is fact and taken from newspaper accounts.

Acknowledgements

My thanks go to the many people who have assisted me throughout the research, writing and publication process for this book, especially beta readers fellow author Jenny Harrison, Carolyn McKenzie, Dr John Reynolds, Bev Robitaille and my eagle-eyed professional editor and designer, Adrienne Charlton. I thank you all for your input and keeping me from straying from the storyline.

Much of the factual information about Bristol was accessed through Bristol-specific websites. There are far too many to list here, but the ones I found the most useful include:

Bristol City Docks hosted by Chris Fewtrell
bristolcitydocks.co.uk/welsh-back/
Bristol Floating Harbour
www.bristolfloatingharbour.org.uk/
Bristol History
www.bristolhistory.co.uk/?s=welsh+back
Bristol History and Genealogy, people and places (and more)
www.bristolinformation.co.uk/
Know your Place – Bristol maps.bristol.gov.uk which provided me with an interactive map of streets then and now to help with locations and settings
About Bristol
www.about-bristol.co.uk

Bristol Archives
  archives.bristol.gov.uk
Clifton Suspension Bridge
  cliftonbridge.org.uk/completing-the-bridge/
Bristol's Lost Pubs
  bristolslostpubs.com/central/g-j/

General websites covering Victorian domestic life, their houses and kitchens, funerals and the position on women, as well as *Mrs Beeton's Book of Household Management*, were accessed through Internet searches, as were websites dedicated to the Bristol dialect, manner of speaking and words unique to the city. Online newspapers were a valuable source of detail about inns, licences, fires, courts and people.

The genealogical details of Sarah's life were ascertained through Ancestry, Family Search, census records, Birth, Marriage and Death records, and newspapers of the time. My thanks to the Bristol & Avon Family History Society for answers to my questions.
bafhs.org.uk/?v=c97b334ffd41

Last but not least, I thank my family for putting up with my thoughts being in another place and time more often than not. I couldn't do what I do without their love and support.

Printed in Dunstable, United Kingdom